MW00915244

Snow Angels

Silver Lake Cozy Mysteries, Volume 2

Sophia Watson

Published by Cozy Mystery Publishing, 2017.

This is a work of fiction. Similarities to real people, places, or events are entirely coincidental.

SNOW ANGELS

First edition. September 2, 2017.

Copyright © 2017 Sophia Watson.

ISBN: 9781520183107

Written by Sophia Watson.

Also by Sophia Watson

Silver Lake Cozy Mysteries
It All Comes Out in the Wash
Snow Angels
That Summer in Silver Lake
Solstice

Watch for more at silverlakemysteries.wixsite.com/sophia-watson.

For daddy and his storytelling, with love.

Snow Angels

Silver Lake Cozy Mysteries
Book 2
by Sophia Watson

Copyright © 2016 Sophia Watson

All rights reserved. No part of this book may be used or reproduced in any matter whatsoever, including Internet usage, without written permission from the author, except in the form of brief quotations embodied in critical articles and reviews.

Any unauthorized usage of the text without express written permission of the author/publisher is a violation of the author's copyright and is illegal and punishable by law.

This is a work of fiction. Names, characters, places; and incidents are the product of the author's imagination or are used fictitiously, and any resemblance to actual persons, living or dead, business establishments, events, or locales is entirely coincidental.

Other Books by this Author

The Bonaventura Cozy Mysteries
Jitterbug[1] as Zara Brooks-Watson
Tie Dye[2] as Zara Brooks-Watson

THE SILVER LAKE COZY Mystery Series as Sophia Watson
It All Comes Out in the Wash[3] (Book 1)
Snow Angels[4] (Book 2 - Cyber-Crime mini-series, part 1)
That Summer in Silver Lake[5] (Book 3)
Solstice[6] (Book 4 - Cyber-Crime mini-series, part 2, sequel to Snow Angels)

---

1.   http://books2read.com/jitterbug

2.   http://books2read.com/tiedye

3.   http://books2read.com/wash

4.   http://books2read.com/snowangels

5.   http://books2read.com/thatsummer

6.   http://books2read.com/solstice

POETRY, PHOTOGRAPHY, Short Stories &
  a Children's Book as Cathy Smith
  Waiting for the Sunrise[7]: *The Collected Poetry of Cathy Smith*
  Hidden Treasures[8]: *Seven Short Stories*
  The Tree People, for children ages 6-10.

MOST E-BOOKS ARE AVAILABLE in paperback also.
  See silverlakemysteries.wixsite.com/Sophia-watson[9] *for all book updates & sales links.*

---

7.   *http://books2read.com/waitingforthesunrise*

8.   *http://books2read.com/hidden-treasures*

9.   http://silverlakemysteries.wixsite.com/sophia-watson

Chapter One

It was almost the end of November. The weather had been vacillating between warmth around the sunny afternoons and the colder evenings after dark. At night, the cold circulated around the night sky as the stars spread over the Mississippi River like a tangled archway of far-off candle lights. The winds outward over every body of water in the small town of Silver Lake seemed to sweep the cold inland against the windows of the homes near the local farms and forests.

The town was close to the East Cape Girardeau area of Illinois, which was next to the southeastern border of Missouri, which sat underneath the extensive, already snow-covered peaks of the Ozark mountains. The town sat right on the banks of the Mississippi river. Dark cumulus clouds began to gather over the river and drift towards Silver Lake – the home of Central Illinois University (CIU). Soon it would snow.

The lights and electricity had been flickering on and off in Asia's home for a couple of days. Asia had changed all her fuses and called Elton Jamison who was a good friend and an electrical engineer. He said that this situation seemed to be a Silver Lake Electric Company problem and the entire town had been having the same problems of inconsistent electricity delivery. There was nothing wrong with Asia's home.

There seemed to be something wrong with the main. The suspicion was that the controlling computer at the electric company was having "ghost" problems in its programming. In other words, Elton Jamison felt the problem was an internal computer glitch or virus at the Silver Lake Electric Company that was defying a solution.

The problem was irritating but did not injure commerce since the blackouts did not last for more than approximately thirty seconds to one minute. Aggravating – definitely yes.

Local computer experts had been called in to try and solve the difficulties. The local guess was that it was a hacker problem – maybe just a local kid messing around. But others felt it was far more serious than that, including the police department.

Before the torrents of winter landed upon the waters of the Mississippi, there were a few warm days left to harvest the local farms and gardens and begin fall canning. Asia Reynolds, locally celebrated documentary filmmaker, took the last of her tomatoes into her kitchen and put them into a colander in her sink.

She turned the cold water on them and rolled their nice, firm flesh over in her hands. Wiping her wet hands on a dish towel, she walked over to the back door and grabbed her log-splitting ax.

She looked forward to savoring the end of her chores for the day, so she could enjoy one of her favorite seasonal treats – just a plain tomato from her garden, sliced and doused with a smattering of sea salt. Eaten plain, it was a piece of heaven to her.

That would be her reward for completing the preparation of some of her winter firewood. When Asia had quit smoking, she became a sugarless lacto-vegetarian, which was why her dog (then a little puppy) was named Zucchini. Not only her favorite dog, but one of her favorite vegetables, as well.

She was a big woman. Splitting logs was her version of eighteen holes of golf—splitting a cord of wood in the Illinois fall twilight. She put a light jacket on. It had the large brown letters of the SLPD (Silver Lake Police Department) stenciled on the back.

The jacket belonged to her friend Sergeant Sheila *"She-she"* Rodriguez of the Silver Lake Police Department. Asia had no guilt over borrowing the jacket that Sgt. Rodriguez had left behind. It fit perfectly and was light enough for the extensive physical exercise that log-splitting required. Otherwise, she would be too hot.

Asia walked outside and over to the wood pile, driving the log ax into a small piece of wood – say about six inches in diameter. She picked up the wood with the sharp end of the ax and banged it on a larger stump embedded in the hard-packed earth of her back yard. An apple fell off a tree a couple yards away. She smelled the fine, fruity fragrance of the other over-ripe apples. It made her hungry for some Apple Betty with cinnamon and freshly grated ginger. Her stomach growled. She promised herself she would go down to her root cellar and bring up some fresh apples to do just that.

She thwacked another log and it split in half. She easily thwacked it into quarters. She split a small stack of logs, which soon grew into the usual square, eight-foot-long, four-foot-wide neatly stacked cord. The wood was very dry (which was good for splitting), so it took her only about four hours to complete her task.

As the sun slowly set into darkness and the air got colder and colder with the rising of a full silver harvest moon, she went again into the kitchen, rubbing the bunching muscles on her shoulders and pushed the buttons for the outside lights. Now sweating despite the ascending coolness, she took the SLPD jacket off and placed it over the back of a chair.

She looked out the sliding glass doors in the back of her house at the cord of split wood she had just finished and blew the damp curls on her forehead back, swiping them with her hand. She smiled, estimating the size of the cord with her eyes. She'd be warm and cozy until the serious snow started. She could prepare wood even after the snow started but preferred to do this chore in the drier weather of the fall. The snow created an impediment and the ground became treacherous with ice. The unsplit wood would be packed into her barn to keep it dry. She could split more cords in there, and even chainsaw smaller pieces from a few large logs if she needed to while she was protected from the weather.

Her carefully insulated barn had a large oil-barrel wood stove in it, too. A couple of neighborhood boys, teenagers, had come over while she was resting inside, and packed her Silverado with the split and unsplit wood and drove it up to the barn, loading most of the wood into a wood storage area inside. This was one chore she liked to have help with. She grabbed her jacket and went outside again. There were some advantages to being almost six feet tall, 200 pounds and still looking slender. She could easily use an over-the-shoulder log ax and would split the other cords when she had the time.

She had already hired these two local teenagers to move and stack most of the wood neatly in her barn, like she did almost every year. She usually left a cord close to the house within easy reach and just covered it with a tarp when it started snowing. She didn't need all *that* much exercise. She did plenty of swimming at the heated local indoor pool.

She now helped the boys load the back of her Silverado double-cab pickup and supervised backing up to her barn doors. That was work enough. Three sets of hands made moving 1,000 lbs. of wood (or more since she had almost six cords already split and ready to be stacked) way easier. They were done within a few hours. She went back inside her warm kitchen and walked back into the dining area.

Elise Snuggles, local African-American cable news anchor and good life-long friend, walked into the room, after not knocking on the open front door. Asia switched on the large standing fan in her dining room which started up with a loud, audible *zoom* and started rotating a fine breeze, making the fronds of her Boston ferns wave back and forth. After all that hard labor, she did not need that much warmth, it just made her sweat. Just a little when she came in was enough right now.

Elise answered Asia's querulous look with, "Doors usually only open one way around here – and that's usually *in* –

so one can get out if the snow piles up against them." Making herself at home at her friend's houses had been her habit since elementary school. Asia still did a double-take when Elise just walked in and made herself at home, although she really would not have it any other way...especially since Elise was so instrumental in detecting that she had been in trouble during the kidnapping affair with Talbot Patterson and his accomplice Kinsey Nesbitt last summer.

"*Jeez Looeez,* Asia! It's going down to the 40's outside, you're spouting sweat like a fountain *and* have the fan on! Choppin' wood like a lady, again?"

"Yes, darlin'," said Asia as she threw herself down in a dining room chair, enjoying the breeze from the fan until she cooled off.

"The meteorological department at KANU is predicting snow tonight."

"How much?"

"Just a dusting. Starting at about midnight."

"That's kind of nice. Makes me sleep more deeply."

"It looks like an early honey harvest this year."

"How are your bees?"

"They're okay. We moved them into the barn with gear on and we'll light the wood stove and generate a little heat tonight. Can I take a trunkful of wood just to start up?"

"That'll cost you two jars of honey."

"Sure. Thanks. Elton has been busy with work and helping me. We have some very fresh honey. The last of the raspberry honey. We did a small honey harvest before we moved the wooden hive frames inside, so they would be lighter. We have to leave some honey in the frames so the bees will have enough food for the winter and make Candy Boards out of sugar. Elton is a jewel – so careful. Didn't get stung even once."

"The bees like him."

"They're nice bees."

"*You* get stung."

"I get tense sometimes and the frames can be heavy for me."

"You should go swimming more and do a sauna."

"Yeah, I know. I still have my two year membership for the Spa. Call me – I'll go with you some time."

"Okay, buddy. Will do."

"I go with Elton sometimes. Not often enough, though. But he gets tired from work. Two black folks in the pool (or more if he brings his friends) is a favorite of mine. I don't like being the only black person anywhere, you know. I want to rent the whole place for Elton's birthday in November. I fig-ure I can run a cash bar and help pay for the party rentals and catering."

"Taking over?"

"Yeah. Make it a fine, black evening for our intelli-gentsia. Brown people in a lighted blue and purple pool. As Harry Skylar says, *'sweet!'*. We can serve dessert from the café/bakery downstairs from the pool. They also fix party platters."

"Mmm..." hummed Asia. "Get the Almontes to donate an organic, honey-sweetened chocolate ice cream cake."

"Now you got it, girl," answered Elise with a grin. "Every-thing's gotta be chocolate for that evening."

"We need something like a celebration since we are at the end of the summer. Even the Ferris Wheel is coming down."

"Ferris Wheel?! The roller coaster is almost packed up into eighteen wheelers, too. Thank God and Jehovah!" responded Elise with enthusiasm, being famous for her small-framed timidity. "Elton never got me to ride that thing with him. Probably never will. He doesn't need all that to make me hang onto him. Not at all. I will do that for free. I don't need to be scared to do that. *No, sir!* I have no need to scream from the threat of danger. I've had enough of that. I like my life real – peaceful – and danger-free."

"I'm a bumper car person, as well," said Asia, with understanding.

"Me too, for the kiddie rides. I even like miniature golf. Miniature is my middle name."

"You can use your smallness to your advantage. I'm too tall to play that. To me, it's like playing golf with a toothpick."

"Boo *hoo*," commented the tiny Elise.

Asia went into the kitchen and brought out a plate of fresh oatmeal-raisin cookies and some hot lemongrass tea. She had fixed a plate of garden-fresh, sliced tomato for herself. Tomato and tea went down just fine for the vegetarian in Asia.

"Yum," said Elise. "Got here right on time." She let the fine lemony fragrance waft into her sinuses, pulling her chair up to Asia's dining table. "You make those?" she asked, pointing at the large cookies.

"Yeah. Grew the raisins, too."

"My Snuggles honey?"

"Yup. Buckwheat honey from this summer."

Elise finished a cookie and slurped some tea, loudly. "*Yum!*" she complimented her friend.

Asia caught a sparkle from Elise's left hand and gasped. She saw a large sapphire set in gold and smiled. "Elton gave you an engagement ring?!" she asked, pointing at Elise's ring finger.

"Yeah, sis, he did. He's so considerate. Truly, the man of my heart."

"Have you set a date for the wedding?"

"Not exactly. It looks like a winter ceremony. Boots and a long dress."

"Don't you want to wait until spring?"

"Naw. I don't think so. Easier to get the babies to show up in the summer this way. I don't need to slide on any ice while my tummy is the size of a basketball, trying to get to the hospital."

"Hmm...true."

Zucchini, Asia's huge Husky/German Shepard walked into the room and rudely snatched an oatmeal cookie from the table.

"*Hey!*" exclaimed Asia. "*No*, Zookie! *Bad girl!* No, no..."

"Well," responded Elise. "At least it's not a sugar sweet."

"True. But she usually doesn't do that. She's generally not allowed to eat from the table, let alone grab anything from a serving dish."

Asia reached over and smacked her dog on the behind. Zookie dropped the remnants of the cookie on the floor, belched loudly and licked the crumbs up quickly, sashaying out of the room with an air of accomplishment and disgust at being hit on the ass.

"Damn," said Elise. "She sure burps like a human."

"She just started doing that. I don't know where she got it from."

A timid knock came from the front door.

"Come in!" said Asia and Elise simultaneously. Asia gave Elise a look.

"Sorry," said Elise without much sorrow. "You know this is home to me, too."

Asia smiled and replied, "This place and the Almonte ranch, as well."

"Friends are family, too," said Elise as she took the empty plate from the cookies into the kitchen, washed it and put fresh cookies on it, bringing it back into the dining room. There was another, louder, knock at the front door. A man's voice called, *"It's me, Harry!"*

Both Asia and Elise (of course) said again, *"Come in!"* Asia shot Elise a slightly hard look that said she felt that her friend had scaled up her chummy overly-friendly enthusiasm to a gentle type of dominatrix activity. It was a joke between them, letting Elise know that Asia sometimes thought she was a little on the pushy side.

A long-haired hippie boy in bell bottoms and an Indian *dhoti* walked into the house. He had a long, light blonde mustache and a guitar case slung over his shoulder. He smiled broadly when he saw the cookies and sat down at the table.

"Hi, Harry!" Said Asia. "There is some fresh lemongrass tea on the stove. Go ahead and pour yourself a mug and have some cookies."

"Oh, joy!" said Harry, grabbing himself a cookie. "I love raisins," he continued, his words muffled inside the cookie as he chewed. He pushed his chair back, went into the kitchen and got a mug of tea.

After finishing his tea, Harry opened his guitar case and took out his guitar, starting the intro to John Lennon's *Imagine* beautifully – picking out the complicated tones and singing in a high, clear falsetto, as Elise and Asia listened.

Zucchini walked in and wagged her tail at Harry. She trotted over to Harold and nudged his hand, ignoring the fact that she had knocked his hand clean off the guitar. He strummed the air for a beat.

Asia said, "Stop it, Zookie! You are such a bad girl today! Go into the other room."

Harry stopped playing and said, patting the pretty bronze-ruffed dog on her broad head, "Oh...that's okay. She just needs a few strokes. Lay down, Zucchini." The dog responded quickly, and Harry picked the song up where he had left off. After he finished, he paused for a sip of tea and another cookie.

Elise asked, "Do well today, Harry?"

"Oh, yeah," the musician answered. "Made my usual fifty dollars. I played in front of Zinski's Bagels all day. It's a good place to get something to eat. Not bad for street music either. They seem to like me. I think I must get them a few extra customers. There was a new guy down the street. A homeless panhandler. He did well, too. An older guy."

"The end of the season's a little better, eh?" commented Elise.

Harry blushed, remembering the trouble the beginning of the summer had caused him – and the hunger.

"*Way* better," he mumbled, sipping more tea.

"That was a mess. I'm glad to be back in school. I left a few days each week free of classes so I could do some street music until it gets too cold. When the weather changes, I'll play in the mall. They usually let me."

"By the way, Elise," continued Harry, I assume you heard that someone hacked into the town computers. I assume everyone knows since the wireless is down on top of the electrical problems in part of town. Any news?"

"We are investigating that right now along with the Silver Lake police department. My station, KANU, is getting updates on that regularly," replied Elise.

Asia asked, looking upset, "Any idea what the hackers are looking for? I am guessing it is probably not just kids messing with the electricity. It is more serious than that."

"The newsroom will know as soon as the cops do. Most folks suspect they are looking for some easy cash in payrolls, the banks or the ATMs. The electricity in part of town is coming back online. I suspect yours will too in a couple of days. The cops are pretty sure the electrical problems were only a test run for taking out the internet."

"You like your new job as news anchor?" asked Harry, looking at Elise and pulling on an end of his new drooping mustache.

"Yeah, Harold, of course I do. I have my ear to the pulse of Silver Lake. I have become omniscient. I know all. There isn't any important scooby that doesn't come my way. In fact, Harry, we can use a musical interlude for our end of the summer tourist season Op Ed. Wanna be on TV?"

Harry flashed a brilliant smile at Elise and said, "Sure!"

"Well then, you need to call me at KANU tomorrow and we will set up a news crew to film you either at work on the street or in our studio."

"All right!" exclaimed Harry, clapping his hands in excitement.

"It'll be a Harry the Hippie special."

"I'll be famous," said Harry.

"Almost," said Elise.

Zookie wagged her tail and nudged Harry's hand again. He scratched her head, taking another cookie. Wagging his head back and forth in pleasure as he chewed, he said, "These raisins are so plump and juicy. You raised these, Asia?"

"Yup," said Asia, shaking her finger at her dog as Harry illegally pushed a subversive raisin into Zookie's willing mouth.

"Say," said Asia, chewing on another cookie herself and turning towards Harry. "I heard you have a cute, little girlfriend."

Harry raised his light blonde eyebrows at her and answered, "Boy, the gossip really travels fast in this town. I only met her a few months ago. She's sweet. Her name is Sage and she's from Denver – goes to Colorado State."

"Don't you miss her after the summer's over?" asked Asia.

Harry shrugged and put his guitar away – giving his attention to the rest of his tea.

"I'm used to it. It's hard to meet a local girl in the summer. There are so many people from out of town. Sage and I have plans to see each other over the Christmas vacation. I've heard Denver is very cool – very New Age. Great music there. Might even make some money playing gigs during the holidays. Sage sings and plays piano and keyboard, so she knows some good places."

Elise frowned and said, "I've got to have my man next to me. Guess I'm just lucky to have met a local."

Suddenly, Harry looked a little sad and slightly forlorn, saying, "Guess you are. I've met Elton. He's extremely nice. Good looking, too."

"Got me a honey of a man," Elise responded. "You still on probation, Harry?" she asked.

"Yeah," he said. "Until I graduate next year. Sergeant Rodriguez is my Probation Officer and

she has already given me permission to go to Sage's house in Denver."

"They ever find out who put that assault rifle in your tent last summer?"

Harry looked embarrassed and said, "No. The evidence on the shooting of Congressman Harrison is a little cold now. They arrested Bill Tuttle but couldn't extradite the Swedish doctor. They said the rifle was underneath a blanket in the back of their truck. Anyone could have seen them put it there. Could have been anyone who was harassing hippies at the time that put that thing in my tent. As you know, there was a lot of harassment towards the hippies, artisans and street performers that summer.

"The cops and the judge both thought that having an open, unlocked living area like a tent was the problem – so they just forbade me to carry any guns and put me on supervised probation. Besides being a vegetarian, I am also a pacifist.

"Of course, I do not need any guns, so I will not get in any trouble as long as they do not find any weapons on me. And they won't." He paused and continued, looking down at the floor, "I, personally, have no idea who put the rifle in my living space."

A Downy woodpecker tapped on a tree outside the glass doors of the dining room as a couple Mourning doves echoed their melodic calls giving Asia's home a sort of ethereal other-worldly feeling, drifting into the darkening mist of the evening.

Harry continued, "I moved indoors to Sage's a few months ago. She had three roommates, so it was a little tight – but they were nice folks and it was fun. Now I've got my old dorm room back since school started."

"A little safer – staying inside. Warmer, too," said Elise with a kind smile.

Harry nodded his agreement, got up, went into the kitchen and heated the tea, bringing the fresh pot on a metal trivet and placing it on the table. He poured himself a cup and did the same for Asia and Elise.

"Thanks, Harry," said both of the women.

Elise sipped her tea and then complained, "I'm freezing." She got up and turned the large, revolving fan off. "Right now, all you have to do is open those glass doors. It must be about 50° F out there. You still hot, Asia?"

"No. I'm fine now," answered Asia. "I just split a cord of wood," said Asia, turning to Harry.

"You're lucky to be inside, Harold," said Elise. "It's supposed to snow tonight."

Harry laughed and replied, "I usually move inside by the end of the summer – at least to a cabin with a wood stove. That's Illinois for you. You can count on this state for unseasonably early weather. I moved into a dormitory in September, as soon as Sage left. School started about a month ago. All of my needs are covered by my scholarship, now. We have a new vegetarian/organic section in the Central Illinois cafeteria which I am really enthused about. It is based on the café/cafeteria design of Boston University. I even got a part-time job over there."

"You can come over here and eat with me any time you want to," said Asia, kindly.

"Thanks, Asia. The Almontes have invited me, too. I'll bring over some of their organic dairy as a gift whenever they share some with me."

"Ah, ice cream," enthused Elise.

"How you stay so small – I do not know," said Asia with a little envy.

"You're not exactly fat," answered Elise.

"This time of year, all my food turns into muscle," commented Asia.

Harry looked at the clock on the wall in consternation and said, "Oh jeez, I've got to go! I have to be at work in twenty minutes. It's a long walk from here."

"Come on, Harry," said Elise. "I'll drive you."

"Ah, yeah! Thanks, Elise."

Asia went into the kitchen and filled two paper bags with the remaining cookies, giving these to her two friends as they walked out the door to Elise's yellow Toyota.

Elise grabbed a sweater from the back seat, put it on, started her car and backed out of the driveway. She turned around and drove behind Asia's house, popping her trunk open. She and Harry got out and started loading the trunk with some of Asia's split logs. Asia walked out of the back of her house and gave them a hand.

When the trunk was full, Asia and Harry managed to close the lid. Harry got back into the car. Elise laid on the horn and called out, "Thanks, Asia! Call ya' later!" She pulled out onto the dirt road in front of Asia's old Victorian and drove toward the CIU dormitories.

"You know," said Harry. "You might as well drop me off at the cafeteria. I have about ten minutes to get to work."

"'Kay, buddy," answered Elise, glancing at the clouds gathering overhead, glad she wasn't scheduled to work in the newsroom tonight. It definitely looked and felt like snow. She shivered a little.

She was culturally and emotionally a sub-tropical person and started dreaming of a winter vacation in the Bahamas...something warm and sunny with a beach. She pushed a Ziggy Marley CD into her sound system. Harry said, *"Right on!"* and bobbed his head to the beat.

A patrol car pulled up closely behind Elise's Toyota, turning its siren and Mars lights on.

She exclaimed, *"What the hell?!"* and dutifully pulled over to the curb. A beautiful Latina woman in opaque, copper-mirrored sunglasses, knee-high, spit-shined motorcycle boots, and the three stripes of a police sergeant, got out of the cop car and walked over to the driver's side of Elise's car. She smiled broadly and took her shades off.

"That music is up kind of loud," the policewoman said. "Scare ya'?" she asked, with a smirk.

"Damn it, Sheila! What's going on?"

"Just saying hi..." replied the cop with a laugh.

Elise pounded on her steering wheel. "That's what the phone is for! I have three (count them) three message machines! One at work and two at home." She looked back at the patrol car and saw Sheila's beau, Patrolman Chico Almonte covering his mouth with his hand and looking at his feet...possibly laughing or embarrassed. His shoulders were shaking.

"Call me tonight, Elise. Okay?"

"Sure. Can I go? Harry's late for work."

"Yeah. Follow us and you can go over the speed limit. Chico doesn't like it. But, hell, I'm his superior officer."

"Okay, Sergeant," said Elise, saluting and restarting her car.

The two cars raced down Silver Lake Boulevard lead by the cop car, siren screaming – lights blazing. Harry ducked his head so that none of his friends would see him.

Elise pulled up in front of the CIU cafeteria. Harry put his shoulder-length locks into a hair net and giggled, saying, "Gotta wear one. It's a federal health code."

"It's sure not a fashion code," laughed Elise. "See ya', Harold."

"Thanks, Elise. I appreciate the bronco ride."

"No problem, kid. Be in touch."

"I will. I'll call you tomorrow after my first class."
"'Bye!

———————

At approximately midnight a light snow began to fall.
Earlier, Asia had stoked the house's main wood stove in the
basement. The boys that helped her load her wood into the
barn had carried quite of bit of the chopped wood down
to that stove. So, she now had at least a cord of dry split
wood stacked neatly next to it. As the temperature fell – it
got warmer and cozier inside her home. She thanked herself
silently for getting that firewood organized today.

Chapter Two

The computers in the entire town were offline. No wireless was available – no internet would work. Cell phones were scratchy and sometimes did not work at all. The landlines were okay. Cable television was fine except for a couple of channels. Dish TV was down, though. Not too many people still had landlines, so anyone who did, now made a lot of neighborly friends who needed to make a call outside of Silver Lake. The town's few remaining pay phones were constantly busy.

The CIU computer department had found identical trojans on many machines – but that was only an access virus – like an access code – or corrupt driver, not the actual virus that took all the machines offline.

Boredom reigned throughout Silver Lake. Many of the townsfolk made do with a little fishing. KANU (which was a cable station) played old movies and DVD sales went way up. The local police station had called Northwestern University and the University of Chicago computer departments for help. Their best geeks would be flying into town in about a day. The cops were really not prepared to fight a computer invasion of any kind, and CIU suggested that they get the best computer experts possible. Whatever had happened had left them scratching their heads.

The communication that everyone took for granted had lapsed into silence. Debit and credit cards were useless unless one drove to Missouri or Kentucky – or used cash. There was a general exodus to shop out of state or across the Mississippi river into another town where everything was working.

The non-internet capable cell phones were fine at first. Then, a strange beep invaded them as well and made *them* almost useless. Conversations were broken pretty much into incomprehensibility. Nonetheless, Silver Lake functioned mostly on the basis of old friendships, landlines and sharing.

Some of the few pay phones that still took coins were at the CIU cafeteria and student union. There were long lines at each of these phones all day long and deep into each evening. Instead of cash registers, stores and business establishments used notebooks and cash boxes. Suddenly, the entire town was sent back in history about a quarter of a century.

The university posted security at the CIU phones all night as well – so the lines continued throughout the night and were used as a valued family communications device. It was not surprising that most townspeople did not have landlines. Calling on these phones was limited since so many people needed to use them. Writing via the postal service was an alternative to using the phones or emailing. Just like the old days.

After the computer people from Chicago flew in – the airport was shut down. This flight was the last one for the duration. The nearest airport was St. Louis. So, all folks needing a flight had to rent a car and fly from there or use the park-n-fly lot. Nothing with an internet capacity would work in Silver Lake.

Working around the clock, the personnel from the universities from Chicago decided that the only solution to their problems was to rebuild the local software from Basic on up. The Apple Corporation had been notified and agreed to work on the problem as well, since they had expertise that even the professors from Northwestern and the University of Chicago did not have.

The question remained, though, *why?* And *what* was the cause of this problem that had invaded Silver Lake and nowhere else? Asia Reynolds' cameras were working just fine. She was busy documenting the entire situation and all the weird changes that were taking place and finishing up a local documentary she had started before the shutdown.

The new operating system that the computer experts were inventing was based on a Linux-type system because it had to be something totally different from the old Windows system for numerous reasons. There had to be various virus and intrusion alarms programmed and embedded into the new operating system.

One day, as Asia made her way down Silver Lake Boulevard, she stopped to say hello to Harry and listen to his music for a while. She ran her video camera as she listened, as well. He laughed and said, "Take a look at the old guy panhandling down the block. He says his name is Joe. He's a nice old guy."

Asia looked and saw the old panhandler was holding up a sign. She walked down and put a dollar in his cup, looking at the old man's sign. She read: "***THE END IS HERE – RE-PENT!***"

Asia asked him, "What is your name?"

He answered, "Joe."

She asked again, "What is your last name?"

"Doe," he answered.

She laughed and said, "Joe Doe?"

"You got it. Like John Doe, or 'D-o-u-g-h' as in money," he replied. "Who cares what my name is? The end is here, right now! Won't need a name after Armageddon." He looked Asia directly in the eyes and continued, "And, Armageddon could be tomorrow..."

Asia put another dollar in his cup and wished him good luck. She asked if she could photograph him.

He said, "Sure. Just don't give my picture to the aliens who have just landed in Silver Lake."

"Aliens?" questioned Asia, smiling.

"Yeah. I saw their spaceship land on the lake. I also saw an old lady with seven of them, walking and talking with them late at night."

"That must have been Frankie Franklin. Those were her dogs with her."

"There are aliens from outer space that look like humans and dogs. If you have a dog, be careful what you say in front of him."

"Her," corrected Asia, trying hard not to laugh.

"Ah HA! I knew it! So, there is an alien in your house, too. Do you dream that you have been in a spaceship?"

"No."

"They are here to take over the entire planet, starting here in Silver Lake."

"Oh."

A little boy, maybe about seven years old, ran past the two of them shouting loudly and laughing, "*I'm a Martian! I'm a Martian!* The end is here! I'm taking over! *The earth is mine!* Bee-*BA-deep*. Listen to your cell phone. *Bee-ba-deep.* That is my language. It means the earth is mine.

"Humanoids be gone! The earth belongs to Mars! *I'm a Martian!* Martians don't like the internet or all of you hogging cell phone transmission."

Asia laughed. Joe did not. He looked philosophical and pulled on his beard. "You see?" he commented cryptically.

"That's just a silly, little boy," said Asia out of a need to add some grounding to her shaky mood in this weird atmosphere of wirelessness.

"No, it isn't," answered Joe emphatically. "He is from another planet. Perhaps not Mars, though. Why should he tell us exactly where he is from? Or who he really is? He only *looks* like a human child, like that old lady with all the dogs – who only look like dogs – wear the skins of dogs – but are really aliens out to get us."

"*The end is nigh!*" he shouted at the little boy as he ran past him again. The child threw a dime at him.

"*Hey!*" said Asia, leaning over to pick up the dime, putting it in Joe's cup.

Joe said loudly, "I cannot use a dime made from end-of-the-world minerals." He fished the coin out of his cup and threw it into the street. "That thing has a transmitter in it, so that Martians can spy on me and follow me around. I only accept human money."

"Oh," said Asia. Glad that Joe thought (at least right now) that she was human. "Where do you stay?"

"In one of the shelters or outside. It depends on the weather."

After Asia finished filming Joe Doe, she decided to drive to St. Louis, buy some groceries and a large set of solar panels with lead-acid deep cycle marine batteries and the wiring to go with her new set-up. She hired an electrician when she got home and had him hook up the new panels – connecting her water pump from the well, a small refrigerator and her first floor inside and outside lights, including a couple of outlets.

Elise and Sheila were so impressed, they went out and got solar set-ups too. There was nothing wrong with the town's electricity, at this juncture, but there had been, and that made some townspeople jumpy. Both Elise and Sheila depended on their electricity to serve others, being a cable news reporter and local policewoman, respectively.

Solar panels were always nice for any weather emergency, so that made them even more practical. The four Almonte men: father José – Cisco, Chico and Julio also bought solar panels and batteries to run their creamery-dairy and freezer units – just in case. Living so close to a large bend in the Mississippi river provided its own weather changes often enough.

St. Louis was selling so many solar panels that they went on sale for half price. Just about everyone in Silver Lake ran up there right now for everything they needed – so the idea went viral.

No matter how much the Chicago computer geeks researched the local computers, they could not find a cure for them other than rebuilding a new town-wide operating system. The local computer experts could not find the worm/virus that had caused the initial crash in the town's electrical delivery system. It had just solved itself.

When the wireless went out, the electricity was fine. Perhaps the electrical outage had been simply a trial run for the type of hacking needed to take out the town's internet. That's what the experts from the University of Chicago and Northwestern thought, anyway.

The researchers also had some problems finding a source IP address for any hackers. At one point, one of the computer experts thought the problem might be sunspots or solar flares – or even a malfunctioning satellite. They contacted their respective meteorological departments and were told that there were no significant heavenly movements that would interfere with wireless transmission in the Silver Lake area. And, by the way, not affect some place else, too.

It was discovered that the name of the one of the malicious invading trojans or possible worm was *.mbezzl*, although there was no way to check if anything was missing initially from the local banks or pay rolls until their intranets were back online. This was not published locally (although Elise knew about it) to avoid a run on the local banks. The experts discovered the name but could not figure out the programming of the virus.

Joe Doe and Harry were doing just fine – panhandling and street music were doing seriously well and gaining in popularity due to the blackout of other types of entertainment. It takes a lot to make panhandling into a form of community entertainment, but that is not *that* farfetched with no television.

The Central Illinois cafeteria was running, although the phones created continuous lines all the way out of the buildings and down the block.

The Chicago computer people were finally able to remove the *.mbezzl* worm and other trojans or boot viruses, but within 24 hours they mysteriously re-inserted themselves, with changes, like magic, which increased the suspicion that the controlling hacker was using a satellite connection or at least a large dish transmitter, since no IP address could be connected with either *.mbezzl* or a major new variation of the same worm/virus called *.Change-O*, possibly delivered by an infected satellite.

NASA was called in and three space station scientists began to search the orbiting communications satellites for signs of technical corruptions that could cause these intrusions.

The key was the fact that the internet outage was accompanied by a Dish TV outage, as well. Dish operates from satellite transmission. Cable, for the most part, does not. That was the clue to a satellite outage.

Day by day, the weather got colder, and it began to snow in earnest. Ice formed universally as the snow melted and re-froze. The pace of the town got slower as people walked more carefully, like they were on tight-ropes, balancing to avoid falling. Die-hard jet-setters began to come into town by train, car and RV. Flying in by plane was still impossible. The annual snowmobile race was set for the middle of December, and it looked like it would be as successful as usual – despite the internet problems.

The race went through part of Asia's land. The noise was a little irritating, but she usually went out to the cabin on the edge of her property to watch the excitement with Zucchini once the real competition began.

Joe and Harry finally moved their panhandling and music, respectively, inside to a large shopping mall common area. Folks felt so sorry for good, crazy, ol' Joe, that no one complained about his indoor panhandling and regularly took him to the food court and bought him winter clothes, boots, and a down sleeping bag, as well. There were reports about how he was doing on Elise's new late, late night news show, *The Mississippi River Journal.* Although, Elise Snuggles was only being nice by including him.

———————

"Pu-leese..." said Elise when she viewed the first Joe Doe segment when Asia submitted it. "*Is* this a *small* town?" she asked her editor sardonically.

You could use your cell phone – but it was like a really bad police scanner. Elise picked up her cell when it vibrated, and the conversation was chopped comically into one word segments. The call was important to the late-night journal. It was a roving reporter's news about the start of this winter's extreme river sports.

"What?! What happened over by the river? *Blip, beep, squeal. Long squeal.* "Hunh?! Say it again," asked Elise with irritation at least twice, possibly more.

Speaking very slowly with plenty of spaces between the words, you might get a sparse message. Or build up enough frustration to simply text your message. This, combined with no email, made KANU's international and national news almost non-existent.

WATR radio was snail-mailing thumb drives and using landline telephones creatively for their out-of-town reports. Soon KANU was doing the same thing.

The competition between Alphonsine LaDuque and Elise Snuggles did not end when Alphonsine was fired from KANU. Elise had to eat some humble pie in order to admit that snail mailing thumb drives was pretty clever. But business was business. So, as we said, KANU did it too.

Suddenly, folks started getting messages in .html on their Explorer programs, even though they, themselves, couldn't get online. These were messages from nowhere and turned their computers on automatically – then off again. Ego calls from the hackers, rubbing in their intrusion so that it hurt even more.

By now, the Chicago computer experts were closer to feeling that the interference was coming from a communications satellite or satellites. This narrowed the options concerning who had the background to re-program a satellite and get through all the security that surrounded such an endeavor. The police ran their felony program through Chicago by landline phone, looking for previously arrested scientists with questionable scientific work. They got a short list of less than fifty people.

The Silver Lake Police Department hired an outside forensic psychologist to profile all of them. There were obviously not that many scientists willing to risk their credentials and research even for a few million dollars in stolen bank and payroll funds. But there had to be at least one person that was doing that. And making ego calls over the town's PCs as a challenge to anyone that thought they could shut them down.

The .html grandstanding got the investigative team in Silver Lake closer and closer to the solution, cryptic though it was. The messages seemed to be "borrowing" a different IP address for each individual "delivery".

The computer team felt that that could only be done by hacking the entire IP system. This left them shaking their heads in frustration.

Chapter Three

Asia Reynolds got home from her daily filming and tromped into the kitchen. She heard a whine on her back porch and the sound of her dog scratching on the kitchen door. She opened it. Zucchini limped in with several large gashes on her face and legs. She laid down on the floor after drinking about a quart of water.

"What happened to you, my girl?" asked Asia in horror, stroking her dog gently. "Did you get that from a coyote?" Zookie just whined and licked at a long gash on her leg. Asia got an old beach towel and went outside, putting it over the seat in the cargo section in the back of the double cab.

She went back into the house and put Zookie on her braided tie-dyed leash. Zookie looked at her dolefully and staggered onto her feet, stumbling behind Asia out the door. She gave the dog a boost into the truck cab. At which Zookie yelped in pain.

The Silver Lake veterinarian's clinic was still open when Asia parked near the door of the office. Dr. Hannah Steiner grabbed a wheeled animal gurney and she and Asia carefully lifted Zucchini onto it. The doctor examined Zookie's wounds as they wheeled her in. Zookie remained her patient, obedient self during the whole ordeal – even on the slippery, stainless gurney.

Dr. Steiner said, "Doesn't look too bad. The wounds aren't deep. Do you know what bit her? These are definitely teeth marks. And large ones, too. Like from a really big dog or large wolf."

"Don't know," answered Asia. "She's up to date on her vaccines."

"Oh, good. I'll give her some antibiotics, sedation, shave her and do a few stitches. Her hair will grow back in later. This leg wound will need a bandage."

"She won't like that."

"You can take it off in a couple of days. The stitches will do the rest of the work."

"Okay."

Dr. Steiner gave Zookie a big dog cookie, saying, "That should cheer her up a little. I have to put her out with anesthesia for about an hour to do that many stitches. Can you come over tomorrow and pick her up? I want her to rest until then. I can come over and observe her. I live right next door to the clinic."

"Okay. I'll be here this time tomorrow evening. Is that convenient?"

"Yes, that's fine."

"I wonder what happened?" mused Asia.

"Well," answered Dr. Steiner. "There's a new dog in town. Frankie Franklin just rescued a female St. Bernard named Hunny. Have you seen her? She's huge. Even bigger than Big Boy, Frankie Franklin's big Golden Retriever-New-foundland mix."

"Whoa! No! Zookie hangs out with Big Boy," exclaimed Asia.

"Oh, my God! *I'll bet that's it!* I know that Zookie likes Big Boy and has since you've had her, pretty much all her life," commented Dr. Steiner.

"Yeah. Female competition and jealousy. Maybe Hunny's not so sweet about Big Boy hanging out with old girlfriends. Hmm," said Asia, concerned. "I'll have to go see Frankie."

"Good idea. Zookie will be all right. Don't worry," answered Dr. Steiner with reassurance.

As Asia moved towards the door, Zookie whined again and tried to get off the gurney, but Dr. Steiner held her still with quick, loving hands. The hands she was famous for locally. As Asia walked out of the veterinary clinic she began to cry. She started her Silverado. The road to Frankie's blurred in her tears. It began to snow. She turned into Frankie's driveway and laid on her horn.

Frankie came out of her house followed by a few dogs – including a large, red and white full-size St. Bernard. She came over to Asia's window. Asia pulled the window down.

"What's up?" questioned Frankie, pulling her coat collar up against the gusts of cold and snow. "Crummy weather," she added with a frown.

"I think your new St. Bernard beat up my Zucchini."

"Really?" commented Frankie with even more of a frown, making her dark brown face look like thunder, glancing behind her at the dogs from her small rescue who started to surround her as usual. The St. Bernard walked over to Frankie and, looking up at Asia, began to wag her large tail, spreading the still falling snow to either side of her furry

body. Frankie Franklin called the dog closer and introduced her to Asia.

"This is Hunny. She is my newest rescued animal. Can you imagine birthing and raising a St. Bernard and then expecting a regular dog shelter to take her when you cannot keep her anymore? I did notice that she has a small gash under one of her eyes, in terms of any fights."

"Maybe you should tie her up for a while."

"You know I never tie my dogs up."

Now it was Asia's turn to frown. Frankie was not known for taking suggestions easily about her animals – unless you were the Forest Service or Humane Society.

"Wait a minute, Frankie," said Asia. "I have an idea. I'll bring Zookie over here and tie her close to Hunny – but not close enough to reach her and vice versa. Then, maybe you can tie Hunny up in

order to give both of them some time to get used to each other."

"Maybe they'll become friends," answered Frankie. "Okay," she said decisively with a small grin, as if *she* had thought of it. "I'll do it."

"Oh, good. Thank you, Frankie! Zookie's getting some stitches tonight. I'll bring her over in a week or so when her wounds are healed over."

"That bad?"

"Yup, Frankie, 'fraid so. Hunny got her pretty badly."

"Oh, shit, I'm sorry..."

"We'll work on it. That rope trick has worked for me many times before."

"Okay. Hope it works this time. It's hard to give away a St. Bernard."

"Bet so. See you later, Frankie."

"Bye."

Asia cut out quickly, sliding sideways on the slush as she hit the curves in the dirt roads on the way home. Her nerves were ragged. She was not looking forward to a night alone – without her dog. The only good thing was the snow. It was coming down harder now. That and some chamomile tea would help her calm her nerves and get to sleep. The silence that came from a heavy snowfall deafened her worries and soothed her loneliness.

She called the vet from her landline as soon as she got home. "How's Zookie? She asked nervously when Dr. Steiner answered.

"Oh, I stitched her right up. Looks like she didn't contract any diseases that I can see."

"Hunny only has a scratch."

"Guess we can figure from that who won the fight."

"*Ow*. Frankie and I are going to tie them up close to each other until they accept each other peacefully. Then we'll see if it was a fight between Hunny and Zucchini. That might be all it was and not a coyote, wolf or some other wild animal. It is serious enough if it was between those two, anyway, since we are neighbors."

"Inventive idea about tying them close to each other. It might work. The bite marks seem to have been from dog or dog-like teeth. I have seen quite a few bite marks in my day."

"Hopefully, the rope thing will work. It has before. I'll see you tomorrow. Don't spoil my puppy too much."

"Big puppy. I just have a thing about giving away doggie cookies."

"Me, too, actually. I'll be over to pick her up tomorrow. Thanks, Doc. Bye. See you then."

"Bye, Ms. Reynolds..." The sound of barking dogs echoed in the background. _____

Joe Doe shuffled across Silver Lake Boulevard as Asia roared past him the next day. *"Hi Joe!!"* she shouted at him as she raced over to the vet's clinic, anxious to have her dog back to lean on. It is surprising how much a silent partner can support one's emotional needs. A good dog like Zookie was solid gold as far as Asia was concerned.

Asia slid into a parking space as Dr. Steiner appeared in her clinic doorway with Zookie limping after her. She wagged her tail and barked as Asia walked over to her and gave her a head rub. Dr. Steiner handed Asia packets of antibiotics and pain pills, with the admonition, "Follow the instructions on the labels. Zucchini is a super patient. I let her sleep in my bedroom last night. She's very quiet. Didn't even snore."

"She snores sometimes, especially when Big Boy stays overnight. You just got lucky. She also snores when I don't give her enough dry food to wet food. I think it is the excess of animal fat. Stuffs her up."

"Bring her back in a week so I can take the stitches out. Take the bandage off in a couple of days and call me when you do. I left an obvious tab on it. Just pull on that and it should unwind easily. I'll mail the bill to your house. You can use Bacitracin if you see any infections – and call me."

"I usually open a large capsule of Vitamin E. It works better."

"You do? Are you sure it works?"

"Big time. Bacitracin has given me infections, so I can't use it. Dogs can use most human herbal and alternative medicines. But they use less, of course, depending on their size."

"Okay. I like alternative medicine, just be careful and call me if you have any problems with her lacerations."

"Of course, See you next week, Dr. Steiner, and thanks for working overtime."

"No problem, Ms. Reynolds. Zookie is an easy animal to work with. She's one of my absolute favorites."

When Asia and Zucchini got home, Zookie went right over to her dog bed and curled up as best she could with her bandaged leg sticking straight out awkwardly. She seemed glad to be home. Asia got down on her hands and knees and looked closely at her dog's wounds. She reached under Zookie's ear flap and ran her finger gently back and forth over her inner ear cartilage. Zookie groaned with contentment. She loved interior ear rubs – even with all of her wounds.

"Happy to get home. Eh, Zookie?" said Asia softly. Zookie stretched her legs out and groaned again, obviously glad to be back to her familiar digs – her own bed and her own home. She looked sad with all of her lacerations shaved.

Asia went upstairs to shower and get her pajamas on. Zookie fell asleep when she heard the water running. It was another comfort zone for her. She did not think Zucchini could climb the stairs until her leg healed a little bit more. It might take about a week. Asia liked her upstairs at night, but at least she was home now. She was way too big for Asia to carry her up.

Asia was startled on the way down the stairs after her shower by a commotion coming from the kitchen. Zucchini was barking, growling and whining. As Asia rounded the wall between the dining room and kitchen, she saw that her dog was also running as she lay in her bed. But, all of this in her sleep.

Asia went over and knelt down, putting her hand on Zookie's shoulder, using some pressure until the dog opened her eyes. Checking Zookie's bandaged leg, she noted that the tight pressurized bandage held just fine.

"Bet you'll be glad to take that off, eh, girl?" said Asia, smiling. "Me, too," she added, blowing the still-wet curls off her forehead as Zookie bothered the bandage and tried to take it off...unsuccessfully.

Elton Jamison's surprise birthday party was this weekend. Sunday, to be exact. It was to start with dancing at the Civic Center and move over to the conference room at the California Spa for a desert buffet ending with a pool party and an open gym.

The pool party was also concurrent with the dancing. So, the swim in the heated pool could last all evening if one so chose. Food was available at both the Civic Center and the California Spa, but only in the café/conference room. Of course, Tobias Smart, (gay, handsome, obese, owner of the California Spa), forbade any kind of food near his precious heated swimming pool. Elise argued with him for an hour. He wouldn't move on the issue.

The music was programmed to start with a soft live jazz trio, featuring a fine saxophone player, bass and guitar. Then, a local Hip Hop band was to provide the dance music. Then soft jazz again and an invitation to cool off at the pool. Elise would be running the Public Address system, a fact that made her chortle with elementary school glee. Running the building PA system meant to her that she was at the top of the food chain. She might even broadcast a video of the party on KANU.

Tobias was giving away complimentary one year Spa memberships as door prizes for everyone attending the party. Far be it from him to pass up a large potential crowd membership even if it was just advertising. Off-duty SLPD cops were to provide security and lifeguard services. They were also offered complimentary Spa memberships.

Elise was inviting all the black professionals from Chicago, St. Louis to Rolla, that she knew from cable and her student days at Central Illinois. Asia opted out so she could watch Zucchini. Elise would give the camera to a professional videographer from Chicago that would be attending. Sheila and the Almontes were invited. The rented cops from the SLPD were mostly the station's African-American reps. All of them were known locally and generally respected. Sheila Rodriguez was supervising the security for the night, besides being a guest.

Elise's distant family from around Silver Lake and Chicago were invited along with Frankie Franklin's kin who were old friends of the Snuggles family – especially Elise's parents. Friends of the band were also invited.

Zucchini lay with her legs spread out and had started snoring and clattering her paws back and forth again like she was running outside. She gave a loud bark and woke herself up as Asia walked into the kitchen dragging her sleeping bag behind her so she could sleep with her buddy tonight. Zookie had jumped up on her bad leg when she barked – so Asia rushed over to her and lay her back down on her side, cooing sweet nothings into her ear.

Zookie groaned but did not whimper. Asia spread her own thick cotton sleeping bag right next to Zookie and fell asleep listening to her dog's deep, warm breathing, with Zookie's bandaged leg up on her sleeping bag so she would know if Zookie was starting to move around again.

Chapter Four

"*Surprise!!*" shouted everyone as Elton walked into the Civic Center ballroom, thinking that he was just going to a community dinner. The jazz trio started a quiet version of the "Happy Birthday" song. Laser lights lit a message on all four walls that said, *"From Elise to you, Sweetheart – Happy Birthday, Honey."*

Sheila Rodriguez walked over to Elise, wearing her uniform. She was heading security at the Civic Center tonight. She put her arm around Elise with a sparkling smile and pulled her aside – off the dais with the words, "I'm going crazy trying to keep everyone safe without most of my communication equipment. We've gone from massive controlled computer surveillance to almost no surveillance at all unless it is here and now and done by hand on a walkie-talkie or over a wired-connection telephone – most of which do not exist anymore. Lucky for us the police department has a landline and the Civic Center office does also, as well as the kitchen."

Elise commented with excitement, "Did you see the movie *Net* with Sandra Bullock? They take everything from this poor innocent female computer-programmer geek. They take identity theft to the *n-th* degree. You don't really realize that computers control a huge amount of records. Scary...isn't it? But here, folks *do* depend on more closed systems than in the city. We can catch these demons. *We can.* So, maybe we need a new satellite with a better lock on it."

Sgt. Rodriguez answered, "Yeah. I saw that movie. What made the identity theft so easy was the fact that the programmer was always alone with her computer. No one really knew her. To top it all off, her mother had Alzheimers, and she was her only living relative. Even her close neighbors did not know her even to see her.

"People are flawed – but computers are not flawed in the same way. This film shows our vulnerability to using records – which can be too easily hacked and changed to suit an unscrupulous purpose."

"It is our closeness that saves Silver Lake," responded Elise strongly. "We *need* each other. We are family, a pretty close-knit community. Joe Doe needs us; Harry Skylar needs us. None of our close friends are as isolated as the programmer in *Net*. We can use our feet, hands and minds to communicate even on the street during the day. As much as I don't like gossip, it could come in right handy now if it wasn't untrue or destructive." Elise did a double-take and added, "Morse code would work."

Sheila answered, "That takes a wire, besides like how many people know Morse code? Smoke signals would be a better idea, except like how many people know that either?"

"Actually, we could make up our own emergency smoke signal system. You know, just in case."

"Hmm, Elise, I will think about that and take it into consideration. Might be a good emergency backup. I mean besides hanging around the Post Office, Silver Lake Public Library, Piggly Wiggly grocery store, or Dollar Heaven."

Elton was motioning Elise to come over by the dais in the front of the ballroom, the caterers were starting to bring out the refreshments and the cash bar had just been set up. A large chocolate birthday cake, the size of a three-tiered wedding cake, was wheeled out as the jazz trio again played the *"Happy Birthday"* song.

Elton waved at Elise again and started moving towards her in the crowd. Elise said, "Sheila, I have to talk to Elton. I mean, it *is* his birthday. What kind of fiancé would forget their intended?"

"*Fiancé?* You all are getting married? For sure?!"

"Yeah. This is sort of our engagement party, too. We are getting married as surely as the sun rises in the east."

Elton reached Elise and put his large, strong hand in the middle of her back. She gave a little shriek and whirled around to face him.

"Nice to be so appreciated that you scream when I touch you!" said Elton, sardonically.

"Oh, Elton. I didn't see you come up behind me like that. You could have been a masher gettin' ready to mash me."

"Oh, shoot, well sorry to disappoint you. I'm just getting ready to marry you."

Elise laughed and threw herself into Elton's arms. He gave her a warm (and passionate) bear hug. She cuddled closer to him as the mellow saxophone played softly in the captive, dancing laser lights of a twirling mirrored ceiling ornament sending rainbows around the room. Other tiny colored lights sparkled around the romantically darkened room as if the stars had reached down from the sky and been invited to celebrate with smaller fires than usual right here in the ballroom of this close-knit, rural farming town.

"Elton, honey, come with me. I have to tell everyone the good news about our engagement."

Elton kissed her and grabbed her hand as they both walked up towards the dais.

Elise climbed the makeshift stage stairs and grabbed the microphone. She blew into it until she could hear the volume accurately and everyone's attention began to focus on her. Elton moved closer and put his arm around her waist.

The saxophone player looked at her in silence as she indicated that he should pause the music. Some guests had been slow dancing and they, too, stopped, looking at her expectantly.

She could hear herself blow into the mike clearly this time and said, "Hi, y'all! We are not only celebrating Elton's birthday today, but another lifetime special event. My engagement to him!"

Loud applause erupted into the room. Elise spun on one heel and took a bow with the microphone, raising it over her head like a victory sign. "Oh, yeah!" she said with a wide smile. She waved at the crowd as they became silent again. "Love you all, too! Yeah, we are starting a new family. Most of y'all remember the old one, well me and Elton are the new one. We are set for a December wedding – crystal Christmas trees – bubbly and a honeymoon in the islands."

A shout went up in appreciation, with more applause. Elton went up to the mike and cleared his throat, catching the guest's attention. "Yeah, well," he began in his sonic, deep-toned voice. "Guess I'll be doing more than fixin' the town's wiring – gonna make me some skinny babies!" He kissed Elise and said, "See y'all at the wedding!" He cued the new band who had stepped up and changed places with the jazz trio. They struck up a fast dance tune, a favorite of Elise's *"Got to Be Real"*—and changed the atmosphere from intimate to *git down time.* It was now time to get funky.

_____

Across town in the deep silence of the first real snowy night of the season, Asia Reynolds woke up and sat down at her kitchen table in the comfort of her flannel pajamas and plush slippers, took a sip of steaming chamomile tea and opened her laptop.

She loaded her most recent videos of Joe Doe and local interviews containing townspeople's reactions to the loss of their Wi-Fi and local internet, and musingly listened and re-viewed all the film – making a few small edits and changing her file extensions to broadcast-compatible files. She could complete polishing her editing later in those formats with a larger screen.

She forgot and mindlessly looked for her emails out of a late-night habit. It slipped out of her consciousness that the whole town was still off-line, regardless of the fact that she had just viewed a film segment about that issue. She just dang forgot. That's how ingrained the habit was. Frowning she tried again to connect to the Net.

Zucchini got up too, padded over to Asia, and settled warmly on her right foot, curling up as best she could with her injured leg sticking straight out. Asia dropped the slipper off her other foot as she crossed her legs, she scratched her dog's downy fur with her toes as she brought her leg down in a stretch. Who needs a slipper? Her dog's soft mane was better by far than acrylic plush.

She powered down her laptop and closed the lid. She took her mind off the party at the Civic Center (which she really *did* want to attend) and put her bare foot deep into Zookie's fur, smooshing into her soft skin with affection.

After Zucchini's fight with Hunny, she really did not feel like going out into the snow to go to the party, which was deep inside the town center, and leaving Zookie alone while she fought with the slippery slush in the streets. No. Not really.

She would be at the Jamison wedding anyway. Asia looked out her back picture-windows through the entryway to the dining room. The snow was coming down just as heavily, if not more so, than it had been doing earlier in the day. Just as she had predicted, the snow from earlier that week had melted into a sheet of ice giving the picturesque present snowfall a treacherous underbelly.

The boys who had helped with the firewood, would be over to plow her driveway in the morning. They plowed all winter and shoveled her front and back pathways and the front and back verandas. They were very dependable, and she paid them well and usually had fresh homemade cookies and a hot drink for them when their work was done. They liked both coffee and chocolate – so she kept that for them, and some of her friends, although she herself didn't drink it.

_____

Zucchini staggered up onto her feet, whined a little and nudged Asia's hand with her large, moist nose. The dog went over to the back door and scratched at the floor in front of it.

"All right, my dear, sweet girl. I will walk you tonight. I want to watch you and make sure you don't slip and hurt your sore leg again."

The big Husky snuffled as if to say in indignation, "You don't trust me to take care of myself?"

Asia got her braided tie-dyed leash and put Zookie's slip chain on her neck. She pulled her knee-high gum boots on and took her parka off its peg on the back wall – not bothering to change out of her 'jammies.

Clipping Zookie's leash to her slip chain, she walked her limping dog out into what had now turned into a full-blown blizzard. The snow had risen from five to ten inches. It blew into her face and up under her collar onto her neck as well. She shivered as she looked at the hazy night sky covered with descending sheets of percolating ice crystals and snow. She blinked as the flakes scored her eyes and heard the roar of a snowmobile as it foolishly flew through the back fields braving the storm with the loud rising tide of hilarity that the first real snow brought out among the youth of Silver Lake. They shrieked along the trails like they were puppies.

The annual snowmobile race would take place when the snow was not in any danger of melting. She shook her head, loosening the snow on her shoulders. The temerity of the snowmobilers never failed to completely amaze her. They were great in an emergency, though. They tended to accumulate a lot of bravery and skill during their rides in storms like this.

The blinding dark and ferocious wind impacting the snow into her face and turning Zucchini into a round, moving white mound – did not seem like an invitation to risk the ungroomed snow sled trails and hazards of fallen logs. She thought she was already pretty adventurous slogging around in all this weather and snow with her dog on foot. The snow was now up to her calves.

She was startled when a large, overhanging drift of snow and ice from her porch roof slammed down right behind her and Zookie. Her dog practically jumped into her arms. Zucchini had taken care of her doggie needs, so Asia turned on her heels and went right back into her kitchen—to warmth, dryness and safety...giving thanks that the overhang did not hit either of them.

She added a couple of split cedar logs to the wood stove in the kitchen, dumped her gum boots in the boot tray—shook her parka outside on the porch, rubbed her frozen hands together and wiped Zookie down with a clean "dog" towel. Zookie clumped over to her bed and lay down with a large groan. "Not exactly spring outside—is it, baby girl?" commented Asia softly to her dog.

If Zookie could have said a few choice words and a loud *"No!"*, she would have. For a dog, she was sensitive to uncomfortable weather and would just as soon spend her time indoors, in her own home and her own bed...or Asia's. Although, she could express exuberant joy by racing around in the early snows with Big Boy or another dog friend. But not always and not when she was injured.

A deep, dark frozen night in the midst of mountains of snow would not be complete without the sound of the town's snowplows raking the curbs of the streets and clearing even the town's public dirt roads in the farming areas. And also, the sound of Sheila Rodriguez's police siren and her Mars lights cutting the darkness with red and blue and reflecting all over Asia's living room windows—turning her walls fuchsia and lightened indigo in turn. Flashing on and flashing off. Zookie barked once.

Sheila struggled up the unshoveled walk to Asia's front door and banged on it. She banged again. Asia opened the door still clad in her pajamas, with Zucchini at her side. She had even walked the dog in her night clothes. They had gotten a little wet but were almost dry now. Wood stoves tend to make air drier and much warmer than oil heat. Although Asia had the capacity to use oil heat, she preferred wood, since it was warmer and cheaper as well.

"Oh my god, Sheila, what is it?"

Sgt. Rodriguez hesitated and then asked, "How are you?"

Asia frowned and looked down, "Uh. I'm okay. I was just outside walking Zookie. I have a hole in one of my gum boots. Darn things are great—the best for water-proofing, but they only last about one winter of hard labor before they spring holes. My foot is still cold. Other than the fact that I am still defrosting from my short walk and I can't stand not to open my emails, I am fine. Is that all?"

A rough blast of wind moved a spray of wet snow all over Asia's night clothes and Sheila stepped through the door unbidden with her hand on Asia's shoulder and a laugh. She pulled Asia inside and closed her door against the wind, shoving a small pile of snow to the side of the door jamb with her foot.

Sheila took her SLPD parka off, shook it into the snow pile on Asia's parquet floor and shrugged her boots off into the tray at the front door. She rubbed her shoulders, then dusted the remaining snow off her fur police hat, hanging it on the coat rack next to her coat to dry.

She invited herself into the kitchen and set a wooden chair next to the wood stove with a loud sigh. "Just got off work," she said into the next room as Asia made her way into the kitchen—still with a startled question on her mind. "I spent the whole evening on a cheap walkie-talkie. I am used to a wireless ear bud. I had to spend hours of party time sober and using my eyes instead of a set of LCD screens and roving cameras. Just glad the whole thing is over. No fault of Elise's."

Sheila hesitated and looked out the kitchen window at the mountain of snow on Asia's windowsill which was due to get even bigger.

Asia grabbed a broom and mop and went to clean the snow that had blown in with Sheila at her front door. When she got back, she looked at her friend in askance. Sheila rubbed her face with reddened, chapped hands and responded, "Guess you want to know why I'm here." Asia nodded.

Sheila went on, "I just could not drive the last mile to my home. The snow, regardless of the fact that it had been plowed, got to me. The township will have to plow all night to get it all cleared. I don't think they can stop until those torrents of snow stop."

"You can stay here, Sheila. Anytime. You know that."

"Yeah. We are practically family. It doesn't hurt that we are the same size minus four inches at the bottom of your pants."

"You still have clothing stashed here."

"It comes in too handy to bring it home. If I remember correctly, I even have an..."

"...extra uniform in my bedroom," joined Asia with a smile. "All washed, ironed and hanging neatly in my closet along with your 'jammies, robe and slippers."

"Friends are heaven."

"Back at you. Want some tea?"

"Yeah, your famous homegrown Valerian, Skullcap, Chamomile combination."

"Sure. That is what I call 'Knockout' punch. Sleepytime brand tea is for nerds. Besides, it doesn't always work."

"As tired as I am, I can still use a push towards the pillow. A slow night still can produce too much adrenaline in a cop."

Asia put her teapot on to boil and got out two super-sized mugs that doubled as soup bowls. She prepared her 'Knockout' herbs, mixing them to a fine powder with a porcelain-coated mortar and pestle.

Sheila had taken her wet socks off and put them (temporarily) on top of the hot wood stove. She did not look like she needed anything to help her sleep. Asia could swear she could hear an intermittent blasting snore just as Sheila's head would nod. But she was always wide awake when Asia whirled around to look.

A loud banging echoed from the front of the house just as the teapot began to whistle. Asia swore a little and took Sheila's now steamy hot semi-wet socks off the stove. "Who the hell can *that* be?" said Asia with a little irritation and fear. "It's after midnight!" Sheila withdrew her service weapon and looked wide awake and alert.

"I'll get it," she answered. Asia was in no mood to argue.

"Get behind the basement door. Stand on the stairs if you have to."

Remembering this summer, Asia ran to do what she was told.

Sheila approached the front door with her revolver's safety off—pointing it ahead of her. She switched the light off in the kitchen and the hallway to the second floor. Moving in the shadows, she called out, "Who's there? What do you want?"

A man's deep basso voice answered through the closed door, "I am looking for Sgt. Rodriguez of the Silver Lake Police Department."

"Why? Can't you go to the department tomorrow? She should be there."

"I can't wait that long. Let me introduce myself, my name is Dr. Rainier Voss and I represent the scientists from NASA that Sgt. Rodriguez has contact with. We are responding to the intrusion emergency in this town."

A howling noise like the sound of a lone wolf accompanied a huge wave of snow and sleet slamming into Asia's living room window, painting it with an opaque icy white sheen.

A groan came from the other side of the door and the man's deep voice pleaded again, "Please let me in. It is terrible out here and I don't relish driving into the heart of this ice storm to find a motel in a town I have never been to before. I have some urgent news for Sgt. Rodriguez but the rest of it can wait until morning."

Sheila softened a bit but asked, "How do you even know Sgt. Rodriguez is here? This is Asia Reynolds' house. Do you have an ID that we can check? We have a landline. So, does the police station, so we can check your story right now."

The man did not hesitate and said firmly, "Yes. Yes. I have a NASA ID with me. And my Florida driver's license. I just came from the Almonte ranch and they said Sgt. Rodriguez was on her way here. She called from the station to let them know."

Sheila lowered her 9mm and opened the door. The man from NASA handed her his identity card and rushed in with a gust of solidly wet snow. He coughed and began brushing himself off, shivering. Sheila went into the kitchen to get the mop as she read his ID card. It seemed genuine to her. She told her visitor to sit down in the living room and dialed the police station. They confirmed that Rainier Voss, their late-night visitor from NASA, was the real deal and Chico Almonte confirmed that he had visited the Almonte ranch earlier looking for her. He had double checked with NASA about Voss's identity at that time.

Voss was okayed by NASA who knew he was in Silver Lake. They also gave the police department his NASA ID number, since they could not send a photo of him via inter-net. Sheila was then satisfied enough to ask Dr. Voss to stay with them and remain out of the still raging storm. She was in a state of shock that NASA itself had responded to their situation by sending a personal representative, since the police station really was not sure what had caused the problem in town.

Voss had a day pack with him with all his things in it. He said he had another suitcase in his car if he needed more clothing.

Asia timidly entered the kitchen when Sheila beckoned her. She meekly appeared from the darkened kitchen still in her ubiquitous, now rather wrinkled, green plaid flannel pajamas, said hello, turned the light on in the kitchen and plugged her coffee pot in, offering Sheila and Dr. Voss a cup when it was ready.

As they sipped their hot drinks in the living room, Rainier Voss's eyes kept wandering to the brand new Yamaha baby grand piano that Asia had bought recently. Zucchini snored from her bed near the kitchen's wood stove. Her occasional snorkeling buzz carried comically throughout the first floor of the house. Voss began to laugh, and tears of warmth streamed from his eyes.

Asia could not help herself; she began to like this guy. His big news was that NASA was pretty certain that the interference in Silver Lake was caused by a hacked satellite. He was the main scientist that had helped to confirm that at the space agency. He wanted to sit down with the townspeople of Silver Lake and guide them through the recovery process. There seemed to be more than just hacking involved with their situation, so Voss felt getting in touch with Sheila as soon as possible personally was warranted, since the other problems involved concerned the police more than the science community.

Voss's bright red cheeks glowed as he asked politely if he could play her piano.

Asia laughed and asked, "You play?"

"Yes," answered Voss, modestly. "A little. I love piano. That looks like a good one, too."

"It is," affirmed Asia. "Yamaha is a good, solid brand of acoustic piano with impressively full sounds."

The wind took on the persona of a wolf pack again and the old Victorian house rattled like an empty cage falling down a hill, thrumming in its wooden frame with each assault.

Voss sat down at the piano and rubbed his still reddened hands together as Zucchini limped over to Asia and sat down looking expectantly at Rainier. Voss played the opening of Rachmaninoff's Piano Concerto #2 Opus 18 with a vitality that took Asia's breath away.

Rarely had she heard prowess like this outside of a concert hall. She felt tears form in her own eyes. Before she had become a documentary film maker, her greatest desire was to become a concert pianist.

The Rachmaninoff made Asia's heart soar with each chord change, with each deeper and broader arpeggio. Zookie lay her head on Asia's thigh.

The dog looked up at her with fathomless, liquid golden eyes filled with the same pure joy that Asia felt. She acted as though she too loved this music. A tear dropped from Asia's eye onto Zookie's broad, soft, burnished head.

After about forty minutes, Voss concluded the Concerto. He had played the complete piece totally by heart, flawlessly as far as Asia could tell. She also knew most of this legendary, difficult piece, but not to play it by heart. She was delighted by the beauty of Voss's interpretation and talent.

She served some refreshments and had gone into the kitchen to secretly change the SD card in her video recorder which she had set up earlier – before Voss had begun the Concerto. She had recorded this strange, late-night meeting. She could and would get his permission if her taping got serious or she wanted to use it in a broadcast piece.

She always filmed professionally only by permission, usually contractual, written by her lawyer and signed by her notary. There was, though, a difference with a non-journalistic piece – if it was only for personal use. She needed to record what Voss was saying about the satellite hacking. She just lucked into recording his piano playing, too.

After drinking tea and eating some of Asia's delicious coconut-date tea cake, Voss laughed again and smiled at Asia. Sheila had fallen asleep on the couch and was still deeply and peacefully sleeping, despite the music. Rainier sat down at Asia's new grand piano again and played the opening to Tchaikovsky's Piano Concerto #1 which he had explained to Asia was his own transcription of both the piano and orchestra parts (which was necessary to play this piece solo on the piano).

Asia sucked her breath in at the precipitous beginnings. Voss was so incredibly good, that the house resounded with melody, drowning out the still raging, eerily howling ice storm like a concert at Carnegie Hall drowning out the sounds of the New York subway. Voss obviously had a dual profession; he was both a scientist and an incredible musician.

Zookie crawled underneath the sounding board of the piano and stretched out, her injured leg (dressed in the vet's pink, paw-print stretch bandage). The bandaged leg made a show of itself by sticking straight out from Zookie's body in front of the foot pedals. She seemed to really enjoy being closer to the heavy vibration of the music.

Chapter Five

Asia began to doze, her head falling to the side. Sheila was already sound asleep and curled up next to her. Asia had put enough wood in the living room fireplace and both wood stoves (in the basement and the kitchen), to last far into the morning. The thermometer seemed to have dropped to at least twenty below. The snow had stopped - it just billowed up with an occasional gust once in a while from all the drifts scattered near the road. Asia was sharing the afghan on the couch with Sheila.

The fireplace made her drowsy and her half-asleep mind fell into the Tchaikovsky like snow falling off the Ozarks into some deep ravine. She fell into a deep valley of sleep and contentment, a valley like the fulfilling of a long-held wish. Three quarters of the way through the Concerto, Voss heard what seemed to be three explosions on Asia's porch. Zucchini tried to leap to her feet, unsuccessfully, but barked anyway from her supine position.

__2:30 am__

Asia mumbled from her sleep, "Dr. Voss, I'll get it. It must be the door." Voss paled and looked frightened. His music had trailed off with Asia's comment. He looked at the clock and said, "It's 2:30 in the morning...It's a bit late for a normal caller."

Asia woke Sheila who took out her service weapon again and volunteered to answer the door. A loud voice came from the front of the house, *"Open the door!"*

Sheila shouted at the still closed door, *"Who is it?!* What do you want? It is too late. I am a local policewoman and I have a gun."

"We need to speak to Rainier Voss. We spoke to the SLPD and they told us he is here. We are CIA, miss. Open the door, please."

"Just a minute, let me call the station and check on this."

The police station confirmed that the two men at Asia's door were indeed Federal agents. Sheila was upset that the station had not called her first, before the men had gotten to Asia's. They apologized sheepishly, as Sheila gave them a lecture on correct, safe procedure.

Voss looked a bit desperate but straightened his back and put his chin up. He commented to Sheila as she walked past him, "They're supposed to be my backup. But I don't know why they couldn't wait until morning or at least call us via the landline here."

"We'll see what they want," said Sheila, opening the door. The two agents were dressed in deep arctic combat clothing—sub-zero hooded parkas and heavily padded mittens. It didn't help that they both had on midnight black balaclavas with only a slash of an opening for their eyes. Their badges and security photo IDs preceded them. Sheila was confused. So far, all three men had checked out, but why they couldn't wait until a decent, working hour of the morning, she did not know. Unless everyone was in more danger than she, or anyone else, realized.

The two Feds took their face protectors off, smiled at Sheila (who had been sleeping in her uniform), approached Rannie Voss, threw him on the floor, forcing his hands behind his back and his face on the floor. They bound his hands with plastic ties.

"Holy shit!" exclaimed Sheila. "What the hell is going on here? I thought you guys were all on *our* side. The *same* side."

"Don't worry, ma'am," said one of the Federal agents. "Dr. Voss is not under arrest just yet. This is a very dangerous, involved case. It is unfortunate that this is the only way we have of thoroughly verifying his presence. We have to restrain him for an identity check. There is much more to this case than hacking—there are matters of national and international security. You will be drawn into the loop later, Sergeant Rodriguez, but for now we have to do our own job. Sorry for disturbing you and Ms. Reynolds so very early in the morning. We cannot take any chances. I am sure you will understand, later."

Sheila nodded, frowning. Zucchini walked up to the three men and sniffed at the CIA reps, snorted and walked over to Asia.

"We apologize, Ms. Reynolds—we are here on special assignment. Our introductions could not wait. Sergeant Rodriguez, we promise to meet with you at the police station later this morning. Believe me, we'll be awake, and we will be there. The agent then bent over and ruffled Zookie's furry back. He said to Asia, "Beautiful dog. What breed is she?"

"Husky and German Shepard."

"Pretty combo."

"Yeah, she is. And I love her," answered Asia.

3:00 am

Suddenly, two more men walked in Asia's still unlocked front door with cameras and recording equipment blazing. Sheila said something profane, Asia looked dizzy and Zucchini pushed herself closer to Asia, almost under the couch, her pink bandaged leg still sticking straight out awkwardly.

Both men said loudly, at the same time, *"Chicago Tribune!"* They both wore Press tags on their coats. Both of them also forgot to close Asia's front door. It definitely let the cold, snowy early morning freeze into Asia's sanctuary.

"Oh, no you *don't!*" shouted one of the Feds, pointing his gun away from Rainier Voss and into the wide, scared eyes of one of the reporters. *"Outside!"* he shouted at them. "Back in your cars. You can interview us at a decent hour *with* our permission." The same agent walked over and pulled on the arm of a reporter, shoving him through the door. He grabbed the other reporter and did the same, slamming the door and locking it behind both of them.

"You'll see our news van in town, come over and talk if you want to. So sorry." shouted one of the Tribune reporters through Asia's closed door, apologizing. The two men pushed their way through the still unshoveled snow to their news vehicle. They hopped inside, turned their heat on and blew snow out the back of the vehicle in a rising fountain from their back wheels, plowing their way out into the quickly filling front road as the snow renewed its effort to inundate Silver Lake with powder. Wind tunnels shot gunned the freezing temperature at the foolish or suffering residents outside at this early hour. God bless the hospital workers, police and town maintenance crews.

3:30 am

Asia passed out on the couch as soon as she could lay her head down again. Sheila watched as the Federal agents pulled Dr. Voss out the door and into their SUV. Then, she went upstairs to the guest bedroom and threw herself over the bed, not bothering to change her clothes or even get under the covers.

She fell asleep instantly. The house buried itself in silence underneath the muffling effect of the renewed snowfall and the snow-covered roof of the old Victorian. The snow hid every sound—even seeming to blanket the memories of the confusing night in the sleeping consciousness of the two friends and their dog.

Dawn the next day

The sun rose in the morning sweet and warm. Not a late sleeper even today, Asia was up around eight o'clock. Not so for Sheila. Asia had to make coffee, an omelet and cinnamon rolls to let the scents of Sheila's breakfast wake her—which it did. Asia made oatmeal for herself. Sheila took a shower and put on the fresh uniform that Asia had stored in a closet for just such a day. She went downstairs towards the warm, enticing smells.

Sheila ate her breakfast and said, smiling at Asia's oatmeal, "I need to go right to the department this morning and straighten this mess out."

Asia responded, "Call me and let me know what the story is. I have to take Zookie's bandage off and call Dr. Steiner. I might have to put some vitamin E on her wounds, it's good for preventing infections even in animals." Asia paused and turned to face Sheila. She said, "Please tell Dr. Voss he is welcome to stay in my house as long as he is in Silver Lake and let me know when they release him." Asia hummed the beginning of Rachmaninoff's Piano Concerto #2 silently in her mind and smiled a little to herself.

"Okay," answered Sheila, looking curiously into her friend's smiling face. She put her SLPD parka and gloves on, sliding into her knee-high boots. "Bye!" she called over her shoulder as she walked out the front door.

The Silver Lake maintenance crew had done a great job clearing the streets. Jedidiah and Jeremiah Simmons, the two teenagers Asia usually hired to clear snow, had already been there. They had plowed and shoveled the front and back of the house. As a bonus, they had cleared the snow from Sheila's police car along with Asia's truck. Sheila drove off in a cloud of powdery snow—grateful to not have to clear her own car.

Asia bent over Zucchini and sat down next to her on the kitchen floor with a utility knife and a pair of scissors. She smiled at Zookie and gave her one of the dog cookies she had in her apron pocket. Zookie put her big head on Asia's knee.

Asia felt a funny sense of elation. She thought it was because of Rainier Voss's piano playing last night. It was the fulfillment of a dream for her to hear such a talent. She felt an urge to call Sheila and find out what had happened to him. But she knew she should wait until there was verified news of the man. She smoothed the velvet fur on Zucchini's head letting the Rachmaninoff roll through her senses again like the gossamer beginnings of spring – despite the much colder realities of the weather outside. It felt like the budding of her apple blossoms with the promise of their beautiful fruit. She glanced at the steamed-up windows in her kitchen as if she could see this right now.

She gently tugged at Zookie's bad leg and began to feel underneath the garish paw-print bandage and cut into the top part, gently working her way down her pet's leg. Zookie was so good, she only pulled away a little and made no sounds at all. Asia managed to get the entire bandage off and slathered vitamin E oil on the stitches, thinking that she had better make an appointment with Dr. Steiner to remove them. Asia rubbed the oil in deeper so her dog would not lick it off. Although, if she told Zucchini to do something, such as not bothering her leg, she would generally do as she was told. She was that smart. The stitches would be removed today anyway. She called Dr. Steiner and made an appointment for one p.m. and told her Zookie was doing fine and did not seem to have any infections.

The phone rang. Asia unconsciously looked at the kitchen table for her cell phone, and then suddenly remembered that it must be her landline—that she didn't need to search for her cell. She got up, stretched and answered her wall phone.

"Hello?"

"Asia. Hi," said Sheila. "I have some news for you."

"How is Dr. Voss?"

"Oh, he is just fine, a little tired, but he is who he said he is. His identity and assignment here has been verified by the CIA. Voss, the Feds and the Silver Lake police department are now working as one unified team. Feels real good to have that backup, now that we are sure who we all are."

"I see. that's good. did you tell Dr. Voss he is welcome to stay in my home for as long as he is working in Silver Lake?"

"Yes. He said he would be delighted to stay at your house. He will call you when he is done at the police department for today. He will be at your house some time tonight."

Asia felt a small thrill of joy and looked forward to more musical evenings. Zucchini whimpered a little and scratched at the floor in front of the kitchen door. Asia smiled, ran her hand down Zookie's injured leg, noticed no unusual sensitivity or open stitches and said, "Okay, sweetie. Stay in the yard," She knew her dog would obey. She opened the door and let her trusted companion out into the knee-high snow.

Asia got on her wall phone and called Dr. Steiner at her veterinary clinic. "Dr. Steiner?" she said.

"Yes, Ms. Reynolds. How is your dog?"

"Very well. No signs of infection. I don't relish going out into this snow this afternoon. I think Zucchini can wait a week or so for you to take her stitches out. The weather would have a chance to change, by that time."

"Well...okay. Just promise you will call me if Zucchini is in any discomfort."

"Of course."

"Is the same time, 1 pm, a week from today, Monday, all right with you?"

"Yes. Fine, Dr. Steiner. The vitamin E is working well, also."

"Wonderful. Bye, then." The sound of barking in the background of their conversation came through clearly on the phone line.

"Goodbye, Hannah"

Asia started baking one of her specialties: carob-molasses-walnut baking soda tea cake for another anticipated evening of splendid music with Dr. Voss. She called Chico Almonte at his dairy and asked if he could deliver a carton of his honey-sweetened French Vanilla ice cream by six o'clock when he got off work. He said he would do so.

Chico Almonte was a Mexican-American patrolman with the Silver Lake police department. He is the brother of Cisco and Julio and son of José Almonte, owner of the Almonte Ranch and Organic Dairy. Maria Luisa is his mother and estranged (divorced) wife of José, living in Mexico. She is also the mother of Cisco, Chico and Julio.

Sergeant Sheila Rodriguez lives with Chico at the Almonte ranch and is his girlfriend and intended fiancé. Chico, Sheila and Asia along with Elise Snuggles went through school together from the first grade onward.

Asia put on a CD of Vladimir Ashkenazy playing Chopin *Mazurkas* and the famous Chopin *Grande Valse Brillante* and *Polonaises*, followed by a favorite of hers: Daniel Barenboim playing Chopin's Minute Waltz, and another interpretation of the *Valse Brillante* with an hour-long recital of Chopin by Barenboim. She went upstairs to her third floor crawl space to search for her old sheet music.

She opened an old trunk with broken hinges and sorted through bunches of family photos and keepsake travel postcards until she got towards the bottom and began to discover her treasured collection of Mozart's complete sonatas numbers one through eighteen. She even found her piano transcription of Mozart's *Eine Kleine Nacht Musik*. She remembered how difficult it was to learn these pieces and how long she worked on them, never really satisfying herself that she was competent in playing them. But, never losing her love for this music.

As she pulled out the sheet music, she could remember the feeling of the counterpoint running through her fingers like silk. Her inner ear played each melody and harmony as her memories followed the dynamics of each piece. She could smell the musky scent of old paper and cloth and watched the cold sunlight travel through rising dust motes as she stacked the long-forgotten reams of music on the wooden floor of the attic.

She laughed a little in excitement and anticipation of the lyrical evenings this could produce. Zucchini walked in and bumped her hands with her cold, moist snout and lay down next to her, surprising her by having walked all the way up to the third floor for the first time since she had been in the dog fight.

She commented to the dog, "Feeling better, eh girl?" Zookie groaned in contentment and licked her hand. Asia then ran her hand gently down the dog's injured leg, checking it again, and saw that Zookie's pink scar was getting tighter as it healed. She kissed her dog on the head, closing the trunk. She picked up a large stack of sheet music and stood up, ducking her head to avoid hitting it on the old, exposed rafters of her roof. She made her way down the attic stairs and shut the door after her dog.

As she passed the hall window, she heard a loud buzzing whine and looked up—surprised to see a large helicopter drone with a camera flying up against her round third floor staircase window. She startled and almost dropped her music.

Zucchini growled and barked loudly in response to the drone's noise and tried to leap up at the window and bite the drone. But leaping was still too much for her. Asia caught Zucchini's large chest and steadied her, putting her down on her feet gently. This helped avoid having her dog lose her balance and fall down the stairs or come down too hard on her leg, injuring herself again.

As Asia and Zucchini reached the ground floor, her doorbell rang, scaring the bejeebers out of her after the intrusive sighting of the camera drone that was obviously spying and taking pictures of her. She thought of her 9mm Glock that was hidden in an end table drawer in the living room. It was loaded, with a full extra clip sitting next to it and a box of bullets. After her kidnapping last summer, she was taking no chances. She reached over and pulled it out of the drawer and stuck the gun into the deep patch pocket of her Victoria's Secret thick cotton robe. Zucchini stood in front of the door.

Someone knocking suddenly rattled the door impatiently. Zookie barked back impudently. Asia glanced at her wall clock. It was noon.

The rich, deep basso voice of Rainier Voss reached her through the door. "Ms. Reynolds—do not be afraid. It is me. I should have called first, but the lines at the police station were busy, so I decided to ride over here and see if you were home. The streets are pretty clear, so it wasn't difficult. In fact, it is quite picturesque out here. A real winter wonderland coated in a velvety white powder. As long as it is easy to get around, one can enjoy the sight. It is not something I am used to, being from Florida." Voss laughed his warm, deep laugh.

Asia quickly unlatched her thick oak, windowless front door and let her guest inside. She smiled at Rainier and gestured to the couch saying, "Take a seat, Dr. Voss." Going over to the fireplace, she put a couple of thickly cut logs on the smoldering flames immediately warming the large room.

Voss reached out for the sheet music that Asia held in her arms, and she put the large stack of paper next to him on the end table. She apologized for still being in her pajamas from last night and promised to make lunch and a pot of spearmint tea as soon as she showered and changed into her jeans and a sweatshirt. Voss smiled as he sunk into the large sheaf of music, starting to hum a familiar tune from the sonatas to himself and sorting out a couple of his favorites.

Zucchini lay down close to his left leg in a very friendly way. He patted her huge, fluffy head and gave her floppy, folded over ear a scratch. A great way to win her love since she greatly liked her ears being scratched gently. She tried to lick his hand.

"Just a minute," said Asia. "I will be right back with a hot pot of tea and some freshly baked tea cake. Then I'll run upstairs and get cleaned up and dressed." Thinking about the scary appearance of the drone she added, "I also have something to tell you." Voss looked up at her with deep concern written on his face.

Asia padded into her kitchen and put more wood into her kitchen stove, thinking she'd better run down to the basement and add some wood to that stove as well, so it would be nice and warm in her house until the evening. She let Zucchini out the back door again with the usual admonishment, warning her to stay in the back yard. She put her handgun in a kitchen drawer.

As she began fixing a tray of cut up tea cakes, she heard the beginning melody of Frédéric Chopin's Waltz #6 in D flat major Opus 64 #1, otherwise known as the Minute Waltz or *Valse du petit chien* (Waltz of the Little Dog) which she had not included in her stack of sheet music.

Rainier Voss was full of pleasant surprises. Including telling Asia the story of how he was named by his mother for Mt. Rainier in Washington state, and that she would call him "Rannie" (which was his nick name since Rainy was a bit too weather-oriented).

After Asia put out the tray of tea cake and the pot of spearmint, she excused herself and went upstairs to shower and change. As she was coming back downstairs after her refreshing bath, she noticed with joy that Rannie Voss was still at her piano, this time playing Pachelbel's Canon in D, another favorite of hers. Voss had let Zucchini back in the house, too, which Asia noted with added pleasure. She felt he was very considerate and sensitive to the needs of others.

Chapter Six

Later, right before a golden sundown lay itself down across the pristine, sparkling farm fields filled with snow in Silver Lake, the roar of engines broke into a quiet nap Asia had been taking upstairs. Dr. Voss had moved into her guestroom and was sleeping downstairs on the couch in front of the fireplace after making several phone calls. She groaned and went over to her bedroom window, looking out over her acreage in the back.

She saw a line of snowmobiles racing along the packed down snow trail (groomed). The township had provided this for the possible contestants of the upcoming Annual Silver Lake Winter Sports snowmobile race. She grabbed a camera, adjusted the zoom, opened her window and got a great long shot of part of the line of snow sleds. She yawned and sat down at her desk, resting her tired head in her hands.

Her doorbell rang and she groaned, making her way down the stairs. She got to the door just as Dr. Voss awakened. She apologized to him and opened the door to Jed Simmons who had a big, wide, gap-toothed smile on his face.

"Hi, Jed," greeted Asia.

"Hey yourself, Ms. Reynolds. I wanted to know if you wanted me to shovel the roofs over your back and front porches."

"Sure, Jed. That's a great idea." Asia smiled and looked out her door at a brand new bright red Yamaha Viper 162 SE. "Wow," she exclaimed, in admiration. "Is that snow sled yours?"

"Oh, yes ma'am. I just bought it from last year's savings. I want to compete in this year's race. If I win the race, I can pay my college fund back the money I spent on the snow sled. A beauty, isn't she?"

"Yeah, it is," Answered Asia.

"I can get around to my jobs a lot easier with that machine." Jed usually used Asia's shovels and equipment, so she watched the young man traipse around back to her barn to get the long-handled roof scraper, ladder and shovels. With a tired but warm feeling, she saw Elise Snuggles pull up to her home in her yellow Toyota Camry. She waited on her porch until Elise walked over to her.

"So, I hear you let the Chicago Tribune scoop me last night when I was the most vulnerable," said Elise, half joking, half not.

"*Really*, Elise. I didn't have much of a choice they actually forced their way into my living room through an unlocked door."

Elise snapped back, "You'd think after last summer, you would know to keep your doors and windows locked."

"Actually, it was the CIA that so carelessly left the door open."

"*Harrumph*," grunted Elise, indignantly, "*You'd think...*"

"One might."

"Anyway, I have news for you and your guest from NASA. Things are just getting nastier and nastier."

"I know, I was photographed through an upstairs window by a camera drone this morning."

"Yeah, people have noticed several of those things flying around town. We think they might be spy cams, if they are not just a teenage prank." She paused, then said, "I have even more news."

Elise made herself at home and chose a large over-stuffed chair next to the fire, hanging her coat over the back of the chair. "So, for the news," she said, leaning towards the now fully awake, upright Rainier Voss. "Someone passed counterfeit bills at my cash bar last night—big ones. We got at least two hundred dollar bills. We didn't want to change them, but everyone at the party was known to us and a friend. So, it felt funny to refuse them."

Voss's eyebrows went up and he leaned forward, his elbows on his knees.

"The counterfeit machines at the bank are still running and they caught it. They are on high alert anyway—so all hundred dollar bills are being checked for authenticity on their counterfeit machine right now. They advise larger businesses in town to get a machine if they routinely receive hundred dollar bills, and they advised smaller businesses to try and refuse large bills.

"They said they expected some fraud problems in this kind of atmosphere, without the safeguards that internet news and emails can provide. So, we are out the money for the drinks and also the change we had to give those people.

It is possible though, that they did not know that they were passing counterfeit money. In fact, since I grew up—worked with, or went to school with most of my guests, I am willing to believe that they definitely did *not* know that those bills were counterfeit."

Rainier Voss cleared his throat and spoke up. "The drones are something within my expertise. The fact that some of them can run without GPS or Wi-Fi is exceptional. They can run on visual alone, from an LCD screen in the controller. We cannot tell what the far-reaching effects of this blackout are until the town Operating Systems are changed and wired for invulnerability. Obviously, whoever is running these drones has the ability to exempt themselves from the blackout. That is not too unusual, since smaller drones can run on 2.4 gigahertz radio waves like a walkie-talkie. If the drone is built with a large capacity lithium ion battery, it can run long enough to give the operator a chance to hide. I will advise the local cops and the Feds to try and net one of these machines...literally.

"Shooting them down will prevent us from discovering what they run on and possibly who is running them. Although it might take NASA equipment to trace the drone back to its operator if it is running without Wi-Fi or GPS as I suspect.

"As far as the counterfeiting goes, we have notified the radio and cable stations to advise businesses not to accept hundred dollar bills. I was speaking to the police department earlier and Elise had already given them a heads-up about the counterfeit bills. True, we cannot stop these thieves from passing tens and twenties but making the public aware will slow them down on the hundreds.

"The combination of counterfeiting with technical skills (even flying customized drones) seems to point to gangsters, a large mob. I suspect an international connection, as well. It must be quite a challenge to take over a small town this way. It takes a lot of technical skill and money.

"We cannot tell the full effect of this attack, like I said, until the Operating Systems used in this town are repaired. As you know, Northwestern and the University of Chicago computer departments are working out a new OS for the people of the town already. It should be ready soon. The international aspect of this takeover is why the CIA is here. As well as, oddly enough, to protect me and anyone else who might have to travel to do research on this case internationally.

"Catching the IP address that this group is operating from is that much harder, since not only do they change their IP every time they broadcast—but, because of that, their physical location could be anywhere in the world. As you might know, an IP address is supposed to be the exact physical location that one operates a computer in. It is the internet provider's electronic address. NASA, though, has helped me equip the Silver Lake Police Department with new equipment they can use to more accurately try and capture their broadcast location or locations. Or help trace them anytime they use any kind of electronic equipment. The perpetrators' habit of leaving messages on computer desktops might eventually help us catch them. That is a useless and stupid form of grandstanding."

"Such as the drones," Elise broke in excitedly.

"Ah, yes," answered Dr. Voss. "But I must warn you, Ms. Snuggles, not to broadcast anything that either me or the Federal agents in town have not officially released to you for publication."

"Yes, of course, Dr. Voss. The Silver Lake Police Department has already explained that to me. I came over here tonight to invite you to be a guest on my late night show, *The Mississippi River Journal,* and I ordered dinner out from the Metaxas Greek restaurant. I ordered Souvlaki for the two of us and got Organic Soybean Stew for Asia from the Harvest Restaurant, one of the local vegan places."

Dr. Voss smiled and said, "I would be honored to be on your show, and I love Souvlaki. Just give me the time of your taping and I will be there."

Elise answered, enthused, "I will call you tomorrow about that. We will want you on this weekend's segment. This Souvlaki has a special yogurt-garlic and tahini sauce not just tomato sauce. I think you will like it."

Asia was relieved that she didn't have to cook tonight and went to the basement to put more wood in the stove down there and get some previously frozen vegetarian lasagna for tomorrow. Most of her friends could not tell the difference between that and the meat-filled version, and it gave them a fat and cholesterol break. She loved to watch people's faces when she told them that there was no meat, cheese or dairy in the dish.

Elise and Rainier Voss were deep in conversation when Asia re-entered the room after putting some coffee and tea on and setting the kitchen table. Voss looked up at Asia and included her in their conversation. He said, "I am going to spend tomorrow on the telephone to the SLPD, NASA and the CIA trying to coordinate our analysis and approach to this problem. There seems to be a general consensus that building our own satellite is the best solution. Since there is more than one dish TV company involved, that will help. Companies can always use an upgrade in their equipment and the federal government is also going to partially subsidize us. Any company that uses the satellite that we think is affected has been having some difficulty broadcasting.

"One interesting aspect of the case, especially for you Ms. Reynolds, being more familiar with the international scene, is that the federal government feels that there is a strong indication that one of our suspected hacker bases of operation might be the city of London. If they are operating from London, we still haven't a clue as to *exactly* where they are located within that city."

Asia raised her head towards the window when she heard a crack of thunder. It was nowhere near warm enough to rain, but it was not unheard of in the rural Midwestern plains and farmland to see lightning and hear thunder during a snowstorm, as well. Although, it was just a little unusual. The daily silence of winter was broken vociferously now. Occasionally, the snowstorm lashed a huge sound wave across the vast cap of a no-longer clear sky. The clouds grew quickly as this new snowstorm rolled in over the tree-lines from across the plains. Lightning flashed as the first snowflakes blew across the already drifted snow of yesterday.

Never a hearty soul during a bout of thunder, Zucchini whimpered and went upstairs on her stiff leg to climb into the bathtub (barely), where she would hide behind the shower curtain when she heard thunder or the sound of deer rifles too close to the house. The recent increasing roar of snowmobiles did not seem to bother her, though, which Asia thought was contradictory. But she was glad that her dog could stand that noise without being scared enough to run for the tub again or stand trembling with her huge 120 pound frame brushing up against Asia from behind her legs where she would go, like a puppy, looking for protection from any loud, blasting noise. She did not like to see her dog become frightened.

She had almost forgotten to work on her new documentary which was about the history of the Mississippi River in the Cape Girardeau area (their area). Even without the internet, she could still film, do research in the Central Illinois University library, the local library and historical societies and film interviews. She could also edit whenever she needed to. She missed researching online, but she took notes and those questions could wait for later inclusion. She was glad most of her work was not internet dependent. She also sold quite a few still photographs to the local and national newspapers and (unfortunately right now) on her own website online. But she sold framed photos at local camera stores as well. With the year 'round tourist trade that did pretty well on its own.

Her cameras worked just fine without Wi-Fi, but she would not have her usual backup technical capacity until the local wireless was repaired. This backup function sent video segments and photographs back from her cameras to her desktop or email automatically. Not having the backup was okay as long as she didn't lose an SD card or camera, which she was careful not to do anyway. Elise answered the door when their take-out arrived just as another crack of icy winter thunder made her jump a couple of inches off Asia's parquet.

_____

After a normal evening and a lovely dinner, Voss, Elise and Asia sat by the fireplace as Rainier explained that he had been on the phone all day researching new angles to their dilemma. It had been weeks since anyone had the convenience of wireless. Rainier, of course, got on Asia's piano again and played the first three Mozart Sonata's flawlessly. This time, surprisingly, using Asia's sheet music.

Elise left later, and Asia excused herself to get some sleep. Voss went on playing and volunteered to fill the house's two wood stoves and to put a couple of logs in the living room fireplace. Asia gave him a small hug across the shoulders, smiled to herself, relieved not to have to do that work, and went upstairs with Zucchini.

A group of cross-country skiers glided silently across a packed down skiing trail in front of Asia's stately remodeled Victorian home, sending a few crystal showers into the air behind them.

_____

The next day dawned full of sun and a fresh foot of new-fallen snow blowing up in Asia's face as she took Zucchini out to the mailbox with her. She looked up at the sound of a single truck making its way down the dirt road in front of her property. Jed and Jeremiah Simmons's pickup truck let their BOSS plow down with a jolt and started clearing Asia's circular drive, waving at her as they passed. Jerry jumped out and started shoveling the asphalt walk from the street (and mailbox) up to her house. She met him at her door when he was done, paid him for their work of this week, and slapped him on the shoulder, saying she would make both of them some hot chocolate.

Before they shoveled, she was able to get through the snow by letting Zucchini go first and using her as a sort of trail-breaker or animated "snowplow", walking directly behind her. Zookie made a great snowplow, hopping through the snow ahead of her. Rannie Voss met Asia in the kitchen still clad in his plaid robe and pajamas. He had made coffee, scrambled himself some eggs and toasted some of Asia's whole wheat bread. He had even remembered to make her some organic oatmeal, since that was what she liked for breakfast, not being an egg eater, which was one of the many vegan aspects of her chosen diet.

He had also filled both stoves and made sure the fireplace got a couple of logs too. Asia felt he must be the best house guest she had ever had, or perhaps an angel. She didn't need to do much for him other than show him where the washer and dryer was and give him some fresh towels. She was fairly sure Voss would wash, dry and fold *all* the laundry downstairs, not just his own. He seemed like that kind of guy. She had left some fresh linens on his bed yesterday and he had changed the bed himself. He was that gosh-darned helpful.

For a physicist, he had a bit of a glow about him.

Rainier did not disappoint. Between his advisory phone calls from NASA and the SLPD, he did all the laundry and also warmed the lasagna, a loaf of frozen garlic bread from her basement freezer and made a pot of Asia's favorite spearmint tea.

Asia had left with Zucchini to go to Dr. Steiner's veterinary clinic to get Zookie's stitches out and get her wounds checked. Dr. Steiner gave Asia the news that Frankie Franklin's St. Bernard, Hunny, was pregnant. She was a newly rescued dog, so her pregnancy was a surprise to everyone.

Frankie was glad she had gotten Hunny inside before she gave birth. She had taken the big dog in for her shots and Dr. Steiner heard the puppies through her stethoscope trying to examine the dog to see why she was gaining so much weight. She estimated that Hunny had about four weeks left to the big day. Frankie was glad Hunny was not over-weight and started making a soft, warm space in her living room for the new puppies. She began putting Hunny in her wood-heated barn at night to avoid any messes should she give birth. She filled an area with clean, old blankets to provide a space for the birth if it should happen out there.

When Asia brought Zucchini home, she was able to sit right down to dinner. Zookie lay down in her bed and licked her healing leg, which was still a little pink and scarred from the wound that Hunny had inflicted. Zucchini had been beat up by a big mother-to-be, who might have been using Frankie's dog Big Boy (a mix of Golden Retriever and New-foundland) as a surrogate husband/father. Dogs do things like that. The Simmons boys had witnessed the fight. She would tie Hunny and Zucchini close to each other (but not close enough to fight or bite) as soon as she could now that Zookie's leg was pretty much healed. Big Boy was spayed. All Frankie's dogs and cats were. So, the father of Hunny's puppies was a mystery presently...some dog in her past life.

As Asia put her feet up next to the fireplace after dinner, she heard a a loud braying noise. She frowned and fell asleep, exhausted by struggling through the snow and her long day, happy that someone else had cared enough to wash the clothing, make dinner, feed the dog and stoke the stoves. *Yay!* she thought. She had put the afghan over her legs and her hand under her chin and fell asleep sitting up in front of the crackling blaze of the fire. The plaintive braying started again and entered Asia's dreams, as Rannie Voss went outside to investigate what the noise was.

He turned on the outside flood light over the back yard and the barn, but a heavy winter fog had rolled over everything covering all visuals with a creamy whitewash that eluded reality. Even the way to the barn was an invisible obstacle course. Good thing the Simmons boys had plowed earlier and spread sand and gravel over the icy sub-strata. The braying seemed to be over by the barn, but Voss was afraid his feet might hit a stray piece of firewood or something else, so he put his arms out in front of him and waved them back and forth as he traced his way back to the house in a slowly blinded sort of way. He had seen nothing, and the plaintive call continued to shrilly cut though the curtain of fog.

Voss called the Silver Lake Police Department when he finally got safely inside again. He got patrolman Chico Almonte on the phone. "Any news from NASA?" Almonte asked.

"No, sir. The fog seems to be hiding some sort of animal out in back of Asia Reynold's house."

"What kind of animal? A coyote, wolf, buck in heat, horse, or dog from Frankie Franklin's place? Did you see it?"

"No. I couldn't see it. The fog was too dense. It sounded like a wounded buck or a frightened bear cub. I didn't want to get too close in this fog. It might be dangerous. I don't know what kind of animal it is."

"Sounds like a job for the Forest Service."

"I don't know their number."

"That's okay, I'll call them and send them over. If the animal needs trapping or tranquilizing, you will need them."

"Yeah, that's great. If it is an injured animal, I would want it taken care of right away."

"The Forest Service has access to a wildlife veterinary. They should be there within the hour."

"Wonderful, thank you Officer Almonte."

"You're welcome, Dr. Voss. I will be following them on Niño, my stallion, before I go home."

"Bye, then."

"Bye..."

———————

About forty-five minutes later, a green Forest Service vehicle showed up with its Mars lights blazing. They pulled around behind Asia's home. The loud braying complaint escalated in volume.

Asia finally awoke from her nap with the renewed braying and the sirens from the emergency vehicle. She hurriedly threw her parka, gloves and boots on and went out back. Zucchini followed her despite Asia's command for her to stay on the porch. Zookie had a way of trying to look invisible when she disobeyed, so she sheepishly stopped behind a large snow drift and peeked around it to see what was going on, hopeful of not being seen. After all, despite her uncanny intelligence, she actually *was* a dog.

The fog had lifted by about fifty percent, which was enough to see about three feet in front of one. Asia heard a guffaw ahead of her and frowned in confusion. She did not see anything funny about some injured wild animal hanging around in her yard. When she saw the two green-uniformed Forest Service officers and came face-to-face with (of all things) a rather pretty brown and tan, very cold and shivering, medium-sized female donkey, she got the joke. The guffaw she heard had come from the donkey. The officer with the tranquilizing gun put it away, and the other officer put a rope around the cooperative, but scared, donkey's neck.

The braying now made perfect sense, but who would release a donkey in weather like this?

Anything that small should be inside a warm stall. The mystery was how she got loose. Asia quickly opened her barn doors as the sound of hooves came up behind her.

Zucchini quietly and unobtrusively slipped into the barn behind Asia and stopped behind a large stack of hay, sneaking a peek like before.

Asia stoked the barn's barrel stove and lit it. She dried the little nervous donkey with some old worn out towels and put a thick blanket on her. She grabbed a square bale of barley straw and spied her dog hiding, laying down and shrinking from her as she looked away with a guilty expression on her fuzzy face and devious, squinting eyes. The dog refused to look directly at Asia.

Patrolman Chico Almonte walked in after he had tied his stallion Niño to a hitching post outside. Asia put a water trough near the burro who brayed again and knocked it over after a couple of sips. The donkey squealed like a pig. Animal Control promised to send a vet over in the morning, since the animal was really their responsibility until the owner could be found. They agreed to leave the donkey in Asia's care until the vet decided that it was a healthy animal. Asia tried to put an extra pony halter she had on the new animal who was having nothing to do with it, and almost bit her for all her troubles. Asia saw her coming and moved her hand out of the way too quickly to connect with those sharp donkey teeth.

Zucchini slunk forward on her belly, using Chico to hide behind. The donkey flared her nostrils and actually quieted a bit with a big sigh. Zucchini moved forward, sniffed at the now silent donkey and lay down between her and the blazing hot wood stove, putting her head underneath the stove bottom. It was one of those weird dog things, liking to be near a burning wood stove, even liking to stick her thickly furred head underneath the stove. Otherwise, Zookie panted throughout the hot summer season, being a long-haired dog. But, being near the hot wood stove seemed to give her an odd sort of comfort.

She once played hide and go seek with Big Boy in Asia's kitchen. Asia startled when she saw her dog jump up and start to land on the hot kitchen stove top with both her paws trying to get Big Boy's attention in a triumphant *"gotcha' now"* kind of a way. She got a very strange look on her face when she landed, got down immediately without yelping, and never did *that* again. Her thick black paw pads were not even scorched. It must have been doggie-mind-over-matter. Since then Zookie had been very careful around the stoves and never got close to burning her flesh ever again. She occasionally singed the hair on her sides, though, by passing too close to the stoves. But, outside of the rather rancid smell of burning hair, nothing was injured. The same when Big Boy was visiting. Both dogs were wary of the stoves. It was an issue that the dog owners, and parents of small children in Silver Lake knew all too well.

The burro walked over to Asia's large dog, nuzzled her with a good, friendly sniff and made gurgling noises, licking, delicately this time, at the remaining water in the plastic trough that Asia had refilled.

She now let Asia stroke her and put the halter on, tying the rope they had put on her loosely to a post. Niño, Chico's large, midnight black stallion, echoed the burro's gurgling noises with his own gentle huffing through the barn doors and pawed the ground as if to ask if he could get closer to the little burro. Asia turned towards Chico, who knew the entire town like the back of his hand, and asked, "Any idea who this donkey belongs to?"

"Possibly," answered the officer. "It might belong to Bertha Mason. She has a smallish dark brown and chestnut mule that might be this donkey's daughter. It is a lot like Bertha to have both a donkey and a mule. That is a little unusual for this area, but an interesting difference and a change from horses, cattle and chickens. As far as I know, though,

Bertha is out of town visiting relatives on the East Coast. If this is her donkey, she must have gotten herself loose and started wandering around town. I can ask around and see who is tending Bertha's animals while she is gone."

Asia decided to temporarily name the burro "Pumpkin" (which seemed to suit the animal's slightly orange sheen) until they found out who she was, since Chico did not know her name. She patted her and brushed her with a long, soft currying brush and made sure the pony blanket she had put on her was secure. The wood stove in the barn gave off adequate heat if one was heavily dressed. The barn was insulated enough to keep water liquefied if the stove was hot enough. Asia put more wood in the stove and invited Officer Almonte in for a cup of coffee or tea. Zucchini made no move to leave, so Asia smiled at her, patted her head and left her to comfort her new friend.

The donkey did not complain when Asia and Chico left and shut and latched the barn doors against what was now becoming a vicious winter wind. The night was filled with stars over the blowing snow and the silver moon was almost full, shining brightly over the driveway, lighting the way up to Asia's back door.

When Chico got to Asia's kitchen, he asked to use the phone. She, of course, said yes and he called Bertha Mason's home. She was not there, presumably she was still traveling. He left a voice message about the donkey. Until the owner was found, Asia said she would care for the little burro. She did not own a horse. She used to own a Shetland pony, so she had halters, leads, brushes and all the equipment needed for an ungulate of Pumpkin's size including a nice, little, light-weight red decorated pony cart she could use to exercise the donkey in the summer. Until then, Zucchini could keep Pumpkin company. Asia knew that if Zookie befriended an animal, they were friends for life. Zookie had a loyalty streak.

Later, that night, Rannie Voss and Asia settled in the living room and turned on the television to watch the *Mississippi River Journal.* Voss had recorded his segment in Asia's house earlier that morning. It lasted only fifteen minutes. Asia had been at Dr. Steiner's with Zookie and missed all of the wires, cameras and lights that KANU had crowded into her living room.

The theme music to Elise Snuggles *Mississippi River Journal* came on and the cameras focused first on the beautiful framed photos of the Mississippi river and Mingo Wildlife Refuge that hung on Asia's living room wall, which she had taken herself. The cameras refocused on Rainier Voss seated in front of a blazing fire in Asia's fireplace. The interview began with Voss giving the television audience a quick overview of his reasons for being in Silver Lake and his scientific credentials. Asia was shocked to learn that he was a former anti-government computer hacker who had learned his lesson in jail and been hired first by the FBI, later earning a Ph.D. in physics from Yale before being hired as an intern in NASA's satellite program. It was he who first diagnosed Silver Lake's problem as a hacked communications satellite. He first noticed that the satellite in question was not responding to his routine computer maintenance program. When he received a call about the problems in Silver Lake, he suspected that the two were linked.

On the *Journal* news, Voss mentioned the counterfeit bills floating around town and gave some information that Asia had not been aware of. He stated that the FBI and CIA had jointly been dredging a certain perimeter along the Mississippi river for counterfeiting equipment that the local police suspected had been dumped there.

He said that it would take a rather wealthy group of thugs to just dump expensive equipment like that, but that the SLPD had discovered some suspicious comings and goings at a local warehouse. The police found no equipment when they had raided the place.

The joint investigative agencies had found nothing in the river so far.

Elise asked Rainier how far NASA and the Feds had gotten with their investigation and wireless repair. He said that the new satellite was almost ready for launching from Cape Canaveral. The internet protections, especially the new operating system that the University of Chicago and Northwestern were working on was not ready for distribution. It would take at least another month to finish. By then, the law enforcement agencies working on the problem hoped to have the group of criminals that were perpetrating these crimes in custody. Then, it would be safe to launch the new satellite. The cameras faded out, away from Dr. Voss, and some guitar music was heard as the KANU logo canoe floated across the screen, then the camera shifted to Harry (the Hippie) Skylar launching into *Alice's Restaurant* and another song by Joni Mitchell, *The Circle Game.*

The camera then swung over to Elise who was sitting in front of a panoramic photo (Asia's of course) of the Mississippi river with the title and credits of *The Mississippi River Journal* superimposed over that.

Asia clicked the TV off, said goodnight to Rannie and went upstairs for what she felt was a well-deserved sleep. Zucchini left the barn through the dog door and Voss let her into the house. She went upstairs and hopped into bed with Asia where they both reveled in the comfort of each other's company and hugged each other in sleep.

No noise from the donkey in the barn. She must be learning to trust Asia and her dog and find some comfort in doing so.

Chapter Seven

Asia got up early and took Zucchini into the barn with her. Pumpkin seemed glad to see both of them and was very gentle with the dog. Donkeys are very sociable animals that are prone to loneliness, so making quality friends was a priority with the new animal. Pumpkin was careful not to step on the dog. She nuzzled her and made snorting noises. Asia noticed that the pretty burro had a bit of a hay belly from lack of exercise. At least she was not underfed, but this was not good for the health of the donkey and showed that the previous owner had not paid enough attention to her care.

Asia was hoping she could keep the little burro and planned on getting Jed and Jerry Simmons to make a small light-weight sled for her to take her out for short rides, which besides being a lot of fun, was great exercise for the donkey.

Pumpkin was young and strong and obviously was not averse to cold or snow. The Forest Service vet had given her a clean bill of health and some de-worming paste (which was standard). Asia pulled one of her hooves up and looked at it for herself. The donkey was really well-behaved, and her hooves were clean and well trimmed. Asia had seen all four hooves. She was obviously a standard-sized donkey and not a miniature, so Asia felt confident that she had the strength to pull her in a small light-weight cart or sled and also that she would enjoy walking alongside Zucchini who would want to go with them and not be left behind.

The dog and the donkey not only hit it off right away, they seem really companionable and Asia felt that they were bonding. She stroked the pretty burro gently on its head. The donkey nudged her back in affection.

Asia thought it was a good idea to get her out to exercise right away as soon as the sled was ready and the roads clear enough, with a small layer of snow for the sled—or perhaps they could use the groomed cross-country ski trail. Pumpkin did not seem to dislike snow and Asia could tie a rope to her halter and lead her around in the open area in front of the barn for some early exercise and fun. She accepted the lead and halter easily to Asia's delight.

Asia had gotten a load of barley straw and grass hay from a neighbor and this provided the donkey with some proper food that did not induce her to gain any more weight. Donkeys do not need cereals or grains such as oats, barley, wheat and corn. These are too high in sugar and starch for a donkey and could cause obesity and certain serious diseases. Asia was getting a delivery of dry, clean Timothy hay bales this afternoon. Pumpkin was expected to eat about 3.5 lbs. of that per day after she lost her hay belly.

This was not much, but anymore and she could suffer from over-feeding. Asia had another stall and planned on locking the Timothy in there so Pumpkin would not have too much access to it.

She gave Pumpkin a couple of apple slices for a treat. Her lips were soft. She was sweet and did not try to bite. After that, Pumpkin let Asia brush her coat a little. The donkey seemed to enjoy being pampered and brushed and made little contented noises which was a good sign and made Asia chuckle and pat her on the neck. As far as vaccines went, they would need to speak to Bertha Mason or whoever her former owner was if they could find them. She should not have been wandering around loose and that was now an issue for the Forest Service or Animal Control depending on whether or not they thought she was wild in origin. Obviously, she had been domesticated even if she was feral originally.

She had been moderately well cared for—her teeth and hooves seemed fine, although Asia would need an equine dentist to take a professional look at her back teeth. But her coat was in need of regular brushing and she seemed to exude a need for companionship. Donkeys can get lonely, and it seemed that Pumpkin had been that way for a while. In that sense, she might have been neglected somewhat, but she obviously had some good early training.

Asia heard the barn door slide open a little and turned to see a rather good-looking, blonde woman in a full-length, black, down coat and a thickly knit wool hat wave at her. Embarrassed by the sudden appearance of this stranger, Asia's first reaction was fear. All she could remember from last summer (which flashed back at her suddenly) was stranger danger. She faltered and dropped her horse brush on the floor and stuttered a weak, "Hello? Can I help you?"

She thought that maybe the woman had slid off the road in her car and was in need of a tow. Or a landline phone, since the cell phone service in town was almost useless right now. Sliding around on the slippery back-country dirt roads was a seasonal hazard in the winter.

Pumpkin's huge, feathered left ear wobbled towards the lady near the door like a radar dish, and the donkey moved closer to Asia as she slowly swung her head to look at the new woman. She made a moderately loud hooting sound like a baby elephant. It was half a bray. Asia laughed and stroked her again, commanded Zucchini to stay with the donkey for the burro's comfort and went over to the lady standing rather awkwardly by the opened barn door.

Asia pulled her visitor outside and shut the door so that no more cold would get in. Pumpkin didn't seem sensitive to cold, and she had grown a winter coat, plus the old pony blanket was tucked around her snuggly. But Asia did not want her over-exposed to any drafts.

The woman smiled and held out her gloved hand and said, "Let me introduce myself. My name is Lilah Aylward. I am the CIA operative assigned to security for you and Rainier Voss."

Asia felt suddenly depressed. *A beautiful woman like this? Her Rannie?* she thought. A stab from the green-eyed monster shot through her like an arrow. She longed for the soft, simple touch of her donkey and her dog and tried not to think of the warm, joyful evenings with Rainier playing the piano and his helpful, quiet, undemanding presence in her house.

Lilah seemed to notice the change in Asia's mood and said, "Rainier is still welcome to stay here, but I will need to work with him during the day. I must ask if it would be all right to sleep on your couch if things get rough. I will offer protection to you as well, of course."

Of course, thought Asia, meanly. "Yes, Ms. Aylward. You are welcome at any time," she answered hypocritically, without enthusiasm, hoping her real attitude did not show. Three's a crowd, she thought, looking at the snowy ground, not hearing a peep out of her now obviously contented donkey. She wished that she felt the same contentment.

"Would you like some coffee or tea?" offered Asia who could not help being hospitable despite her unwarranted feelings of hostility. She was Silver Lake born and bred and no one here would refuse hospitality to a guest or even a stranger who seemed to be caught out in the middle of a such a ferocious snowstorm.

"Oh, yes! I did not take the time for breakfast this morning. I wanted to catch both of you at home. I could use something hot."

The two women made their way into the warmth of Asia's kitchen. Of course, Asia offered Lilah some of her fresh baking soda coconut-date tea cake, without even a hint of bitterness. *Who was she anyway to feel jealous?* Rannie could not know she had a hidden crush on him. She anxiously rubbed her reddened hands together near the wood stove. *Now, he might never know how much she was attracted to him*, she thought, feeling like crying.

The bright warm kitchen drove the cold darkness of the winter morning away as the wind howled even louder outside, working its way up to another blizzard. Rainier came into the kitchen in his pajamas and began to fill the wood stove. He smiled at Lilah quizzically and began to fry some bacon, asking her if she would like an omelet. She indicted that she would. While he did this, he began to wash the dishes from last night. He smiled at Asia and looked with a question towards Ms. Aylward again who quickly introduced herself. Rainier did not seem any happier to see this representative from the CIA than Asia was, but did not show his feelings, except to Asia when she glanced at him when Ms. Aylward wasn't looking.

Asia made herself a steaming cup of spearmint tea. Ms. Aylward took some too. Asia sat sunk into a deep silence while they drank tea and ate the cake. Rainier set the table for the omelets and bacon. He smiled into Lilah's sparkling emerald-colored eyes. Asia got up suddenly and started washing the pots and pans, banging around with a lot of noise while the two of them ate. After all, she was a vegetarian and was satisfied with the fresh tea cake and tea for breakfast, and, maybe, a glass of Almonte organic milk.

The phone rang. Not used to the sound of the wall phone anymore, Asia startled and spilled some wash water on the floor. Felling like a clumsy dork and an uncoordinated idiot in front of the stunningly beautiful and elegant Lilah Aylward, she lurched to the phone.

It was Bertha Mason who sounded short-tempered as usual and a little put upon having to call Asia, whom she had never gotten along with. She considered Asia a lesbian because she never had a boyfriend that Bertha could recall, not that Bertha would know anyway. And Bertha did not speak to lesbians.

"Ah hear y'all got my burro," said Bertha in her Texas accent.

"Hello, Ms. Mason ... and, why yes, I do. We did not know who she belonged to. So ... she is yours?"

"Sure is. Eleanor escapes all the time. You'd think this weather would keep her indoors."

"Eleanor?"

"That's her name. She's named after an aunt Ah did not like very much."

Asia sneezed and then shivered at what she considered a rather inappropriate name.

"Actually, Ah'm downright surprised that she's stayed inside *your* barn. She's a real Houdini when it comes to barn doors and locks in general. Too much of a smart ass, so to speak. She bites through her lead and unlatches my barn doors all the time. Ah cannot use a combination or key lock because Ah lose the key and forget the combination. Slides away from me. Getting' older, Ah'm afraid."

Asia coughed and smiled to herself. "No, Ms. Mason, the donkey has not tried to escape. She seems happy here."

"Anyway, Ms. Reynolds, Ah've about had it with her. Either Frankie Franklin or somebody else has to adopt her or Ah'm going to put her down. At my age Ah cain't be chasin' her all over town. You have a cold? You keep sneezing and coughing. Is Eleanor sounding off and complaining a lot?"

"No to both questions. I do not have a cold and the donkey has not been making any noise. In terms of running away, I think she likes the exercise, fresh air and freedom."

"Well, thanks for your opinion, but Ah just want a day of peace and quiet and less of Eleanor's complaining."

"Donkeys do take some work. You can't just stable and forget them."

"You're just full of advice. Why don't *you* take her? You can do all the grooming and care-taking and try and keep her away from the door. She is, by the way, up to date on her vaccinations. The Animal Control wanted me to tell you."

"I would be happy to keep her."

"You just do that. Ah don't want no Forest Service or Animal Control bothering me just because she used to be wild. She ain't been wild in five years."

"I don't think the Forest Service will bother you if you let me keep her Ms. Mason."

"You're welcome to her. Ah might still want to visit her though. Regardless of what you thought of my donkey-caring abilities, Ah still loved her, the silly thing."

Asia was surprised at the offer of a visit and felt warmer towards her elderly neighbor. She said, "Of course, come over and see Pumpkin whenever you wish."

"Pumpkin?!"

"Oh, yes, we gave Eleanor a new name. We call her Pumpkin because we like her smile and she is a little bit orange. She sort of looks like she's smiling most of the time. It's her slanted eyes and upturned lips, I think. Also, she seems to have bonded with my big Husky Zucchini."

"I think you like squash ... Oh, yeah," said Ms. Mason, practically shouting into the phone due to her, not Asia's, deafness. "You own that dog with the funny name. Ah seen her around town. Beautiful dog – big as a small pony."

"Thank you, Ms. Mason. I think Zucchini and I will make a good family for ..."

"... *Pumpkin!*" shouted Bertha Mason with a laugh. "Goodbye, Miss Reynolds. Ah will sign the donkey over to you as soon as the Forest Service veterinarian contacts me."

"Thank you so much. Bye, Bertha."

There was a loud braying noise from behind Asia's house. She put her boots and parka on quickly, holding the door jamb for balance. To her surprise Lilah Aylward slipped her winter wear on also and followed her out to the barn.

Ms. Aylward said, "I guess your donkey needs you."

"Guess so," answered Asia.

As soon as the two women started talking outside, the braying stopped with a loud, wet-sounding snort. Zucchini ran past them and disappeared into the doggie door with a zip. Her feathery tail swooped in with a flourish just as Asia slid the bolt on the two doors. There was more expressive snorting from Pumpkin and a muffled bark from her new "sister".

"What's the matter, sweetie?" asked Asia as she and Lilah entered the barn. Pumpkin had a very expressive face and she looked forlorn at first and perked up as soon as she saw Asia. She snuffled and pushed Zucchini gently with her big nose. Asia gave the donkey a couple slices of apple, walked her around the barn for about twenty minutes, making her trot a little by running a bit herself.

Even though it was a gentle exercise, it was a good start for Pumpkin's mood and over-weight condition. The new sled that Jed and Jerry Simmons were making should be ready in a week or so. Zucchini walked next to the donkey as they went 'round and 'round in the large barn.

Asia brushed Pumpkin for a few minutes which made the donkey's coat shiny and silky. This finished cleaning up the mess that her coat was when she had first gotten to Asia's. It was obvious that Bertha Mason had not groomed her hardly at all.

Asia gave her some more barley straw and would feed her later (with a few pounds of Timothy hay) after some more simple exercise when she got back from her experiment with Zucchini and Hunny at Frankie Franklin's. It was about time to try and promote a friendship between the two rivals. Asia waited until Pumpkin was absorbed in her barley straw and happily munching away. She let Lilah (who was becoming kind of helpful and had a pleasant personality) take Zucchini outside and pack her in the back of Asia's double cab, starting the engine and warming up the Silverado. Asia grabbed a steel cable dog lead and Zookie's leash and got in her truck as Lilah scooted over to the passenger side.

The roads to Frankie's were slick and tough to drive, Asia drove slowly but still slid from side to side. It was a good thing Frankie's place was close by. When it became obvious that Asia was driving to Frankie's, Zucchini began to whimper and complain, acting skittish. She pawed at the window in the back. She never did things like this unless she was disturbed—and she usually liked to go to Frankie's because of Big Boy. Hunny had really gotten to her.

Asia pulled up in front of Frankie's house. Of course, Hunny and Big Boy came out to the truck first. Hunny growled and barked and jumped up on the truck in a very threatening way when she caught sight of Zucchini. Zucchini cowered under the back of the front seats on the floor of the truck. Frankie appeared on her porch and called Hunny who came to her obediently. Asia marveled at Frankie's skill at training even her newly rescued dogs—all her animals, actually. Her warm, affectionate, caring ways made them respond in a loving way, too. She sent a worried look towards Asia and put Hunny inside her home, shutting the door.

Big Boy came over, wagging his tail in a friendly way, and waited patiently while Asia and Lilah opened the door of the Silverado and jumped down. Zucchini slunk off the truck apprehensively and stood up against the back of Asia's legs, wagging her tail at the big super-sized Golden-Newfoundland mix, Big Boy, who was her boyfriend of many years.

Lilah Aylward sniffed and put her hand to her nose, commenting, "Whew! That big gold dog smells funny."

Asia laughed and answered, "Yeah, he spends almost all his time outside. He's smelling better than he used to. I know he smells a little like horse shit, but he's the sweetest guy you'll ever meet. A truly gentle dog."

"A *little* like horse shit," laughed Lilah.

Frankie came out and introduced herself, giving Lilah a quick hug and making a joke about her real name, which was Louise, saying she liked her nick-name "Frankie" a whole lot better. And, since the name was given to her by friends, it meant all the more to her. Big Boy went over to Zucchini and played with her, goofing around near their legs.

Asia brought out her light steel cable lead and tied Zookie to a post on Frankie's porch so she could get under the porch for shelter if she wanted to. Frankie shook her head but got Hunny and tied her to an opposite post just short of where she could have physically connected with Zucchini. The two dogs growled and pawed at the ground in front of each other but were not close enough to bite.

Hunny bared her teeth and got nasty at Zookie. Zookie looked at her with mild disinterest, climbed up on the porch and lay down, sniffing at Asia and giving her fisheyes of disdain and disapproval. Hunny went and did the same, minus the glaring fisheyes.

Frankie laughed and said, "Whoa! Guess this thing is going to work. I will feed Zookie tonight. Those two can stay out on the porch for one night. They are big and have heavy coats. I don't think the cold will hurt them, just makes their coats grow thicker.

Asia wished she didn't have to leave her dog somewhere else again, but it was important to make peace between Hunny and Zucchini. The fighting between the two dogs had to stop and stop now. She said she would pick Zookie up the next day. Frankie said she would call if there was anything that she needed Asia for.

Asia answered, "Sure. Looks like they'll be okay, though. When they lay down and just look at each other like that, it is close to making peace. Next, they will try and lay next to each other, then you know they are getting friendly. When they are loose again, they might even play a little with each other. Just make sure you leave Big Boy outside, so they learn to share him. Right now, they seem okay sharing his attention. The best thing would be if Hunny lets Zucchini get near her puppies when she gives birth. I pretty much think she'll let Big Boy care for them and puppysit."

"We'll hope for the best," said Frankie. "By the way, I heard that you adopted Eleanor, Bertha Mason's bad-girl donkey. She never looked after her properly anyway. Her age is no excuse. I'm ten years older than she is. Her health, though, I guess, is an issue."

Asia tensed a little when Frankie insulted her new, sweet donkey. She answered, "We call her Pumpkin now, and she seems happy. Zucchini spends a lot of time with her and they have become buddies. I might even sleep out in the barn until Zucchini gets home."

"That reminds me," said Frankie, blinking up at the snow that was still falling. "Have you seen, uh, Pumpkin's little bitty friend yet?"

Asia registered surprise.

"That donkey never goes anywhere without her little Fuzzy Bud, even when she runs away."

"Her *what?*" responded Asia. Lilah started to laugh at the funny name.

"Fuzzy Bud is the puppy that Bertha got for Eleanor-Pumpkin. I'll bet she shows up. You'll love her, she is the cutest little long-haired Chihuahua in town. Not that there are that many."

"She can get through all this snow?" asked Asia, concerned for the little thing.

"Oh, sure, she follows the donkey everywhere. If a fox can jump through this snow, little Fuzzy Bud can do it, too. Just keep your eye out for her. She is sure to show up. You know donkey's get lonely. I guess Chihuahua's do too."

Asia smiled and nodded, worried she might have to break up a friendship, Bertha might want Fuzzy back if she showed up at Asia's barn. She and Lilah petted Zookie good-bye for now and got back into the Silverado, slipping and sliding their way back to Asia's despite Asia's new studded tires which cost her enough. Nothing, including chains, seemed to work on these icy back-country dirt roads.

Pumpkin was silent when she parked the truck and got out to see Jedidiah Simmons plowing her drive and Jeremiah cleaning her walks and porch roofs again. Jedidiah yelled at her from his plow truck, "Watch for the little red fox! I saw it about an hour ago."

"Oh, okay, Jed, I will," yelled Asia back at Jed as she went inside her home. Lilah said goodbye and got in her government issue SUV, taking off for her motel.

That evening, Dr. Voss was playing from Asia's Mozart collection when she started reheating some of the vegetarian spaghetti with soy nuggets that he had made. Rainier was adapting to Asia's vegetarianism by liking all-vegetable or vegan meals from time-to-time. He was a pretty good vegetarian cook, she had to admit. His use of spices was exquisite. He had made soy "meatballs" perfectly. He was a sort of vegetarian *Cordon Bleu*. Such a sensitive, considerate gentleman.

Asia had told him where the rest of her sheet music was up in the attic on the third floor. It sounded like he had found her music to Beethoven's Piano Concerto #5, the *Emperor* Concerto which she had a fantastic transcription to since it was usually played with an orchestra. She had a great recording of it with a young Vladimir Ashkenazy playing with the London Philharmonic Orchestra. Rainier Voss was in fine shape this evening and was obviously painstakingly careful with the breathtaking dynamics of this wonderful piece, without which the concerto would sound like mush in Asia's opinion.

All was quiet this snowbound evening except for the resounding music coming from Asia's Yamaha. She had been out to the barn and found Pumpkin contented and quiet, already laying down with her head on the ground. She got up when Asia came closer and nuzzled her when she brushed, stroked and gave her a hug. Asia had no plans to use a bit with her, only a soft halter which she was having a crafts person custom make for Pumpkin. She knew donkey's needed REM sleep and was glad Pumpkin was comfortable enough to lay down and put her head on the blanket. It was surprising since donkeys generally will not fully lay down unless they are sleeping with a companion.

There was a rustling noise in a back stall. Asia just assumed it was mice nesting in a warm, dry place in some hay like they did every winter, to have lots of mice babies. To boot, it was snowing again. Asia would have to walk Pumpkin in the barn to exercise her. She wanted a local farrier to put new winterized shoes on her donkey so she could grip the snow a little better. And, of course, trim and file her hooves. The sled and halter should be ready in a couple of days. Pumpkin was only 12 hands high which was big for a standard donkey, but too small for anyone but a child to ride.

She was big enough, though, to pull a lightweight cart and sled even with Asia in it. She had very thick strong legs. The back stall rustled with activity again. Asia made a mental note to get some mouse traps.

Rannie was upstairs asleep when she got back in the house. She did the same as the new snow lay a blanket of deep quiet around her home. Rainier had stoked all the stoves for the night and Asia smiled to herself as she dug underneath her quilts. The moon rose in an almost clear sky and seemed to throw hundreds of stars around it like a wreath.

When Asia went to pick up Zucchini the next day, she felt ecstatic to get her dog back. The Annual Silver Lake snowmobile race was starting this afternoon. The weather was clear, although there was still a light snow and snow blowing up from the ground and drifts. Zookie was glad to see her. She had been laying right next to Hunny. Hunny was glad to see her too.

The St. Bernard was a beautiful dog. Frankie had taken some time to brush her which brought out her natural red color and made her thick winter coat silky and shiny. Frankie came outside and waved at Asia as she went over to Hunny and unclipped her from her lead.

Asia did the same for Zucchini, giving Frankie a worried look. She needn't have worried, though, the two dogs ran around in the new snow side by side and played a game of tag together. Obviously, they were now friends. Asia was relieved and surprised. This process usually took up to about a week or more of separation. But Frankie was an unusual soul and an immensely gentle handler. She had told Asia that she had sat down and given Hunny a long talk about what she expected of her. She and Asia both believed that animals could understand far more language than most people thought they could.

Frankie gave Asia a hug and left to go to work at her rib joint. Even at around eighty, Frankie still worked at her family's small but popular take-out. She was a spit-fire of energy. She had fed the dogs, including Zookie, and took off in a spray of snow in her pickup.

Asia gave Hunny a hug and ruffled her back. The big dog licked her hand and put a large paw on Zookie's back as if to say, 'We're friends now.' Zucchini hopped in the back of Asia's double cab and they made their way home. Asia went into her barn to exercise and feed Pumpkin. Zucchini went with her. She put Pumpkin on a long rope and lead her around in a circle inside the barn.

She still used the pony halter, but it was a little too tight on the donkey's large head, so she would be glad when she got the new custom halter. She cleaned Pumpkin's area and gave her fresh water. She readjusted Pumpkin's blanket and stoked the barn's barrel stove. The farrier had been there this morning when she was at Frankie's, so the donkey's hooves were freshly filed, clipped and cleaned. Her new "winterized" shoes were nailed expertly onto the burro's newly groomed hooves. The farrier was well-known to Asia, so she trusted him and would mail him his fee.

She felt Pumpkin could take a short walk outside down her driveway and on the cleared road in front of her house. She looked for Zucchini who had disappeared somewhere in the back of the barn. She called her to come with them, but the dog had disappeared—maybe she had gone outside already. Asia frowned and secured Pumpkin's blanket again, leading her to the barn doors. She opened the doors, called Zucchini again and led the little donkey outside.

The donkey ran a very short distance and kicked sideways playfully. She seemed happy to get outside.

Asia jogged to the front of the house with the donkey running beside her. The small ungulate definitely did not seem averse to the cold or the snow. She seemed to like it and was enjoying her romp down the road. The donkey's blanket and halter were bright red and Asia had put a bell on the halter, so the little burro was a cheerful sight.

Since Pumpkin had a reputation for running away, Asia thought this was a wise idea. The bell was new, but the blanket and halter had belonged to Asia's old Shetland pony who Asia had gotten in her youth and had lived many long years, passing away at the age of twenty-five. Asia was also going to microchip Pumpkin as she had done with Zucchini, just in case she wandered off or was stolen.

Zucchini mysteriously had not shown up for their morning jog, so when Asia and Pumpkin got back to the barn, Asia got a little concerned when Zookie was still nowhere in sight. She called for her dog again and used her silent dog whistle. She heard Zookie whimpering somewhere near the back of the barn, as if she couldn't move. The dog sounded like she was very upset. Then, she heard a very tiny bark. Going to investigate, she saw Zucchini with a very small, very red, fox who was cowering in some hay in the back of the stall.

Zucchini stood between her and the fox. Asia tried to get her dog to move away, but Zookie would not budge. Asia was concerned about Zookie getting bitten and maybe contracting some disease or just getting hurt again. Although, she had to admit that the two animals seemed to be friends and Zucchini seemed to be protecting the fox from *her*, not the other way around. Thinking she would call Fish and

Wildlife in the Forest Service to trap and release the little fox, she walked towards her house, musing.

As soon as she got inside and put her boots in the boot tray and her parka on a hook, her phone rang. It was Bertha Mason. This woman seemed to be psychic. She always knew when Asia had just arrived home.

"Yes," asked Asia.

"Ah heard my little Fuzzy Bud was seen around your yard."

"Your *what?!*" exclaimed Asia, puzzled, not remembering her talk with Frankie.

"Fuzzy Bud is my Chihuahua. She actually belongs to the donkey. They are inseparable. The dog is only six months old. Eleanor used to have a horse to keep her company, but the horse died, so Ah got her Fuzzy Bud and it seemed to make her happy."

"There was a small red fox around here," answered Asia. "In fact, it got into my barn through Zucchini's dog door. The door is purposely kind of difficult to push open, but the little fox did it."

"Was the fox red?"

"Yes."

"That's probably Fuzzy Bud. She is a long-haired Chihuahua and bright red. She is often mistaken for a fox—but if you look closely, you can tell she is just a dog. Well, congratulations Ms. Reynolds—you have inherited my dog along with the donkey. I don't think you can break them apart. They are practically relatives. That donkey really likes her dogs. I think she thinks she *is* a dog."

Asia smiled and said, "Okay, Ms. Mason, thanks for telling me. I almost had the Fish and Wildlife people pick her up. That would have been an embarrassing mistake. I will go out to the barn and check again, but I think that must be Fuzzy Bud."

Okay, so now you know. Glad Ah called to give you a heads-up. Don't expect Fuzzy Bud to sleep anywhere but with the donkey."

"Thanks, I won't. I'll go out and check on the situation right now. Bye, then."

"Bye."

Asia went to her back door and called for both Fuzzy Bud and Zucchini. They both came running together this time. The tiny Chihuahua and over-sized Husky made a comic pair. Fuzzy hesitated at the door while Zucchini went right in. Fuzzy Bud then turned around and headed back to the barn.

She sure did look like a fox.

"Hey Fuzzy!" called Asia, hurriedly putting on her boots and parka and following the little dog back to the barn where she was headed. She watched her push her way in through the dog door with an unusual amount of determination and gusto. Asia followed the minute puppy into the barn, grabbed a clean pony blanket and put it down near Pumpkin who squealed with happiness when she saw the little red dog. Fuzzy was not much more than a puppy and lay right down on the folded, warm blanket.

With the additional heat from the barrel stove, it was warm enough for Asia to sleep there too. Pumpkin lay down next to the Chihuahua and put her head on a corner of the dog's blanket, closing her eyes. Asia laughed and went back to her house.

She had planned on going out to her cabin today with Zucchini to watch the start of the Annual Silver Lake Snowmobile Race. But before she packed Zucchini into her truck, she put out a bowl of fresh water and some dry food mixed with wet food for the new puppy who was not shy or hiding anymore now that she was sure Asia would not drive her away from her donkey friend.

Not a problem. Asia had taken a liking to the tiny red dog. She would not deny Pumpkin anything. Everyone who knew her knew she loved that donkey and would do anything she could for her.

Rainier could not come. He had to stay close to the phone. He promised to make dinner and perhaps call Lilah Aylward to drive him over to the cabin later. Asia told him that she might be back that night or possibly stay over until the next day. She would be back to feed and take care of the donkey and the new puppy, although Dr. Voss said he could do that for her if he couldn't make it out there. He seemed interested in the new dog and said he would go out and take a look at her.

Chapter Eight

Asia was glad to get to her cabin. It had been a full year since she had seen the place. She had brought her cleaning equipment. Good thing, too. The cabin needed a thorough sweeping and dusting. She needed to turn the water back on and let it run in her tiny rustic bathroom sink, shower and kitchen. She lit the wood stove so that the entire cabin was warm and cozy by the time she turned the water on.

She was happy that the Simmons boys had brought two cords of nicely cut and split wood small enough to fit her miniature *Jotul* stove. They had stacked it neatly on her porch and covered it with a heavy tarpaulin so that the wood had remained relatively dry. She stacked an armload underneath the now roaring stove.

It would dry out even more under the stove, but it was not close enough to the stove to alight. She smiled again because the Simmons brothers had kept the road to the cabin open as she had asked them to. She warmed a bean stew on the wood stove and sat down to eat after feeding Zucchini and filling a bowl with dry Science Diet kibble. She could hear the roar of snowmobiles in the distance. The cabin was only about twenty feet from the groomed trail that the contestants would follow. The sound of the snow machines was getting louder and closer.

The stew tasted superb. Rannie had prepared that and some organic, heritage cornbread for her, plus some Apple Betty for desert, as well. She blessed him. He was the only visitor she had ever had (including her childhood friend, Sheila Rodriguez) that had cooked, cleaned and tended her animals for her, at least in her own home. Her friends would do those things but only when she was being pursued by a bad guy and staying in *their* homes, or sick, not simply because they were there so much, which they were.

Dr. Voss was faithfully looking after Fuzzy Bud and Pumpkin for her while she was watching the racers pass by and staying in her cabin for a short time-out. She set a rocking chair by the side window facing the snowmobile trail.

Two little boys about eight and nine years old respectively, chased each other in the snow, yelling and falling over, laughing loudly. One of them started pulling the other on a sled, turning around occasionally to throw snow at the little boy in the sled—both of them still laughing.

The boy pulling the sled, Izzy, pulled his younger brother up a hill and got into the sled too, snuggling close to his little brother with one of his arms tightly wound around the other boy's waist, his legs on top of his brother's legs, toboggan style. Izzy pushed off the top of the tall hill with one arm and the two little boys went whizzing down the hill towards their home. It was a great ride.

The snow was packed down due to other kids on sleds doing the same thing. It was not the same trail that the race was to take today, but it was close by. It was slick and perfect for a ride in their smooth-bottomed sled. Both boys were hungry, and their mother would be making lunch soon.

They screamed with delight on the way down and hit a soft snow drift at the bottom of the hill. They jumped off the sled and chased each other around to the other side of the snowbank.

Tuffy, Izzy's younger brother, yelled, "Look, Izzy! *Look!!* A snow angel! Someone made a snow angel!"

"Aw, Tuffy, someone just laid down in the snow here. Don't know who would do that. It ain't nothin' much."

"Yes, it is! Don't matter what you think. It's good luck! Come here and look! Wow, Izzy, the hole is so deep, wonder how he did that? It was a big guy, maybe a grown up, too. The snow angel's real big."

"Lemme see, Tuff..." replied Izzy as he shoved himself through the deeper drifts at the bottom of the hill.

A loud scream made Izzy jump a full foot above the snow. He yelled, "*Tuffy! What's wrong?!*" He ran to where Tuffy stood over the snow angel. Tuffy whispered to his brother, "There's someone down there, Izzy. See, look, you can see his boots—over there." Izzy gasped when he saw the buried man's legs in the bottom of the snow pit.

He turned to his brother and said, "Come on Tuffy, we gotta tell mom or someone. *Come on!* I'll pull the sled. You think he's dead?"

"Yeah. No one could lay in this cold, wet snow for that long unless he was dead."

"Maybe he is just knocked out." Izzy threw a small rock at the man and yelled, "*Hey, Mister!* You still alive?" The man did not move. Izzy reached down in the hole and put his hand over the still man's face after sweeping away some of the snow over the man's unmoving body.

There was no breath. "Yeah, I think he's dead all right. Let's go home and have mom call the police." The two children held each other's hands and walked to their house which was not far. The smallest child was still shaking with fear.

Izzy turned to his little brother as they walked into their home and said with a cynical tone of voice, "Some good luck that was, Tuffy! A dead man?" His little brother shrugged his shoulders, answering, "I thought you would think I was just being a baby getting excited about a snow angel thing."

His brother swung his arm around the smaller boy and said, "Naw, Tuffy, I wouldn't call you a baby. You're my best friend." They tromped into their kitchen after taking off their wet snowsuits and boots.

The sound of an emergency helicopter broke through the noise of the passing snowmobiles next to Asia's cabin. She was querulous at the sound. The machine landed, lights flashing, near Izzy and Tuffy Ritter's house, which was also close to the cabin. Zucchini started barking. Within a half hour, a knock came at the cabin door which made Zookie start up again. Asia called out, "Yes? *Who is it?*" a little fearfully.

"Ms. Reynolds? We're from the State Police. May we come in? We need to ask you a few questions."

Asia opened the door and let the two State cops inside. They seemed happy to warm up near Asia's wood stove and gladly accepted her offer of some hot tea. She kept some Earl Grey tea in the cabin kitchen for such occasions.

"What is the problem officers?" Asia inquired after the two men had warmed up.

"Ms. Reynolds, have you seen anyone walking around here recently?" asked the smaller of the two men.

"No. No one," answered Asia.

"Any children?"

"No. I have only seen the racers on the trail. No pedestrians."

"Trucks? Other, off-trail vehicles, snow sleds not on the trail?"

"Nothing. I have only been here since this morning, though."

Both officers looked at each other.

"What happened?" asked Asia.

The larger policeman looked at her intensely and answered, "Two kids found a dead man in the snow near here."

When Asia recovered from her shock, she asked, "Were the two kids Izzy and Tuffy Ritter? They are the only children that live near here."

"Yes," answered the smaller cop. "They were playing on their sled and found a frozen corpse at the bottom of a hill."

"That's terrible. I hope it doesn't traumatize them."

"Their mother called it in. Seems they prefer to play video games since the sighting."

"I don't blame them," responded Asia, shaking her head.

A fine-looking man with long, dark curly hair sat in a custom designed chair molded specially to his own back.

He wore two diamond stud earrings and a dark Armani suit jacket with khaki pants. He faced a wall covered with six large screen TVs being used as computer monitors. He was one of the world's most infamous computer hackers and was wanted by almost every national security agency in the Western world and some Eastern security agencies as well. He tended to listen to Opera when he worked and used headphones so as to not disturb his crew or pilot and also to keep his enjoyment of this media to himself. This afternoon he was listening to Giacomo Puccini's *Madama Butterfly* with enthusiasm.

This setup was airborne and so helped the cartel escape detection. The man at the computer was the mega-wealthy hacker Jake *"The Joker"* Wheeler. He was programming another worm that would infect major targeted cities and take down their wireless internet. Silver Lake, Illinois was only a trial run for an even larger cyber assault.

Jake was angry and getting angrier by the moment as he sipped his hot espresso. Why on earth drop a dead Team member right in the middle of Silver Lake so the locals (and the cops) would all know there had been a murder?

He was secretive by deep inner nature. He had hidden the full spectrum of his computer skills from everyone except a very few, trusted—usually life-long—friends. His family only knew he liked video games and could build a computer and program applications, all of which he had done since he was a young child. Because of his talent, he had inherited over a hundred million pounds Sterling from a supportive and admiring grandparent. He had made even more from his illegal enterprises. His wealth had bought him worldwide freedom. He smacked his lips again on his imported Greek espresso. He never used anything unless it was what he considered "the best".

He felt that dropping a dead man in Silver Lake was a violation of his secrecy policy and vowed to terminate the men aboard his private jet that were responsible for this mistake. They would have no more fun with *his* money and their payments from all their embezzlement activities would also end. His plane would also have to be broken down as soon as possible and sold for parts after all the identification was removed. He could not afford to have his plane traced.

He was not sorry for losing this jet, because he could upgrade and buy something newer. There were other planes flying over Silver Lake, including the private jets of wealthy vacationers who came to Silver Lake for the winter sports, but had to land in St. Louis or elsewhere because of the wireless blackout. The fact that there was still plane traffic over Silver Lake was Jake's only protection.

Jake was frustrated at his loss, anyway. He was obsessively careful about his possessions. He never permitted waste, even in his kitchen. When he got back to his private air strip, he would have to start hiring to fill the positions he would lose when he let those responsible for dumping this Team member over Silver Lake and creating a security risk by doing so.

He was furious about it. Maybe those responsible just wanted to piss him off. He thought so. He would get them back for it. He would.

He saw his reflection in his closest TV monitor, smiled at himself and loosened the large diamond and turquoise clasp on his string tie. The last act of the opera began increasing his usual joy while programming something new. He was wearing a black silk shirt that had nice temperature flexibility with the strange shifts in air pockets that occurred while flying, despite the jet's climate control. When he finished his espresso, he pushed a buzzer and a Team member approached him with a questioning air. Jake said, "Sit down and finish building this worm. It will build itself but will ask you the usual questions to proceed. Just answer the screen as usual. I need to shower and eat some lunch. It should be finished programming itself by the time I get back."

He patted his stand-in on the shoulder despite his revulsion towards this worker who had deliberately not pulled him into the loop about dumping a body they could have discretely put into a deep freeze and flown back to their home base in Europe. The man who was killed was obviously suspect among some Team members.

That did not mean he had done anything wrong. No one had asked him about committing this action. So, he thought some of his volubly discontented Team members had allegedly committed the murder.

The stand-in sat down and adjusted his loose, gray designer jacket, sitting up with interest as he observed the worm creation program that Jake Wheeler had designed. No one, except Wheeler, knew the inner workings of the complicated program. Not one programmer in his personal Team could even guess. That was the beauty of the cocoon that Wheeler had built around himself. Jake smiled warmly at the man in his chair and smugly walked away to his private quarters, sure of the fact that he had everything over his soon-to-be-former Team members.

Three Cyber-Team Wheeler members sat together as Jake completed his toilet and put on some mascara and eye-liner as a personal servant blow-dried his shining, curly shoulder-length hair. He admired himself in a full-length mirror. The eye make-up looked great, in his opinion, with his flashy diamond studs, including a diamond in a piercing under his lip, and full hair.

As he sucked raw oysters (cultivated in his own private reserve in Europe), he was alone with only a waiter wearing a crisp black and white uniform in attendance serving him from the jet's kitchen and walking each course to Jake's table.

The three Team members ridiculed their boss's isolation-ism quietly in a corner of the largest space on the plane. They knew something would come down. They showed their weapons off to each other with a little laughter and a flash or two of the many diamonds they were wearing.

They high-fived each other and went to their own quarters pretty sure that Jake could not replace their skills, and that they were safe to choose anything they wished while still remaining within the Wheeler cartel.

Raphael Case, one of the renegade Team members, wan-dered through the computer room, looking over the shoul-ders of the Team member that Jake had put on the main key-board. He could hear Jake playing his afternoon movie, de-spite the heavy sound-proofing throughout the jet. He really wanted a chance at that keyboard, but his status within Cy-ber-Team Wheeler was not high enough. Egoistically, he was sure he could find a crack in Wheeler's worm program.

He felt his excitement rise as he thought of assuming authorship of the worm. Using the program could bring him a great deal of money, even without using the large internet blackouts that Wheeler had pulled off and had planned for the future of their cyber cartel.

Raphael felt that smaller "hits" would gain him enough money and less negative media or police attention—giving him enough getaway time without using an expensive transport such as the jet. He could buy a simple panel truck and use it both as an RV and carry-all for computers and the counterfeit bills without bringing any counterfeiting equipment from place to place, which he felt was excessively risky and sort of unnecessary.

He felt that Wheeler liked grandstanding for the press too much. Wheeler liked to see himself in the media. Ditching expensive counterfeiting equipment was Wheeler's calling card from his days as a successful professional poker player. His boss felt it was a good diversionary technique and useful to get the cops off his tail for hacking. *Might have been good in the old days*, thought Raphael.

But now, Raphael knew that Interpol, for one, could identify the entire cartel that way—as they did once in Monte Carlo. They weren't caught physically—but they were identified, and their jet was noted—which was why this group of mutineers wanted to do something that would force Jake Wheeler to destroy his jet and buy a new one.

The renegades did not feel the cops would catch them before they reached their home base in Europe. They had plans to blame the murder on Jake. That was one of the reasons they had done it in the first place, saying that the murdered Team member was suspected of being disloyal to the Team. That was just a ploy.

The European security forces had never been close enough to their identities to figure out where their multiple bases were, or what all their cyber identities were. Raphael knew, if he was successful in copying the huge worm program, he would miss Wheeler's wealth. But different parts of their cyber cartel had secure and secret bases all over Europe and finding something for himself, alone, would not be difficult. Or so he thought, anyway.

In fact, he had already started to build a new hide-out with some extra savings he had squirreled away from the last ten years of working as a cyber servant for Jake Wheeler. Everyone on the Team knew that Wheeler was hiding income, and most of them did the same, making plans for their own independence.

Again, he peered at the worm program building itself on all six TV screens in front of him. The man at the computer spun around in his chair and faced him. He smiled and said, "Oh. Hi, Raphael! Wish I could build something like this myself. It could make any hacker as rich as Wheeler." He looked curiously at Raphael who had noted an unusual key sequence the other man had used before he had turned around.

It was not a standard unlock sequence—but it was an unlock sequence none-the-less. He made a mental note to write it down in his notebook with the rest of his notes on this program. Sometimes a simple, yet unusual, key could unlock a hidden program's security and reveal its programming through a code-breaking analysis extended throughout the program by repeating a similar type of keying that the author had used.

It worked on the principal that habits extend to programming. As per the habit of using certain vowels in passwords or certain consonants. Repetitiousness or a habit of using similar keystrokes had opened many a hacker's programming unintentionally.

Case repeated the sequence of keystrokes he had observed with his fingers on the palm of the opposite hand, mouthing the keys silently to himself all the way back to his private quarters.

As soon as he shut and locked the door to his suite, he grabbed a pen and quickly wrote the sequence down. He smiled as he noted that there were indeed similarities with some of the other keystrokes that he had noted from the same worm-building program before. One of the most intriguing facts about Wheeler's intricate worm-building program was not only its flexibility to re-program itself, but also the ability for it to spin-off hundreds of smaller worm programs that were useful to open computers to major intrusions from the Wheeler hacker organization.

Jake Wheeler was playing a game of chess against his own computer program, now that his film was over. He was winning right now, but he knew it was only an exercise and the machine would ultimately win. The uniqueness of his chess program was that it could be programmed by the user to create unique moves or set up to let the human player win or lose. He laughed at his own cleverness at creating *real* games programs – not just some useless chase game created to excite the male ego, although he had done that, too. That and several practical, famous and very successful apps such as radio, exercise, smart temperature controller and music play-back programs. He was a multi-millionaire because of these programs alone.

The money from those programs was still funding such things as his jet, his staff and his computer hardware without touching his inheritance – without even revealing its where-abouts or its ever-growing totals. He spent his inherited money only on himself: fine jewelry, his clothing, his food. It gave him happiness. *His* happiness.

He had done computer application and game program-ming as a child. And now, he was a grown man and he thought as a man – not as a child. He was happy with his success in invading this small town. He was not a man that was known for his mercy. He had no sympathy for smaller peo-ple, or for other people in general. He knew the local hos-pitals, police and fire stations had problems with the initial electrical uncertainties and the consequential wireless black-out.

Too bad, he had thought maliciously. Although he knew that the electrical problems were minor. Thing was, that only *he* had known that. So, the problems in the town at that time were only ones of worry and panic. He thought of the times he was bullied as a child and he felt justified in frightening others. His computers had been his only friends at times.

Perhaps he would lift the wireless blackout. That would help his cartel's getaway, although he had no plans on leaving Europe again and could control the whole thing from there. From his main hideaway.

He and his Team had transferred ownership of much of the Silver Lake banks' investment funds to his own coded accounts. His Team would be paid from that, and his own profits would remain untouched. He had left local monies and payroll alone, although the town did not know it yet, and he knew they were worried about it. The bank's investment capital, though, was now his. The money they had made from their depositors was his. Like sleight of hand. Like a joke.

This was not done out of compassion, but he knew that law enforcement went more lightly on criminals that did not interfere with depositors or show unrelenting greed. He had another, to his mind, smaller, worry.

Anonymous, the famous online hacker organization had messaged him several times. The gist of the messages was something like this:

ANONYMOUS HATES YOU. YOU DO NOT STAND FOR JUSTICE, ONLY THEFT. YOU CANNOT USE THE NICKNAME "JOKER". YOU ARE WAY NOT FUNNY & WE WILL GET YOU.

SMALL TOWNS ARE NOT A REFUGE FOR CRU-
ELTY. WE WILL NOT LET YOU TAKE OVER ANY
COMMUNITY FOR YOUR OWN SELFISH GAIN. WE
DO WHAT WE DO TO HELP OTHERS AND SPEAK
UP FOR THE DEFENSELESS.

REMEMBER ANONYMOUS HATES YOU. **BE-**
WARE!!

How naïve the local people were. He wanted them that way. His hands were covering their eyes, making them blind. He made them slaves to his will and purposes. He was not exactly all-seeing, but he had placed miniature cameras and drones around town. He had GPS on every strategic security element that operated within the township...and, of course, everywhere and everything he thought he should surveille. A Wheeler Cyber-Team member was also left behind in Silver Lake to adjust the surveillance equipment and help out on the ground. He was used to being effective and prided himself on it.

Most of all, he wanted that new satellite that NASA was building. That would be his *coup-de-grâce*.

He worked on putting together some new hardware the rest of the afternoon, as he and his crew flew to Europe. He soldered newly designed printed circuits in the workshop within his private suite. His crew ran the mundane life of the jet and prepared a *Cordon Bleu* supper for everyone.

Asia Reynolds recovered from her shock at the discovery of the body near her cabin, but no longer felt comfortable simply watching the snowmobile race which was almost past her place anyway. She packed her things up, turned her water off and loaded Zucchini back into her truck. It was snowing again, and the Simmons boys had been out there already plowing the road to her cabin. She did not feel good telling them about the new tragedy, so she simply thanked them for their conscientious care, offered them some hot chocolate and gave them some hugs to make herself feel better. She cleaned up again, locked the cabin and drove home in her truck, happy to be going home to her protective environment, Rainier Voss and even Lilah Aylward. She kind of figured that Dr. Voss would have supper ready and hoped that it was one of his veggie days, since he had expressed a liking for vegetable meals. Asia felt a rush of love for him.

It continued to snow, and the wind was blowing the light powder across the road, sweeping it upwards and blinding Asia so that she had to drive at a crawl all the way to her house. Rainier did indeed fix an all vegetable meal. Lilah had been invited to dine that evening. Asia was a little miffed, but gracious.

She went outside again, before removing her winter gear, with a curious Zucchini right at her side. She wanted to check on Pumpkin and Fuzzy Bud. Pumpkin began braying as soon as she walked into the barn. Fuzzy wagged her tiny tail excitedly and came over to touch noses with Zookie, unafraid of the big dog. The barn was nice and warm, and the stove had been stoked recently. Both animals had a clean, full water bucket or bowl with fresh water in it. Pumpkin looked soft, clean and freshly groomed. Even Fuzzy looked like she had been brushed and her kibble bowl was full. Dr. Voss had done a fine job and kept his word about caring for her two new animals.

The biggest surprise of all was sitting in the corner. Besides Rannie Voss putting Pumpkin's new custom orange, bitless soft halter on—there was a brand new, small, brilliant crimson-enameled sled off to the side of the big barn. It had lovely, reflective decals down both sides in a gay, sort of Amish, pattern and several bells decorating the front. It was just large enough for Asia, her two dogs and maybe a couple of grocery bags in a small covered box towards the back.

The driver's seat had a back and was completely padded with padded fold-up armrests. It was even more beautiful than Asia had expected. The Simmons boys had done a wonderful job of crafting the vehicle.

Asia walked over to the glistening sled and lifted the side of it easily with one hand. It was definitely light enough for Pumpkin who was short but standard-sized and hefty enough to pull her in this small conveyance.

It would be good for exercise. The skis on the bottom of the sled were waxed and ready for at least a short run. She patted and hugged both her little donkey and the tiny Chihuahua. She tried to take Fuzzy out with her and Zucchini, but the little dog whined and wiggled frantically, trying to jump out of Asia's arms.

She gave up and put her down, watching her run back to the donkey and lay down in her dog bed at Pumpkin's feet. Pumpkin lay down next to her and made happy snuffling noises. Asia laughed, shook her head and went into her home with Zucchini, sitting down to a lovely dinner with her friends. Rannie had decorated the table with fresh flowers. Asia was hungry and ate quickly, not feeling like discussing the events of the day until she had taken a hot shower and put her pajamas and robe on. She tried to feel positive and looked forward to running the new donkey sled tomorrow with Zucchini and Fuzzy Bud on board. She felt sick about having to talk to Dr. Voss about the discovery of a dead body next to the snowmobile trail. The shower felt divine and she lost herself in it for a few minutes. Zucchini growled from her favorite place on the bathroom floor and woke her up from her dreamy state in the hot water. She laughed.

Rannie had stoked the house stove and living room fireplace to perfection. Asia went downstairs and was surprised to see that Lilah was laying down in a sleeping bag on her couch. Rainier motioned to Asia silently to step into the kitchen. She did what he asked her to do with a question on her face. He grabbed Asia's arm and pulled her towards the back door, holding his index finger to his lips and raising his eyebrows while making eye contact with her.

"Asia," whispered Dr. Voss, confidentially while holding her close, "Lilah must remain here to protect us. We need professional security right now. Ms. Aylward is highly trained in the martial arts and has an arsenal of defensive weaponry with her. There has been another security breach within Silver Lake or aimed at your town.

"There was a murder today as you know. The victim was an internationally wanted super-hacker. It looks as if the cyber-criminal cartel targeting Silver Lake is involved in some serious in-fighting and actually want the security agencies to know this and get a little aggressive in finding the them. This is not contradictory. The increased pressure would help the mutinous group attack their own organization and perhaps help them with some legal immunity later if they were ever asked to testify in court. They are very clever people.

"We also do not think it is an accident that Jason Bing (the hacker that was found murdered) was killed the day before we were scheduled to release the new Operating System for Silver Lake or the new satellite. Both are scheduled for release and launching tomorrow afternoon around the same time."

Asia needed to sit down. She replied, "The Illinois State police interviewed me this afternoon and told me that Izzy and Tuffy Ritter found a dead man in the snow near their house. Is that what you mean? That man was super-hacker Jason Bing?"

"Yes. We think Bing discovered a group of dissenters in the cyber cartel that is targeting us, so they killed him conspicuously as a warning of their power and to serve their own purposes—possibly to throw their action in the face of their leader who may also have been involved in the murder.

"The newly designed, defensive communications satellite and protected Operating System are both going to be operative some time tomorrow?" asked Asia.

"The Operating System will be immediate, but we cannot lift the blackout until we ascertain if the new satellite has strong enough protection to turn its operations on. *That* is what will lift the wireless blackout and put all the towers back into running order.

"We are now on high alert because we think this cyber cartel might make a move on us, the Operating System, and the new satellite – getting so bold as to steal the new satellite before launching. We think they might have done as much financial damage as they are going to do to our own town, but we will not know until our accountants take inventory when the internet is turned back on. We have a great deal of intelligence that says we are dealing with a very egoistic power-oriented group that Interpol has been tracking, or trying to track, for some time. They do things just to get noticed. It is an ego-hacker thing.

"There was a group in Monaco, which might not be them – we are not sure, that was noticed by international security forces last year that fits our identification of the group that attacked Silver Lake.

"We think that Silver Lake's international reputation for extreme sports and jet setter accommodations brought the town to their attention. We also think they have bigger plans than just embezzling our small town or passing counterfeit bills. Our best hope is the fight they seem to be having internally within their own cartel."

"Like they might have *wanted* media attention for the murder of that guy?" questioned Asia, in amazement.

"We think so. We were not even aware that they might have planned to leave this area soon. But Bing's murder indicates they were airborne at the time he was dropped. He did not die from the impact. He was shot. But he must have been dropped because the forensic evidence tells us that the impact was too great for the body to have just been tossed where it was found. He was dead before they dropped him.

"Interpol has tried tracking a private jet (also seen in Monaco) the cyber cartel seems to be using as a mobile command center from time to time. They have been unsuccessful in catching this group because they are very good at using cyber camouflage and blocking tracking equipment."

Asia was a little excited and said, "So we might get our wireless and internet back tomorrow?"

"We hope so," answered Rannie. "They have a lot of access and seemingly limitless amounts of money. We at the United States security agencies and NASA believe they have their own tracking crews, towers, satellites, air traffic controllers and customized computer hardware and software. They are capable of blinding our tracking equipment and they have done exactly that for the many years they have been in operation. Blocking tracking equipment in general, that is.

"Like I said, we do not believe that Silver Lake was their main target, either. We think they might still have extensive surveillance in Silver Lake, though. Even if they have flown away to their main center, which we believe is in Europe somewhere. Their surveillance in Silver Lake is why Lilah is here. She was sent to protect me, but since I have spent so much time with you and because of your international reputation as a documentary film maker, we felt it would be advisable to take you under our protective wings, as well."

Asia tensed, remembering the time she had to stay at the Almonte ranch last summer while in the protective custody of Sgt. Sheila Rodriguez and Patrolman Chico Almonte.

Regardless of the fact that both policemen were very close childhood friends of hers, the threat of being kidnapped was more important than her freedom at the time. She suffered from the restriction, nonetheless.

She commented, "I wanted to take Pumpkin out in the new sled for some exercise tomorrow. I hope that won't mean that my movements will be limited."

"No," replied Dr. Voss. "Our main concern is our presence here. If Lilah and I are too obtrusive in your home, we can move to a local motel. I wanted to stay here for at least another month or until the cyber criminals who did this are under arrest and safely in jail. You are implicated already by hosting me. It was actually a bad idea to stay here and that is my fault because I found you and your home charming. It gives me a much needed rest.

"I might, though, need to move to wherever these criminals target next. Our national security agencies believe they are going to target a larger city." Dr. Voss looked worried.

Asia was shocked and upset that her beloved Rainier might have to leave. She reassured him that even Lilah's presence was no problem and that they were welcome to stay through to the end of their duties in Silver Lake. *The end*, she repeated to herself, not wanting to think that Rainier Voss would ever have to leave. His leaving was an ominous thought.

He saw the anxiety written on her face and threw his arms around her, holding her close for a few minutes and looking at her soften and become pliant in his arms. She felt warmed and even grateful. He kissed her hair and showed no sign of releasing her. She thought, *Never let me go...* Rainier ran his hands up and down her back in a caress.

The two of them crept quietly up the stairs past the sleeping form of Lilah Aylward. Lilah, with all of her combat training, awoke easily to see both of her new house mates creeping up the staircase to the second floor. After they had passed, she stretched and turned over. She was trained to awaken at the slightest passing or unusual sound.

The next day Asia went flying down the snowy road in front of her house, sliding on the new sleigh pulled by Pumpkin. Riding in the sleigh were Zucchini and Fuzzy Bud. The bells on the front piece were jangling merrily. Pumpkin wore her colorful Indian blanket strapped to her belly and seemed happy to stretch her legs and get outside regardless of the cold weather and snow. She would snort and bellow occasionally and even stopped once to look back at her passengers with her eyes slanted in a characteristic smile.

At one point Asia saw Frankie Franklin's St. Bernard, Hunny, galloping up the road, coming towards them. Pumpkin was amazingly calm given the size of the dog. Hunny could have been at least two hundred pounds. Asia sucked in her breath in anticipation of disaster.

But there was no disaster or altercation. Hunny was just bouncing around, happy to see them – even nuzzling the donkey, who nuzzled her back. Zucchini jumped out of the sleigh, ringing the bells with her commotion. Asia looked away and closed her eyes like a coward, still ready to stop a fight. But there was no fight. Zucchini and Hunny jumped into the snow with a flourish and chased each other around, playing get-away, hauling their huge bulks lithely around in-to the deeper banks of snow ... obviously having a great deal of fun.

It was amazing for Asia to see these two huge dogs simply having fun with each other, when they had been out to kill each other so recently. Now, they were the best of friends. Fuzzy crawled up under Asia's seat and stayed there, hidden, pretty much disinterested in the play of the giants. Her being the size of a kitten, that was no great surprise. Asia reached down and scratched the little Chihuahua on the head. She picked her up and put her in her lap. Fuzzy curled up there and watched the other dogs play with more interest from her safe nest in Asia's arms.

Asia spied a pickup approaching slowly from the direction of Frankie's house. In fact, it *was* Frankie. She pulled up next to the sled and powered her window down. Frankie smiled at her and threw a snowball at her from the truck.

"Hey!" exclaimed Asia, laughing and brushing the snow out of her neck.

"Saved that one for you," laughed Frankie right back. For an elderly woman, she had a lot of vitality.

"The dogs are getting along now, Frankie."

"Yeah, it's a miracle."

"Makes for a perfect day," said Asia with a smile on her face.

Frankie looked at Asia piercingly and asked, "You sure are glowing this morning. Is that only from the dogs?"

Asia turned red with embarrassment and hugged Fuzzy closer to her. How did she figure out that there might be something else?

"Cute little dog you have there. That's Bertha Mason's Chihuahua, Fuzzy Bud, isn't it?"

"Yeah. Yes, it is. She comes with the donkey, so she is mine now," answered Asia, grateful for the change of subject.

"See ya', girl," said Frankie, calling Hunny and packing her into the truck. She had to push Zucchini away from the door. Zookie put her tail between her legs and walked ruefully over to Asia who patted the back of the sled indicating that she should jump in. Zucchini barked as Frankie and Hunny drove away. She ran after them a little and then turned around.

"Zucchini!" yelled Asia, a little frantically. Her dog trotted back again and jumped into the sled this time. The donkey stood up and wagged her tail, shaking the snow off her fanny. Pumpkin seemed to be able to guess where they wanted to go and automatically turned the sled around. She started back towards Asia's. This was one smart donkey. Asia figured that Pumpkin had a lot of experience finding her own way around. After all, the little donkey had found *her.*

She grabbed the reins with one hand and continued to hug Fuzzy Bud to her with the other arm. Fuzzy had started to shiver. Chihuahuas, even the long-haired ones, are not known to do very well in the cold or snow. Asia reached down, pulled up a lap blanket and wrapped the tiny dog in it.

Pumpkin didn't seem to need the reins on the way home. Asia used them anyway and made sure the donkey stayed over to the side of the road as much as possible.

Chapter Nine

Jake Wheeler prepared for landing. He sat in the custom high-backed window seat of his private suite, fastened his seat belt, put his headphones on and chose an opera. He listened to *Quando m'em vo'soletta* by Giacomo Puccini in *La Bohème* as they landed on his private air strip in the Southeast English countryside near the National Trust property. Jake loved this area and won popular support here in the British Isles by donating heavily to National Trust maintenance. They landed smoothly, Jake unbuckled his seat belt, and walked to the open door of his jet. Being a big fan of Puccini opera, the aria resounded in his head as he walked down the ramp and over to his home.

His cook had prepared breakfast for the entire crew at his villa. Jake noted with a small amount of anger that there were four crew members missing at the table. He knew one of them was the dead man, but the other three would have to be traced. He ate in silence.

The other crew members knew there was something wrong due to his complete silence. One of them finally brought up his favorite subject—an analysis of their past plans and possible future actions.

"You know," commented one Team member as he chewed on a bagel. "One thing I was worried about was how much that film maker, Asia Reynolds, has on her cameras."

Jake answered him, "Yes, and we will find out at some point. I have also been thinking about lifting that internet blackout over Silver Lake. We really don't need it anymore. Our experiment in terms of money-making and calculating our intrusion capabilities was successful.

"Let Silver Lake, NASA and their computer experts think that their own new defenses worked, even if they actually could not withstand another assault. I feel that giving them some false ego is a good idea, that it is good strategy on our part to pretend we are weaker than we are. I, personally, believe we are ready for the larger take-over plans. How do you feel?"

Jake asked this, addressing the entire crew.

Wheeler's crew was stunned, although they had known all this was a possibility and had discussed it before. Wheeler's youngest computer trainee, Richie Stevens, spoke up, though, after a prolonged and strained silence.

"Mr. Wheeler, I think that is a brilliant strategy. Why waste our larger plans for only small returns? We might even be able to empty America's Federal Reserve. And, by the way, do you still want that new communications satellite?"

"Of course," replied Jake Wheeler forcefully, facing his student. "But it would be better if we found a way to take the satellite so that no one would know that it was stolen. Maybe there is a way to disable it, make them abandon it and then refurbish its software to meet our own needs."

Wheeler's plans had a double edge. Even his crew would not know who disabled the craft if he did it himself in seclusion. After the death of his crew member, he didn't want to give out too much information to his staff. He would need only minimal participation from his Team. That was fine.

He might like to retire to London or travel to see his family for a while and dissolve the Team he now had. He had made sure in the past that he had made each skilled Team member feel indispensable simply in order to protect himself, although he knew none of them were indispensable.

The young man who had been speaking, now clapped his hands together in delight. Most of the Team members around the table looked duly impressed with Jake's clever plans. "Well, Richie," said Wheeler commenting to his young protégé. "I'll be working on restoring Silver Lake's internet this afternoon. This time they really *won't* know what hit them. I don't think NASA, the CIA or any security agency, or computer programmer (except a hacker) would have a clue.

We should wait until they launch the new satellite. The new Operating System designed for Silver Lake should be in place by ten this morning—the satellite by one pm or so." Wheeler turned to one of his staff people and said, "Get my car ready and have Hattie pack a suitcase, groceries and lunch.

"I want to work on this in my London workshop. I can hack NASA from there, so I will know exactly when their new satellite becomes operative. And, you all know we have surveillance inside the Silver Lake police department. That will tell us how many homes in Silver Lake have installed the new Operating System. Then we can synchronize our actions with those events."

Normally, Jake would have liked to at least take Richie, his trainee, with him to show him his new circuitry designs, but right now he did not feel a strong bond with any of his crew. That dead man in the Silver Lake snow could have been him, and he knew it.

The Team at his table looked at each other with a querulous air, since this type of explanation was usually accompanied by a few more invitations. Wheeler continued, "The rest of you can relax. I will call you when I need to consolidate any new plans. I already sent Team Wheeler Security Forces after the three Team members who are absent from this table. If any of you have an idea of where they might be, let me know on my cell phone. You will be highly rewarded and can remain anonymous.

"Their microchips are not transmitting. They have blocked my tracking equipment. Those three people have been severed from our company. They will not be back among us. All of you know who they are. You are now free to go and visit your families or rest here at my villa. It is your own choice. Good-bye for now. And thank you for all your good work on this project. I will be in touch with all of you." Jake Wheeler then rose and went to the back of his villa, entering the garage from there, waiting for his driver to take him to his London condo.

He looked out the open garage door and admired his extensive garden architecture. Even in the winter, it was designed to look lovely. He had the finest gardeners he could find from all over the British Isles working for him. And his garden, even in the winter, was a wonderful show of evergreens and landscaping. The paths, of course, had been cleared so he could walk among his still green and trimmed bushes. Even the Queen had been sent photos of his finely trimmed pathways of evergreen. His evergreens were planted in a traditional garden maze pattern. His stable and kennel also reflected some of the Royals' tastes despite his Grandfather's and his own Scottish ancestry.

He raised his best horses in Kentucky, as did the Queen. He rode every day when he was present in his villa for any sustained period of time and owned several fine, healthy Pembroke Welsh Corgis which he knew was Her Highness, Elizabeth II's favorite breed of dog. At one point, she owned and trained close to a dozen Corgis.

This favoritism towards the Queen, he well knew, did not make him a favorite with his Irish, Scottish or Welsh Team members. Although he had his own favorite choices within their own cultures as well. He had an ego the size of his ambitions, and those where very large and very international. He also had a need to rule. A lot of his hacking had this in mind. He was bullied as a child in grammar school, so he felt success was his best revenge – and controlling others a passion.

He was not like his nemesis, the infamous hacking organization *Anonymous*, who forced disfavored FBI agents to donate to organizations such as the Red Cross from their hacked credit cards one Christmas as a sort of *hacktivist* Secret Santa. He thought the activity was funny, but the charity donation actually confused him.

He did not understand why anyone would take a risk like that and not profit from it. He understood moderation, but only from the standpoint of saving himself or his Team members long jail terms or avoiding too much of a legal hassle.

He giggled to himself about his plans for Silver Lake. He had also been nice enough to relieve about 20 million American dollars from a few local banks there—not counting how much his Team had earned from passing counterfeit bills and cheating at poker.

Jake's driver arrived and packed his luggage into the SUV.

Wheeler was soon enjoying several operatic arias on his way to London as he watched the beautiful English countryside roll by his car window. He listened to one of his favorites: *O mio babbino cara* by Giacomo Puccini from *Gianni Schicchi*.

Sergeant Sheila Rodriguez was trying to survive an incredibly hectic workplace and field hundreds of computer questions within Silver Lake Police Department headquarters. The launching of both the new NASA communications satellite and the distribution of an ironclad new Operating System from many points around town, such as the Public Library, Town Hall, Civic Center, and, of course, the police station flooded those distribution points with confused townspeople.

The IT technicians from Central Illinois and Chicago had to offer their services live at these places for the townspeople who had never installed a new Operating System themselves and did not know how to observe the rather simple steps involved in the installation (and not try the "advanced" buttons). The hardest part of installing was evaluating the required hardware, such as the processor or even video card necessary for the new OS.

In some, rather frustrating, cases a new computer was required. This alone caused a small amount of panic and conflicts. The town was able to offer new laptops that had all of the required hardware at a large discount. A generous wealthy donor (Tobias Smart, owner of the California Spa and Laundromat) gave laptops away for free to poorer folks.

The Operating System was on a CD, so it was easy to give away to those who were computer savvy and the amount of time it would ordinarily take to load (about an hour) was clearly written in the instruction pamphlet that came with each CD. They had put automated voice instructions on several phone lines and on the CD, but cell phones were not really operational yet. The situation almost had Sheila in tears.

Of course, Sgt. Rodriguez and her officers were busy trying to keep the peace and break up any fights that could occur in the process of this type of emergency. *This thing better work,* Sheila said to herself in exasperation many times that morning, getting exhausted by all of the questions and anxiety. On top of that the local Medical Examiner had not finished the autopsy of the dead man who had been found during the Silver Lake snowmobile race.

One thing the local cops *did* know was that a few international security agencies were looking intensively for the private jet they assumed dropped the corpse. Sheila was glad that most of the investigation was outside of her jurisdiction.

This made answering stupid computer questions a little easier. Interpol had some initial ideas about who the dead man was and what cartel they were dealing with. They were double checking the possible identification of Jason Bing.

They had tried to track the hacker jet before around Monaco unsuccessfully due to the incredible computer blind the hackers used to block wireless incursions. It made the jet virtually invisible.

Patrolman Chico Almonte came up behind Sheila and wrapped his arms around her. He said, "I'm cooking tonight."

"Hi, baby," responded Sheila, softly. "You're always cookin'. You can take me home anytime." Chico was her major support. She relaxed into his arms.

Sergeant Rodriguez and Patrolman Chico Almonte had been together pretty consistently since third grade and Sheila had lived with the Almonte family on their ranch for about a decade. Marriage was in the air due to the engagement of Elise Snuggles and Elton Jamison, but Chico and Sheila wanted to wait for professional reasons. Chico was as beautiful physically as a man could be. He was buff and handsome and liked to cook, take care of his family and clean in his time off.

He owned a police steed, Niño, who was as beautiful as he was. Niño stood about seventeen hands (Chico was over six feet), was shiny black and had the personality of a pot of melted butter. The horse was popular with the children of Silver Lake. Chico's popularity as a Community Liaison Officer had led him to consider getting a teaching license and beginning a second career as an elementary school teacher. Neither Sheila nor he wanted to raise children with two officers of the law as parents. Both of them felt that having both parents in possible jeopardy of violent death was not responsible and not what they wanted for their kids.

Across town, Asia Reynolds and Rainier Voss were waiting for news from the satellite launch. They ate sandwiches on freshly baked bread and drank spearmint tea in the living room in front of a roaring fire. Rainier liked grilled organic soy cheese sandwiches with lettuce and tomato, so did Asia. She was almost convinced that Rannie Voss was probably going to be NASA's first vegetarian scientist – or even spaceman. The satellite was due to launch at Cape Canaveral in about ten minutes. Asia turned her TV on, and they finished eating during the countdown. The computers in the NASA control room actually did flash – *five, four, three, two, one* ... and their satellite blasted successfully off the launch pad ensconced in a rocket. A thrill passed through Asia's living room.

"Well," she said. "I guess we're on our way back into this century." She thought it was funny that she took so much comfort in the flames and warmth of her fireplace, but still looked forward to reading her new emails. She also felt a sudden depression because as thrilling as the launch was – it also meant that her recent lover would be leaving.

The announcement came that the satellite was successfully put into orbit and was now functioning. Ten seconds later, Asia's cell phone rang. She thought, *Damn. Time waits for no fool.* "Hello?" she said.

It was her BFF, local news anchor (and well-known pothead) Elise Snuggles, who answered Asia's hello with, "Well, *damn*, girlfriend, my gosh-darned laptop just booted up and got on the internet! I went right to Facebook and told everybody I was back and *still tickin'!* That new Operating System is elegant, sweet and easy. It even has instructions on audio playback. Come on over to my house, bring your laptop and we'll smoke some weed and get drunk on the Net! I still have at least 20 lbs. of weed from my summer harvest and an unopened carton of white Zinfandel from my engagement party. So, get your butt over here before I get so stoned I forgot I invited you. *Better hurry!*"

Asia waited until Elise took a breath and forgot her sadness over Rainier's imminent departure just listening to Elise's usual insanity. "Okay," she said, brightening. "I'll be right over." As little time as she and Rainier had left, she knew Elise would purge her heart and give her a huge stash of joints so she and Rainier could spend their possible last night smoking weed with Pumpkin and Fuzzy Bud in the barn sitting on hay bales by the barrel stove ... Asia's version of an earthly heaven and the best possible memory of someone she had loved for a very short time.

She kissed Rannie on the cheek and explained why she needed to leave him for a few hours. He laughed and walked her to the back door, saying that he had to get online and keep in contact with NASA and the CIA to track everything that might develop moment-by-moment. She hitched Pumpkin to the sled, put Fuzzy in the back on the blanket, lit the bright array of solar lights that detailed every curve of the sleigh and let Pumpkin pull the sled up to the doors. She opened the barn doors and pushed the sled outside. Sliding out into the darkening afternoon, she made her way to Elise's. Rannie waved at her as he closed the barn.

It was only late afternoon. It got dark early in the winter in Silver Lake, like everywhere. Groups of happy young people were out in town singing carols a little early. Asia was amused that the surfacing of the internet and revival of cell phone usage caused such a surge of joyfulness. People waved at her in the sleigh. Pumpkin brayed and smiled at them. She danced a bit to the side and rang the sleigh bells. Children ran over and tried to run with the sled and follow her.

Asia discovered with joy that her donkey seemed to like children. The whole town was lit up with Christmas displays and lights. Even people she did not know waved at her as she passed them. She passed Joe Doe walking up to the Mall, she supposed. He looked horrified at her in the sled and ran away as fast as he could, sliding, falling and yelling some warning about Martians.

Asia came jangling up Elise's driveway. Pumpkin brayed loudly as Asia put her and Fuzzy in the garage. Elise had not pulled her car in, which was great because her garage was heated, and Pumpkin would be comfortable there. Elise came to the door, responding to the noise, and said, loudly,

"What the hell is all that? Sounds like you brought over a baby elephant. You farm folks always be pickin' up some new animal. Lemme see..."

She walked over to the open garage and peeked in timidly from around the corner of the building. "My Gawd, Asia, *what* in tarnation is *that?!*" Fuzzy peeped out of the sleigh and barked at her. "A donkey and a miniature dog? What possessed you? Are you building a manger, too? Are you playing Mary and looking for Joseph and baby Jesus?

"The sleigh's a real knockout, though. Where'd you get it, the North Pole at Santa's Village?" She walked over to Fuzzy, who seemed to give her confidence enough to get closer to the donkey. She patted the little dog, but Fuzz evaded getting picked up. "The dog can come in. You get to clean up after the donkey, though. It can stay out here. She kick?"

"No," responded Asia, wrapping Fuzzy in her lap blanket. The temperature was still above zero and Asia planned on leaving early, so she figured her two new furry friends were good for a couple of hours in the heated garage. She told Elise the story of how she had come to adopt the dog and the donkey, and that the Chihuahua would probably not want to leave Pumpkin's side...as cute as she was. "Jedidiah and Jeremiah Simmons made the sled by hand, beautiful isn't it? You can pet Pumpkin, the donkey, she is gentle."

Elise said, "You know Jed won the snowmobile race?" Elise came over, timidly, and patted the donkey's head and neck. Pumpkin bobbed her head and snorted long and loud.

Elise shrieked and ran out of the garage. Asia laughed and called her back, stroking Pumpkin and telling her Elise was silly, glad that Jed won the race and earned the money for his college fund. She had seen him at the head of the snowmobiler pack but was not sure he had stayed there.

Asia went inside the house and the two friends sat at their laptops with music and partied, cracking jokes at each other as they read their emails and smoked as much weed as possible.

———

Fresh evergreen scented the room at the Caribou Café in Denver as Sage Sommers and Harry Skylar set up their instruments and amplifiers. They had gotten a gig to play at this place every afternoon and evening for the duration of Harry and Sage's Christmas vacation, which was almost a full month. The money would be good, and they put out a tip jar, as well. Harry gave Sage a hug before they started playing and kissed her gently. He was so happy to see her, after waiting so many months. The café was already getting crowded. Sage's singing was popular around town and her fans were curious about Harry.

He didn't disappoint. Their set began with a lovely improvised solo on guitar by Harry. His fingers were light and flew across the strings as if his guitar was a fairy harp. He played the beautiful theme from *The Mask of Zorro* (*I Want to Spend My Lifetime Loving You*) by James Horner. He used some of the Flamenco techniques he had learned last summer from SLPD Patrolman Chico Almonte who was also an accomplished Latin guitarist.

The afternoon, holiday crowd, loved Harry and filled the tip jar. Sage came on stage to welcoming hoots, hellos and enthusiastic applause. The two played the Horner piece again and Sage sang the words in her deep resonant contralto, ending with both of them singing harmony in the famous duet. New customers crowded into the café and the emptied tip jar filled up again. The owners of the place had to set up some folding chairs to accommodate the overflow.

The two musicians then segued into Harry's extensive Joni Mitchell repertoire. But what really brought the house down again and brought the audience to their feet, was a long set of Harry's original songs, especially his love songs to Sage. By the end of their first night, they must have made over three hundred dollars in tips.

They walked back to Sage's parent's house happily, hand in hand. It was the end of a very successful first night of their ongoing gig at the Caribou. Denver was decked out in hundreds of lights. Extensive rows of houses were decorated with hand-crafted evergreen, especially evergreen wreaths with multi-colored bows and bells.

Harry had really never gotten into Christmas very much before. It had been a lonely time for him, even at his family home. But as he held Sage's hand, as they sauntered to her house, he felt warmed by the celebration this year. He had also never traveled to a girlfriend's family home to meet her parents and spend a holiday with them.

Sage's parents, who were vegans much to Harry's delight, offered the two of them sandwiches and hot tea when they got to the house. Everyone sat down together in the open concept pine-paneled kitchen. Sage told her parents of their opening night success. Her folks promised to visit the Caribou when they were playing and listen to them. Sage's parents were both highly successful crafts people. Sage's mother was a potter and their home was filled with her work. Along with the open concept architecture and Native American art, wall hangings, paintings, rugs and pillows—her pottery added some breathtaking beauty to their home. Harry was overwhelmed with the natural luxury.

Sage's dad made rustic-themed handcrafted furniture and sold locally very successfully. Sommers Furniture was highly popular in Denver and the surrounding area. His furniture made the home even more exotic and comfortable. Speaking of exotic, Sage's dad, Antonio, was a former Hollywood stunt man, which was how he built his exceptionally fine house. His specialty was jumping and horseback riding. He had even bought a fine, black Friesian gelding that he had ridden in an action film and needed retirement.

Mr. Sommers had also heard of and admired Asia Reynolds' work. He convinced Harry that writing music for the film industry was a good idea and could help put him through college. Harry was immediately interested. With Antonio Sommers' Hollywood connections and Sage's in-home recording studio, he felt his music with Sage's vocals would make a good audition tape for a soundtrack demo. He was excited and enthused. Harry was tired of being poor and would just love to help his parents. New films used recent and vintage folk music extensively which was a *Skylar and Sommers* genre. They both thought, deep in their hearts, that this profession might help to keep them together.

Antonio Sommers went out the next morning to ride on a trail with Marco, his Friesian. Sage took a video of her dad on the horse, planning to add her music and give it to Harry for a Christmas gift. She had written a new song especially for Harry. She knew he would love it. He was fascinated by Marco. The horse was the first Friesian he had ever seen. He did not even know of the breed. He had never heard of it.

The extra-long curling mane was striking to him. He had never seen a horse with a wavy tail, or even naturally wavy hair. While he was there at Sage's house, he volunteered to groom Marco. And he did it with love. He loved the beautiful, gentle, talented ex-stunt horse. Sage was sure a video of the horse in motion would stun Harry with her thoughtfulness and impress him with her sensitive observations of his like and dislikes.

Antonio stood on Marco's saddle (for his daughter's video and for fun) and jumped off the horse from a standing position, throwing both of his arms into the air straight above his head. Harry's mouth flew open in amazement.

London was Jake Wheeler's favorite city. He loved it above all others. He loved the crowds, buses, parks, stores, everything. He had his favorite restaurants and times of day. His family lived there too. For a hard-assed cyber criminal, he was amazingly loving towards his family. His grandfather, especially, was dear to him. He usually tried to spend Christmas with them, as well.

Jake was watching his computer screen and looking out his third story window at the same time. Suddenly, his screen went black and then came up with a chatroom style set of windows with a little blinking cursor next to something that said: "Type text here..." A message typed itself inside the top box. It said, "No hacker is alone, Jake. No matter what you do or what you have done, we have been there with you, watching you. You know about smart cars? The driverless ones? You don't have to answer – it is a rhetorical question. When do smart cars become stupid cars? Think hard. This is millennially philosophic – sad and real.

"Okay. I'll answer the question for you. They become stupid when some power-hungry person with advanced hacker skills takes over and forces smart cars to do stupid and dangerous things – like those Jeeps in Colorado that were forced off the highway in the mountains by some hacker.

"Like – any crazy post (or even pre-) pubescent teenager could force an automated car to face opposing traffic or even deliberately crash into another car or crowd of people. All it takes is a mania for control and a set of computer skills with the appropriate hardware.

"It is one thing to steal money or ruin someone's credit. It is another thing entirely, to assault someone for no real personal profit, no monetary gain ... just a desire to manipulate. Or, in a more useless manifestation—to rule over others. I mean everyone knows you don't need the money from your escapades."

Jake sat up, feeling furious. He typed, *"WHO IS THIS??!!"* in all capitals.

The chatroom box answered, "I have a bad feeling about you, Jake. Like you are a smart driverless car gone headless and rampantly stupid."

"TELL ME WHO YOU ARE!!" typed Jake, turning red in the face.

A live screensaver of colorful tropical fish in an aquarium flashed onto his screen. Over that in dark, bold poster block letters someone had typed, *"YOU ARE JUST A MONKEY IN A ZOO. WORSE. MONKEYS DO NOT DESERVE THE ZOO CONFINEMENT – YOU DO."*

The screen went black again. Big white block letters spelled out: *"YOU ARE A DRIVERLESS CAR AND I AM GOING TO DRIVE YOU. Enjoy the ride, Jake Wheeler. Goodbye."*

Jake tried to answer on his keyboard. Nothing happened. His keyboard was powerless. He was also unable to get his NASA program to come back on. Frustrated and angry, he decided to take a walk to the local park. He powered down his computer, put on his coat and boots and slammed out his condominium door, pounding down his front stairs to the street. The cold air awoke his senses and he calmed down. He even smiled at a few passersby.

He liked strangers, people who did not know who he was. It made him feel free, as if he was someone else. As if he was innocent, no one special. He felt like dropping the whole thing. The whole hacking thing. It was not like he needed the money, as that intruder had said. He slammed his fist into a brick wall as he walked past it.

He strained his neck and looked up at the sky. It was just starting to snow. He felt a few tentative flurries on his face. It made him calm again. He pulled his collar up and watched his feet as they took him down the familiar route to a small park in his neighborhood.

He saw a cat run up a set of stairs and enter a small cat door. He smiled and sort of missed his horses. Animals made up another society, besides his computer contacts, where he was never left out. In a way, he felt that animals were superior to humans.

He had learned as a small child to never miss anything. After his mother had died, he had learned to be alone.

His dad taught him how to program and build computer hardware—so he always had a communications device and could make friends over the internet without worrying that he would be bullied for being alone, thin, motherless, small or intelligent. A tear ran down his face as he reminisced about his lonely childhood.

He *had* to continue his career as a cyber criminal—there were plenty of people who would kill him if he showed remorse or weakness or tried to quit and reform himself. There were other things he could do to redefine himself. But quitting was not an option. At least he thought so right now.

A sparrow landed on the back of the empty park bench Jake had sat upon so that he could feel the cold coming off the pond in the center of the park. He watched the dark brown and tan bird and wondered at the resilience of such a small being, living in the harsh winds of the British winter.

Why are the small birds, sparrows, so strong, so resilient? he thought to himself. *Why can't I be like a sparrow?* He reached into his pocket and pulled out some of the millet he lined that pocket with so that he could attract birds. His mind returned to the disturbance he felt because some of his Team members had felt it necessary to kill someone. In all the things he had done, he had never done that.

He had never killed anyone.

Chapter Ten: Cyberpunks

Rainier Voss had been on the Net to NASA and at least three national security agencies all day. Things were going well, but there were a few things that bothered him. He felt alone. No one person at any professional agency agreed or empathized with his feelings right now except to give him some more time to explain and prove what he was intuiting. The best thing about what was going on was that he had permission to stay in Silver Lake for a few more weeks and possibly longer. He knew Asia would be overwhelmed with happiness over that.

He was playing Beethoven's Piano Sonata #14, popularly known as the *Moonlight Sonata* on the Yamaha to relax. And, so he would not have to think consciously about his concerns, he worked better while ruminating and playing the piano at the same time, subconsciously at times.

The things he had to connect with needed deep feeling – not only with his conscious thought. It was complicated. At the same time that he played the piano by memory, he had his laptop open to his secure NASA connection and was watching computerized readings of the new satellite's functions. All was well on the surface. Everything was going as planned. He, though, did not think all was well. It was just intuition. The music soothed his tensions and apprehensiveness.

He stopped worrying so much and remembered that he had wanted to clean the barn and leave food and fresh water for the dog and donkey. He stopped playing the piano and logged off the NASA site, powering down his computer and started thinking "food".

He got up and put the chili he had made on low on the stove to heat it up. He enjoyed being a possible vegetarian. It was an adventure for him, and he loved adventure.

Rainier filled Zucchini's bowl with dry Science Diet. The dog woke up at the sound of raining kibble. She still enjoyed sleeping underneath the piano when Rainier was playing. When he stopped, she usually snorted loudly and started snoring. Weird habit, but true. Best way to stop it was to pour kibble, which is just what Rannie was doing. It worked. Zucchini traded her rough snoring for loud crunchy chewing.

Rainier got on his coat and boots and turned the outside lights on. He picked up a small bale of Timothy hay from a closed, unused stall, and put it in Pumpkin's feeder, filling Fuzzy Bud's bowl with small kibble. He also cleaned the animal dirt from the floor. Now, Asia's jobs were all done. All she had to do was pull up to the barn.

Chico Almonte also had a bad feeling about the possible too-quick recovery of Silver Lake's internet. Like Rainier, he had no rational explanation for his intuitive feelings. He spoke to Sheila and she basically told him to be satisfied that their fixes had worked so far. She told him that Dr. Voss also had misgivings and would be remaining in Silver Lake for a longer time.

When his shift was over, Chico decided to stable his horse Niño at home with the family's other horses so he could groom him over the weekend. Instead of going straight home, Chico decided to go and speak to Dr. Voss and rode his horse over to Asia's house. Rannie was washing the kitchen floor and baking corn bread when Chico arrived.

"Say, man, it's nice to know I am not the only guy who likes housework," laughed Chico when he let himself in the back door after leaving Niño in Asia's barn and throwing some wood in the barrel stove out there. "Something smells real good, Doctor."

"Made some cornbread for dinner to go with some veggie chili. Would you like to stay for dinner?"

"Sure. I have to call home first. I'm supposed to cook tonight, myself. I have to get one of my brothers to do my housework. I just came over because I am sort of worried about the new Wi-Fi fixes."

Rainier frowned. Chico looked confused. Rainier said, "Why are you so concerned, Chico? Everything worked out just fine."

"That's why I am so worried. It seemed a little *too* smooth. As soon as the satellite began functioning—everything lit up immediately—all the dish television reception came on right away. The Operating System we programmed was (and still is) perfect. I felt it was all a little *too* perfect. I expected us to be hacked some other way or have another kind of disturbance." Chico paused. "They told me at the station that you are a former hacker. So maybe you understand my feelings of caution."

Voss was a little startled. "I think we are dealing with someone who is at risk in his own organization."

Chico interrupted, "The dead man?"

"That and the feeling that the head of this cyber cartel is trying to hide behind our smooth transition. He might be trapped in the embezzlement business. His teenage fascination with technology is probably getting old. And, probably, so is he, if he is who I think he is. Cannot speak about some of my thoughts, though."

"Too big for a small town police department?"

"Something like that."

"National security?"

Voss looked strained. "Yes," he answered. "What we discuss here has to stay between us and perhaps your partner, Sergeant Rodriguez."

"No problem," answered Chico with a questioning look.

"Way I figure, the leader of the cartel is probably emotionally unstable right now. All of our protective devices must be antagonizing to him and, also, we still have this problem with finding him, confirming his real identity and finding his cartel members," said Rainier Voss.

"Unstable? Do you have any idea who he is?" asked Chico.

"Only a little. Criminally-minded hackers are a weird lot. *"Criminal"* as defined not by simply breaking a law, but more by the type of injury caused. Mostly they have control issues and even Obsessive-Compulsive problems with life and programming. So right now, he would be getting pretty angry and frustrated. Even humiliated. He has just lost control. That is the psychological profile of him that I have assembled, plus the usual teenage obsession with computers."

"Yeah, I agree. It would be a good time to see if he will make a stupid move," said Chico.

"Good point. That is one reason I believe he might have been involved with our success getting back online," rejoined Voss.

"Really? It was odd to me that there seemed to be no attempt to stop us," stated Chico.

"I would love to infiltrate them. Problem is, we cannot infiltrate what we cannot see or find. They are presently invisible."

"We need to design a trap."

"I'm already working on that with the CIA," replied Dr. Voss. "We'll get him."

"We will," echoed Chico, pounding his fist into the palm of his other hand.

Asia got into her sleigh after visiting with Elise. She was slightly inebriated, but happy to be back with her friends online. She let Pumpkin do the driving and take her back to her barn while she hugged Fuzzy Bud in her lap to keep her warm. Pumpkin was unerring.

She had called Rannie on her cell phone and he met her at the barn doors, letting her into the now cleaned, stoked, warm and stocked up area. Voss had made sure everything was clean and in place in the barn. He hauled the sled in and tied Pumpkin up next to her feeder filled with Timothy. She ate three times a day now that she had lost some weight. Fuzzy walked over to her full kibble bowl and started eating alongside Pumpkin. Zucchini wagged her tail and followed Asia and Rainier into the kitchen which was rich with the scent of dinner.

She said hello to Chico who seemed distracted and deep in thought. Voss warned Asia not to repeat anything she heard from him or Chico except to Sheila. He explained with a smile as they ate dinner that he could stay here with her a little longer, because he wanted to do more research on the group that had hacked the systems in Silver Lake.

"But we're okay now. Everything is fine," said Asia, with a small, awakening hope in her heart. Her crush on Rainier Voss grew bigger every day. She felt it might even be true love.

"Everything may *not* be fine. I am contacting our computer experts in Tokyo. Now is the time to go full blast and track this group of hackers. We need to find them before they do something else," replied Rainier. "If we could find a residence, or a work center, we wouldn't even need names. They have too many different identities to track using a name anyway. They can change our *Trapwire* camera security program, so even if we *do* have a photo ID, they can re-program CCTV around the world so as to not identify themselves. Or deliberately *mis*-identify themselves as anyone they want us to see."

"Tokyo?" questioned Asia.

"That is where our best former hacker international informants are."

"Like people who got tired of being chased."

"And needed closure on a former lifestyle, big time."

"So, they change sides. Like you."

Chico looked hard at Asia.

"Yeah," said Voss, looking back at Chico. He said to him, "I thought you knew that I was once an anti-government hacker many years ago. I served my time, learned my lesson, and decided to protect our freedoms by closing our systems to interlopers. My specialty was any hacker that could permit a foreign government to piggyback on our government systems."

"Like whatever protections you are planning right now," commented Asia, thoughtfully.

"About that, yeah." Voss turned to Asia and continued speaking, "I might have to go to Europe to continue setting my traps there. I think that personal contact would be more successful in finding any of these people than looking for them online.

"I can do most of my preliminary work here. We do not even know what country or countries this cartel operates from right now. So, my trap and tracking designs will be mostly computer based with openings for inserting geographic locations. I just have to find their activity somewhere in cyberspace. A signal from a renegade computer, perhaps. Perhaps a familiar virus or worm or even a Trojan."

"Or," contributed Chico, with a mouthful of cornbread. "Another hacker organization willing to help you because they do not like that particular cartel or their activities. The Silver Lake hackers have to have a weakness somewhere."

"We can find that weakness," answered Voss. "It will just take time and the right equipment, and we have both. Like the Rolling Stones say, *Time Is on My Side.* Right now, we are running the government email surveillance program to find keywords that refer to the internet hacking in Silver Lake. It is simple, but it could locate one of their computer systems." Zucchini barked at the back door.

A loud voice announced Lilah Aylward and a male CIA operative. Voss opened the door and let them in. He told Lilah about their discussion. She said, "We just animated a Bot to try and capture at least one logarithm the hackers have used."

"And therefore, triangle a possible location of transmission," said Voss.

"...or multiple locations that they use or have used, " Lilah added.

"It's a start," said Voss, thinking of the piano. "That might only let us in on a conversation and not reveal identities or present-day locations."

"Like you said," repeated Lilah. "It's a start. It could lead us to a source code, and possibly prevent an entire city from being held hostage."

"As the saying goes," said Voss. "Nothing is impossible."

"Hope isn't anyway," said Lilah, sitting down with a sigh to a hot bowl of chili and a fresh piece of cornbread. The other agent, Reginald Poplar, did the same. Voss went into the basement to bring up Asia's folding bed. The two agents could sleep in the living room comfortably. Voss put some cedar on the fire after he made up the new bed. They all sat in the living room with some hot tea and date-nut teacake. After finishing his tea, Rainier played some jazz on the piano, his version of *Chestnuts Roasting on An Open Fire*.

Jake Wheeler rubbed his forehead and neck vigorously. He sprinkled the remainder of his millet on the ground in front of him. He watched a flurry of sparrows and pretty multi-colored finches land at his feet with delight. He did not want to look at a computer screen today, for the most part.

There was a coffee shop near here with live music. He really liked the place. Folks there really did not know who he was, and he used cash consistently when he visited the place so no one could trace a credit card in his name. He decided to walk over there.

He called a lovely girl that he pretty much considered his girlfriend and asked her to meet him there. His Team was on sabbatical, so he did not need to contact them any time soon. He had to think of something to update them on eventually, though. They needed to feel that they were "in the loop" (so to speak) at all times. He needed a show of wild plans for cyber crime to impress them. Even if he was going to replace all of them, he needed to take care. Especially now.

He planned on sending his Team members their share of the Silver Lake bank money. Their share of the counterfeiting money could be added to that. The payments would keep them quiet for the duration of their vacation time. He could send the payments tonight. The three mutineers were getting nothing.

He also planned on giving the three mutinous Team members over to New Scotland Yard. When it came to his whereabouts and programming in his most important worms, etc. they were ignorant.

What they could reveal might harm his other Team members, but generally not him. His villa in Chislehurst had protective designs, so his equipment was safe. His Team equipment was not, but the Team itself could deal with that. He would inform them of his decision tonight. The thought of what the three members would do made him laugh.

Their computers alone would be enough to give them years in prison and a condition that they would not be allowed to ever own or operate a computer again, not even in a school or library. Wheeler smiled. He could start covering up his own trail tonight.

He did not care if they were indicted for the murder of Jason Bing. If he needed to, he would supply evidence to this end. He just wanted those three locked up and silenced for a good long time. As long as possible. In his mind, he had declared cyber war on them.

Jake assumed the American Feds had *nothing* on him. All they had, he thought, was the *effect* of the cyber-attack he had led. He had been careful to hide his code in a confusing pattern. After all, he had helped to create *Stuxnet* (pronounced "Stucks Net" – it is a Dutch word) one of the most hidden worm codes in existence. He had done that when he was in Holland before the code was enhanced by the U.S. government and Israel jointly.

He did not know how long his computers and tablets would remain locked from the hacking invasion this morning. He assumed, due to the style of the hacking, that the intrusion was a private individual and not a government that did the hacking. If he could use his girlfriend's laptop, he could try for any source code that had been used on his computer to lock it up.

It might not remove the lock, but it would verify that his "visitor" was, like he had guessed, a private individual. If the code was familiar, he might even recognize a particular cyber individual or group—that could lead to a code cracker and eventually unlock his equipment. And, he knew, he might *not* recognize anyone at all.

Most analysts could not translate his code to the point that they could find him. But a private individual could stumble upon him in cyberspace and communicate out of curiosity. This is what he thought had happened. Not sure that was the case, Wheeler was determined to investigate his "visitor's" motives. He put his hand into his coat pockets and fingered the new 9mm 6 round Glock 43 and Piexon JPX Jet Protector 4 shot pepper sprayer, hoping only to use such weapons in self-defense, or not at all.

He waited at a café table until his girlfriend, Jessica Parker, showed up. She had no idea who he really was. She didn't even know his real name. She had no knowledge of his computer hacking. She knew he did some programming, but that was nothing compared to his real skills. She gladly lent him her laptop and he went online in the café trying to break the code that had let that person lock up his home computers.

He found the interloper. The hacker was not even in a stealth group, let alone a security agency. It was just a teenager from Brixton that had a head full of code. Wheeler unlocked his own computers and locked the hacker's computers long distance. He copied all the kid's online identities and passwords. That kid would not be going online anywhere any time soon. Wheeler rewrote his own online identities and put his privacy code on his new quantum bit chip as much as he could from the café. This was a processor he had been saving on an exterior drive. He could enhance his RSA encryption when he activated the Q-chip remotely so that any other uninvited voyeurs would find a whirligig of mis-coded junk released into their own computers. *Back at you, kid,* he thought.

Jessica leaned over his shoulder and smiled at him. He startled and hid what he was doing with a quick movement. "Almost done there?" she asked, innocently. She thought his name was Joshua Handlin and that he was orphaned very young and had no other relatives...and not many friends either.

His cloud of anonymity got denser with each keystroke. This would also help him when he disenfranchised his Team Wheeler members. He had homes that only he was aware of. He had condominiums all over the world.

He finished his Cappuccino and kissed Jessica, closing the lid of her laptop. He might feel lonely, but he was so much closer to being invisible—and that brought him comfort. He walked home alone and waved at her as he left.

His computers were unlocked for *him*, anyway, and he laughed to himself over his own cleverness and began packing. His family had an almost inaccessible, remote rural home in the Hebrides and was planning to fly there in his private helicopter. He could fly it himself. It was hidden in a rooftop hangar on top of his condo in London, which he planned on selling. He did not log his flight plan even under the name of Joshua Handlin. He was a citizen of Scotland and thought he could talk his way out of any trouble if he got caught. He was going from his private air pad to his grandfather's private landing strip at the family's island home.

His girlfriend would say nothing. He knew that. He had thought about taking her with him but decided not to. One day, soon, he wanted to tell her who he really was. Not quite yet, though. His Team Wheeler members were free to stay on his estate in South East England, although he planned on liquidating that place as soon as he could sell everything. As soon as he disenfranchised them, they would no longer know his whereabouts anymore. They could be hard to find, but he was much harder to find.

Rainier Voss sat at Asia's kitchen table and looked in horror at his laptop. He saw that the Locating Bot the CIA programmers set loose on the internet seemed to be failing sort of miserably. He looked at its key codes and had a feeling that they had been hacked by some genius with a Q-bit processor.

Someone that was not your average de-coder, but far beyond that. He swore, got up and heated some coffee for himself. He had stopped drinking caffeine due to Asia's influence, but now he needed some nervous energy in order to brainstorm this situation.

He stepped outside without his coat to try and clear his head. It was cloudy and very cold. He did not even have his wool sweater on, just a thin, cotton short sleeved shirt. He was wearing his house slippers in bare feet. The cold was refreshing. He stretched with a groan. Asia came outside and hugged him. She was crying and asked, "Why are you acting this way? You will catch pneumonia dressed like that. It must be -20° Fahrenheit out here."

"Hi, darling," answered Rannie pulling her closer and kissing her passionately. "I think I have some bad news. The CIA Bot isn't working. I need to go to Langley and use their computers to try and triangulate the location of this broadcast—at least get a general idea. There aren't many programmers that can do what this fellow is doing. I need to fight Q-bit with Q-bit, super processor with super processor."

He saw Asia's confusion. He continued, "I mean I need to use equivalent computer power to find this guy. The CIA headquarters in Langley, Virginia has that kind of equipment. Lilah and Reginald will probably have to come with me since they have firsthand knowledge of what happened here."

Seeing Asia's reaction to Lilah's name, Rainier said, "Oh, sweetheart—don't worry about Lilah. She is only my bodyguard. We will see each other again. Maybe when this thing is over. It is too important to catch these people before they can do more damage. If we can catch even one of them, it might lead to the capture of *all* of them. The world will be a safer place when we can do that."

Asia let a stray tear trail over her cheek. She brushed it aside. Zucchini rubbed against her leg and whined at her distress. She reached down and ruffled her silken back. Comforting her dog also made her feel better.

Rainier went inside and poured a cup of hot coffee for himself. He called Lilah and Reginald from the other room and outlined his plans to them. They agreed to speak to their superiors at Langley for him and book a flight as soon as possible.

The next morning Rainier, Lilah and Reginald left before five am. Asia was inconsolable. She hugged Zucchini to her as she looked out the still darkened windows. The weather reports had been predicting a large mid-winter blizzard in her area. Maybe upwards to two or even three feet of snow.

She had just gotten a new load of Timothy for Pumpkin and a couple 20lb. bags of dry dog food for Fuzzy and Zucchini. She had also had her solar panels cleared of ice and snow, but she needed to shop for bulk foods and other things before the storm got too bad. She didn't care right now. She would go later in the day.

She fell back to sleep on her sofa with her head on Zucchini's wide chest. Before she fell asleep, the thought of being alone in the house and the scary memories of last summer caused a chill of fear to run up and down her spine. Despite all that, she fell into a deep slumber.

Jessica Parker felt funny about Joshua (Jake Wheeler). She also knew more about computers than she had let on. There was just something odd about Josh. He obviously knew about code. A *lot* about code. He did not seem like an ordinary person. He also seemed to have too much money to be ordinary. Maybe he was a physicist from Oxford. An eccentric professor or something. She suddenly felt uncomfortable about him as she had watched him prepare to leave the café. She had smiled, kissed him on the cheek, and gone first. She waved at him as she passed in front of him, crossing the street. He waved back. She could look at her laptop later and try and find out what he had done and why.

She, herself, had been a programmer since childhood. After seeing what she had just seen, she did not trust Josh all that much. There was just something about him. He just knew too much without any explanation as to why he knew what he did.

After they split up and went their own ways, Jake felt angry and then hopeless. Utterly hopeless. He felt that Jessica was not just walking out of the café—but saying goodbye and walking out of his life. There was something wrong. Really wrong.

It seemed to him that everything was wrong. The Team was wrong. His life was wrong. His girl was gone. He had made adult enemies for the first time in his life. For all his talent and money, his future was unclear. Feeling foggy as he left the café, he had bought a pint of halfway decent whiskey and a cup of double shot espresso in a large cup to go. He walked to the park again and poured some of the whiskey into the cup with his espresso. He started to cry and called his grandfather on his cell phone.

He made arrangements to visit him for the weekend. He went home, finished packing and bringing things up to his helicopter – especially some of his microchips. He called his real estate agent and put his building in London and villa in the Southeast up for sale. He would hire people to sell his animals – all of them except one horse he especially loved and one of the Corgis. That was all, besides his machines, that he cared about.

He would bring his two favorite animals to the Hebrides in such a way that no one would see him transport them. It was not that difficult if you had the money for it, and he did. He would miss his garden but looked forward to building another one. He had other secret places in England and planned on moving around a little to confuse his possible pursuers, such as the three Team members that had betrayed him. They would be pretty steamed about not getting their share of the money stolen from Silver Lake.

He planned on purchasing hide-away ranches in Canada and America as well. Places he would not need to use a known identity and could purchase with some false papers that he had accumulated in the last few years. His paranoia about the murder of Jason Bing grew in his mind until the need for sleep overtook him. He would disband the Team Wheeler members in the morning, telling them that they could take a month off from their work. They must be anxious to leave anyway, having been paid.

Asia Reynolds was not enthused about being alone. Of course, she had her Pumpkin, Fuzzy and Zucchini. She laughed to herself. She had Jed Simmons take a break from clearing her snow and carry her folding bed out to the barn that night. She just couldn't bear to be alone right now. Donkeys are great company and the four of them would be warm and cozy sleeping around the barrel stove...blizzard or no blizzard. And a big one was brewing.

She brought Zookie's wool bedding out there. She had gotten a handmade wool bed for Fuzzy, too. She placed the dog beds next to hers and put her heavy cotton sleeping bag and woolen Army blanket on the mattress of the folding bed. It had been a while since she had stoked the stove, so she put enough chopped cedar in for most of the night and started heating some mulled cider to soothe her rough edges.

Suddenly, Fuzzy Bud went ballistic and Zucchini got up off her bed near the stove. Pumpkin brayed loudly. There was banging on the barn door. Asia startled, but went over and unchained the doors, peeking outside tentatively.

Frankie Franklin stood there in the wild winds of the initiating blizzard, snow blowing into her face. She had all nine of her dogs with her. Asia laughed and pulled her into the barn by her coat sleeve, waiting until all the dogs got in, too. "Better get yourself in here, Ms. Franklin. That blizzard isn't playing," she said.

Frankie answered, "I was just doing my duty and patrolling the neighborhood with my dogs. My truck did not make it past your house, gosh darn it. Died right here. You know I don't have a cell phone."

"Really, Frankie. I think you should consider getting one. They're great in emergencies like this." Asia brushed the snow off Frankie's shoulders, and offered her a cup of hot cider. She kept a few extra kitchen things in a cabinet in the barn for just such an occasion. All nine dogs, including Big Boy, Hunny and Frankie's two adopted, sleek Doberman circled the stove and lay down next to Zookie and Fuzzy after drinking some fresh water.

They were so quiet, it was difficult to realize there were eleven dogs surrounding the two women and a rather happily contented, pretty, little donkey. Pumpkin lay down in the center of her "visitors" gazing quietly from one dog to the other.

Asia and Frankie sipped their hot mulled cider. Frankie commented, "Guess we could stay here until morning and call triple A then. Would that be okay by you?"

Asia answered, "Sounds good to me. You can sleep in the bunk in the back. I have more clean woolen Army blankets and the mattress and pillow are good. Check it out, the bedding is in the cabinet next to the bunk shelf. We have enough wood in here for most of the winter, let alone right now."

"Okay, sweetie," answered Frankie, slapping her thighs and getting up to examine the back bunk.

"I just prefer to sleep over near the stove and my animals. I'll go get some cheese, apples and crackers and some clean sheets for you in the house."

"You're an angel, Asia."

"Watch my wings unfold as I fly to the house." Big Boy, Zucchini and Hunny went with her. Or rather, they preceded her and cut a path in the already two-foot-high snowfall. And, it was still falling heavily. The dogs made it easier to get to the house.

Zucchini and Hunny had made total peace with each other. They now shared Big Boy and usually flanked him: one on one side and one on the other. Asia hugged herself in the icy wind and snow-swept blizzard air. All these things made her feel whole (as usual): Frankie, the dogs, Pumpkin and sleeping rough next to the barrel stove in the barn. These were her life values. While love meant sharing this – *she* owned all of these things first of all. Which meant she could be happy alone anyway. She thought sadly about Rainier Voss's departure that morning.

Asia entered her warm kitchen and switched the lights on. She filled a wicker basket full of goodies and folded some clean sheets into her backpack. When she got back outside, the snow was coming down even harder than before.

Frankie and Asia had a little party in the barn. Asia had made some delicious fig pastry with whole wheat and multi-grain filo dough earlier. With some more hot mulled cider, they forgot about their troubles and the storm raging outside.

Asia cleaned the bunk area and made the bed for Frankie. Frankie trying out the bunk and bouncing on it, surrounded by some of her dogs, commented to Asia, "You know, you should keep your Remington 338 ultra-magnum handy. A large, male, black bear has been spotted in the area. *I've* seen it myself on my own property, and I live dang close to you."

Asia said she would keep her eyes out and be careful. She figured she could bring her Remington upstairs from her gun locker in the basement. The barn doors rattled, and she assured Frankie that it was only the feral howl of the storm outside.

Frankie said, "You know you should be careful. Bear can open sliding doors. You should have spread sunflower seeds in your driveway just in case. Some people say it attracts bear, but I think it also keeps them happy and occupied so they will not attack."

Asia went over and padlocked the chain on the doors. She would clean and oil her rifle in the morning. She did not relish going outside in the storm again tonight, especially with a bear being sighted nearby.

Frankie went on, "After this bear business passes, do you think Pumpkin would like my goats? You know, I just rescued couple of them from that old man that passed away up the road. I got most of his livestock, not that he had very much. Got a few chickens from him too. He didn't have any kin that wanted them."

Asia replied, "Pumpkin would probably love the goats. She is so very amiable. Bring them over to visit some time when the road is better. They can stay for a while and get acquainted."

"Sure thing, Asia. I just bought a new small livestock trailer. It's even big enough to haul your donkey in."

Asia was impressed and patted Frankie's hand. For a small, elderly person, she had so much energy and gumption. Asia really admired her. Frankie founded and ran a small animal rescue at her home and farmstead. She also managed her family's popular rib shack Bar-B-Que take out.

She had inherited both the business and farmstead from her parents and did pretty well running both. She made a good living from the business. Her family was probably descended from some of the earliest post-Civil War, African-American settlers in the area, like Elise and her family. That emigration had formed most of the black community in Silver Lake.

Asia loved "Frankie" Louise Franklin dearly. She loved her warmth and dedication to animal welfare. She loved her strength, too. After Frankie fell asleep, Asia went back over to the stove. The barn doors rattled again, violently this time, but the chain held them fast against the ravages of this deafening winter storm.

Chapter Eleven

Jake Wheeler had bought two bottles of fine whiskey on the way back to his condominium, since he could not choose between Glenlivet XXV single malt and Highland Park 30 Scotch. So ... he bought a quart bottle of both and spent quite a little bit of money on them. He had started drinking from the Glenlivet right after he had finished the double shot of espresso laced with whiskey and the other cheap pint he had gotten. By the time he got home, he was pretty drunk. He drank himself to sleep after he had finished packing his most precious things into his 'copter. He did not even bother to remove his clothing or boots, falling asleep across his bed, also not bothering to get under the covers.

The next day Jake did not feel like shaving, even for his grandfather. His grandfather was, by the way, his very favorite relative. He loved his dad, but his grand was a teddy bear.

Jake was an only child and a lonely child. His grand was cute and funny and more his playmate than an elder relative. Grand always understood. His grandmother had passed away many years ago and he never saw the relatives on his mother's side of the family. Jake had more Highland Park

30 with his breakfast. He always had liked whiskey with his eggs.

Grand would love a taste of this real Scottish whiskey and there was still plenty left of the two bottles. He had to stay sober enough to pilot his helicopter and visit his grand without getting him worried about his state of mind.

He packed an insulated shoulder bag with both whiskeys. He took a swig of the Glenlivet for good luck, feeling just a bit happier than usual. His grandfather, Bernard (Bernie) Campbell-Wheeler, still held and managed the Campbell Family Trust for him, just as a protective measure and also because he was very good at investing and made money for Jake just as an added gift from the capital he held for him – and had given him. Investments were how Bernie had created his fortune to begin with, along with a large real estate company. Jake especially liked this arrangement right now, since he was feeling threatened and insecure because of the actions of Team Wheeler. His grand could hide his money for him and was used to him going overseas and could send money anywhere if he might need it, no questions asked.

Otherwise Jake had a free hand to use any amount he might need or want. If an unusually large amount should transfer, Bernie Wheeler was also free to inquire about it. Wheeler was a common name and Bernie usually used Campbell as his legal name. He was listed officially as a Campbell (Bernard Wheeler's mother's maiden name), not as a Wheeler, which was why it had been doubly hard for anyone but the Feds to connect Jake to him.

No one suspected his grand controlled Jake's money, so Jake was protected this way. His grand was famous throughout Britain for his investment and financial acuity. And Jake loved him.

Perhaps later, he would find a safe way to control his own estate, or at least, share that control with Bernie. He had ideas, but now was not the most auspicious time for their realization.

His grand never asked questions and did not know about Jake's illegal activities. Jake had never been caught. He thought all Jake did was construct apps and games and invent "nifty" computer hardware. This hidden, rural home in the Hebrides was a place to which none of his Team had ever been invited and none were even aware of. His Team's ex-members owned hidden properties and homes as well.

He warmed up his 'copter and checked the weather on his flight route. He took another swig of Highland Park. He was drunk, but only slightly. He was still, according to him, able to fly.

Jake's grandfather, Bernard Wheeler, managed the family estate in the Hebrides, and was the legal owner of the entire island. Jake was really looking forward to walking with his grand and Adair, Bernie's Airedale. They would walk along the expansive, beautiful beaches of the island estate. It was still a wonderland to him, even though he had been visiting his grand for over thirty years. The majestic mountains overlooking the Outer Hebrides islands and the waterfall near his grand's estate still gave him open-mouthed feelings of awe. He loved his grand's two black and chestnut Fell ponies: Ainsley and Baird.

They could ride the ponies next to the Airedale on the beaches. The cold did not bother him, he had done this so very many times. He took another swig of Highland Park. He shook his head and felt sad that he could not trust anyone to go with him to visit this slice of his heaven and his beloved grand. He had created too treacherous a lifestyle. He drank deeply of his whiskey and turned off the 'copter. He went inside, lay on his bed and put on some light, soft music, falling asleep. He should take a nap before flying. Might want to be a bit more careful about the alcohol.

He slept soundly for forty-five minutes and awoke refreshed. He took another shot of Highland and got in the shower, still not wanting to shave. He kind of liked the shape of his beard and the nice black outline of it. He loved the flight route to the Outer Hebrides. It exhilarated him. And he needed the thrill of it right now.

He was upset about dissolving his partnership with Team Wheeler. They had been together for many years. He had come to an ending point with the murder of Jason Bing and the disloyalty of the three members that had shot him and thrown him out of Jake's plane. He sent severance notices to everyone who worked for him. After his generous payments to them, he didn't think they would give him any problems. He explained that he, himself, was transitioning and probably going back to creating games and applications.

His computer people would go first. His household staff would leave as soon as his villa was sold. New people would be hired under his alias of Joshua Handlin to help him move to his house in the Hebrides.

The house and estate there was beautiful and very isolated. No one knew about most of the property that Jake or his family owned. The Hebrides islands had many hiding places and were completely inaccessible in bad weather. His grandfather was indigenous to these islands, he knew them well.

His grand would calm him. He drank another shot of Glenlivet this time. He got into his 'copter, pulled out of the hangar, and lifted smoothly off the roof of his building, looking at the sights of London on the streets below. The sky was clear and the air over London cold, but he was warm in the 'copter. He drank a little more whiskey and warmed up even more nicely.

It would only take about an hour to get to grand's estate. There was a family landing strip there with several private hangars. He smiled to himself and drank more liquor and was aware he was getting progressively drunker. The 'copter hit an air pocket and pitched downward. Jake's head spun. He cursed his own drunkenness. The 'copter took another ragged jolt downward.

This was the one time Jake wished he could have taken a friend with him. Jake took another drink and took the 'copter up again. He knew he could not afford friends right now (outside of his grand that is). True, he was drinking a little too much, but he would be at grand's in another fifteen minutes or so. The wind seemed a little too heavy, but he ignored it, he was used to the vagaries of flying this 'copter in British weather. It was like a car or even a bicycle to him, he was so used to it. He could fly this thing blindfolded. As drunk as he was, he might as well have *been* blindfolded.

The 'copter went down towards some rocks off the ocean suddenly. Jake had lost control. The 'copter rocketed down and hit a rocky cliff. Jake hit the glass of the cockpit and everything went black. It began to rain. The wind whipped the rain and the ocean became frenzied and crashed over the cliffs at the shoreline, rocking the wrecked aircraft. Jake was still unconscious and had been for the last twenty-four hours. The helicopter teetered on the edge of the cliff it had crashed into.

Slowly, as the pink light of dawn peeked over a thin horizon line, Jake gained consciousness again and tried to stretch to relieve his cramped position. He felt a shock of pain shooting up his leg. The pain was so bad he could not think. He glanced to the floor on his right side and saw that his two whiskey bottles were fine and still nestled in their insulated carry-on bag.

A miracle! Well, maybe some people would not put that in the miracle category, but he definitely did. At almost 462 Euros or 352 Pounds Sterling ($500) per bottle, it was cost effective too. He grabbed the Glenlivet and took a long drink. The heat passing through his throat warmed him, woke him up from his stupor and took some of the pain away from his left side. He could move a little.

The horrid sound that move made drew his attention out the window. That was when he noticed that the helicopter was perilously close to slipping off the cliff and going over the rocks into the ocean. It would be difficult to find a way out of the ocean if he fell, let alone crawl to land. The entire shoreline was comprised of rocky cliffs at least one hundred feet high, some of them sheer. There were no sandy beaches here. He doubted if he could swim in the condition his body was in anyway. There was no way he could get out of the cockpit under water.

THE OCEAN WAS ROILING. The waves were so vicious that when they crashed into the cliff his helicopter was on, he could feel a heavy spray regardless of how high the cliff was. Jake shivered uncontrollably in the cold winter air. He was soaking wet. His fingers were numb. His feet were getting there too.

It was that heavy spray exploding violently over the cliff he was stuck on that worried him. He would have to get out and get out carefully and quickly if he was to save his own life. "*Save his own life*" echoed and re-echoed in his mind. His life was something he had devalued right before the crash. Now, he wanted to be saved.

He noticed that the small backpack with his newly minted Q-bit microchips and some important software and perhaps a few dry clothes and a rain poncho (valuable even at even his grandfather's place) was still wedged next to the bag with the whiskey in it. He took another blessed swallow of the Glenlivet, shut both bottles tightly and zippered the bag closed.

He would have to crawl out the passenger-side door next to him. He looked downward out his door and gasped. Every time the 'copter rocked with ocean spray or was hit with a strong wind, he could see straight down the cliff into the rocks and tempestuous saltwater. He thought crawling to the door opposite him might counterbalance the machine and help him get out.

He felt his wallet in his back jean's pocket and praised himself that he had done the biker thing of hooking it through a metal eyelet to a belt loop with a small, heavy chain. He would need money once he got to a town. He had taken 3,000 Euros in cash so he would not need his credit cards. By the looks of things, he figured he was still pretty far from his grandfather's estate.

His watch had stopped, so he didn't know the time or the date. He imagined that he was very late arriving to his grand's. That was actually good (outside of his grand being worried about him) because grand would have sent search parties out for him right away and known that the weather would have been treacherous for flying.

He swore to himself since he had not filed a flight plan, but grand would have known how fickle the weather was up here – and known it well. And so would everyone else. They would not have argued against search parties or dogs.

Jake fumbled with the door handle. He had put the strap of the whiskey bag over his backpack straps across his chest. Besides his flight bag, he also stowed a survival backpack. It was clumsy but no matter how he landed on the ground, his bags should stay on. He had no intention of losing his stash of whiskey. He hadn't brought much food in his flight bag, but he had a lift top small can of salmon, brown bread and an apple in a waterproof seal-tight soft container.

The survival pack was another story. He had about 15 packets of dehydrated camping food. He also had a flint-magnesium waterproof lighter and a tiny fold-up stove and hammock. There was also a collapsible pot, silverware and his compass, a lightweight waterproof dome tarpaulin, a mag flashlight, waterproof matches, candles and soap. And, many other useful things. He had his Glock 43 and a full box of 9mm rounds for small game and aggressive human intruders. The hammock could be used to net fish. These were standard for his flight gear and weighed under 10 lbs.

Thank Jehovah he believed in survival equipment. He also had a good quality Swiss Army knife and a fold-up wood saw. The aluminum packets of camping food, he could cook when the rain stopped, and he scrounged some dead pine needles and dry small branches. He had also packed a bottle of water.

All this was actually rather small and lightweight and none of it was jammed in the wreckage. Everything in his backpack, which included a set of dry clothing, fit nicely. The survival pack was a waterproof wetbag – the kind that kayakers use. The straps around his shoulders and in his hand seemed strong and undamaged. Unfortunately, his sleeping bag was inaccessible and stuck in the back of the helicopter.

He took a deep breath and inched his entire body closer towards the door. The 'copter rocked back and forth dangerously because he was clumsy with pain, but he reached the passenger-side door handle, close enough to open the door cautiously.

He knew if he flung the door open in this wind, the opening into the cockpit could be his demise. He pushed his painful body closer to the door, hoping to counterbalance the wind with his body weight. The ocean crashed over his head pushing the helicopter onto land, but also rocking it again dangerously in the opposite direction. The machine was going to fall. There was no doubt. When – was the question.

Jake pushed the door open just a crack when the wind lulled and held it there as he inched closer. *Gosh,* he thought, *those bags (especially the whiskey bag) were clumsy.* But he had no intention of losing that precious cargo. He pushed the door to the 'copter wide open when the wind subsided and was calm and threw himself on the muddy, rocky ground face down.

The wind came back with a roar and slapped into Jake's helicopter throwing it over the cliff violently. It hit the enormous frothing breakers of the turbulent ocean after breaking up on the rocks. A wave crashed over Jake's head, but he was safe, even though he was soaked through to the skin and covered in mud with a possible broken leg.

He could crawl despite the agonizing pain in his left leg. He praised his father's ingenuity and the vagaries of British weather for the foresight in getting him a heavy plastic, bright yellow, watertight kayaking backpack, that could also be used as a floatation device if one was drowning. Everything in it would be dry. He laughed and felt a silly sort of elation.

He took his backpack and whiskey bag off and rolled in the muddy ground trying to get up. It was futile. He could raise himself up on his arms, but he could not tolerate any pressure on his left leg. He screamed. Tears rolled down his face and mixed with mud.

He pushed himself up into a sitting position next to a boulder and propped his back up on it. He pulled the whiskey bag to him, unzipped it and took a long, deep drink. That made his leg feel better. He knew he would need to set up some kind of camp soon, just a temporary thing until he could gain some mobility and strength.

A wave crashed over him, soaking him to the skin with icy cold saltwater, making his wounds sting while he shook with the cold. He began to cry again.

He saw a small patch of forest. A large red deer ran from it, spooking a few woodcock into flight. There were boulders in that place, too, which would make a good start for a small shelter and would dry quickly once it stopped raining. He could also cook on one of the flatter rocks. There was some game there, too, obviously. He would have fresh meat with his camping food, shot with his Glock. He fantasized about starting a nice warm campfire and drying out his clothing. He had a roll of plastic rope and clothespins which he used to pin up parts of his tarpaulin but could also be used to dry clothes with. Another wave went crashing over the cliff and slapped him in the face. He *had* to move.

He strapped the closed whiskey bag across his chest again and began to crawl through the mud and smaller rocks. It hurt, but the field of grass was only about one hundred feet away.

The small forest was out of range of the crashing surf, which would grow smaller when the wind died down a little more. The rain seemed to be less ferocious than it was even fifteen minutes ago. He looked at the sky. It, too, seemed to be getting just a bit clearer, less cloudy and ominous. He continued crawling and finally reached an area filled with tall grasses, which was out of range of the ocean spray. He was really filthy and wet – covered in mud.

The rain stopped as suddenly as it had started. It took him hours, though, to reach that patch of forest. A red buck ran right past him, scaring up another bunch of birds. Red grouse, this time, he thought. The deer had been so close to him, he could practically feel its breath on his face. His gun was dry inside his backpack.

He stopped crawling, resting a moment. He felt sleepy and didn't dare try and get a sip of liquor. He must start a fire soon. The sun was receding. It would be dark in maybe a half an hour, pitch black. He could get hypothermia if he did not pitch camp and start a fire as soon as he possibly could. Especially if his leg was broken as he feared it was.

————

Asia and Frankie were enjoying the warmth of the barrel stove and having some fun with the dogs and the new donkey. Pumpkin liked to play catch and some of the dogs did also. As the two women ate cheese, crackers and apple slices, they intermittently tossed a large soccer-type hard ball around the barn and laughed while Pumpkin tried to get it safe between her legs before Zucchini, Big Boy or Hunny got to it first.

Playing keep-away with these three giants was funny enough. The tiny Fuzzy Bud was bravely trying to defend the donkey's position, but the gigantic St. Bernard, Husky and Newfoundland found it relatively easy to bowl her over or step right past the little Chihuahua, which was pretty comic.

The much bigger donkey, though, was another matter. Pumpkin was a gentle being, but like most donkeys (and elephants, too, for that matter) she was skillful at kicking to the side. She would get the ball and deftly kick it to Asia (who usually had a mouthful of crackers and cheese). Asia would grab it and try and throw it back to the line of expectant and waiting animals.

All the other dogs just sort of ran around, confusing the others and creating a sort of distracting scrimmage. Frankie and Asia laughed until their sides hurt, spitting bits of cracker here and there on the barn floor. It was silly and sloppy and fun. Asia stretched and yawned.

Suddenly, the barn doors shook violently, and something seemed to moan and try to push them apart, but there was no knocking, so no one was there.

"Wow," exclaimed Frankie. "The wind is ferocious tonight. Worst I've ever seen, and I've been here in Silver Lake over eighty years."

Asia looked worried. "I don't think the wind could knock those doors down."

Frankie agreed. "They are way too heavy. You seem to keep your place in good shape, so I would expect that they are solidly on the runners."

"The runners are new. So is the beam they are bolted to."

The two women finished the cheese and deserted on the rest of the apple slices. The doors rattled again, and Frankie got up and went back to her bunk with her circle of friendly rescued dogs. Asia heard her begin to snore rather loudly and smiled. She put an armful of sweet-smelling cedar in the stove and slid her boots off.

She hugged Zucchini and told her what a good girl she was and stretched out on her folding bed. The doors rattled again. Asia frowned but ignored the commotion. Several dogs went over to the front of the barn and began sniffing at the bottom of the sliding barn doors. They barked, but soon stopped, taking up residence across the entrance, several of them growling occasionally in discontent. Asia fell into a deep, warm and comfortable slumber. The rattling door and growling, disgruntled dogs faded into the background. The cedar logs in the barrel stove crackled merrily. There seemed to be not a worry in the world.

Dr. Rainier Voss could not have disagreed more. He took this lull in hacker attacks two ways: one, it made him uneasy and two, he took advantage of this respite to profile the group that had done so much damage. Interpol was pretty sure it was the British group that had run a few cons (including passing some rather well-done counterfeit currency) in Monaco a few years back. Voss saw no reason to disagree.

The profile Interpol had given him included ownership of a private jet, counterfeiting and some advanced computer and tech skills – including a rather vast sum of operating money at their disposal. No agency had an inkling as to the real identities of the group's members.

Voss concluded that the only way he and his colleagues at Langley could identify the members of this group was to infiltrate them through another group of hackers with similar skills – possibly a European group.

That action would take a direct order from the President and the head of the CIA. Voss could see no other way. They had to authorize illegal activity in order to trace the group membership down to their human and online identities. Involved, but not impossible. The theme music to *Mission Impossible* played in Rainier Voss's head.

They would need permission to run the U.S. government program that captured phone, email and chat conversations. That program used key words relating to the crimes that were committed and the area they were committed in. And, they would have to surveille the hackers that worked for the CIA. Voss's fingers flew across the keyboard of his CIA computer organizing the sting. Interpol would be apprised of every move the CIA made in this case.

All the analysts were pretty sure they were looking for a group of Europeans and concentrated on trying to organize any information they could catalog concerning well-known or possible hackers on that continent.

Meanwhile, Team Wheeler members that were still residing in the comfort and luxury of Jake Wheeler's villa were dining on Wheeler's best cuisine and drinking his finest wines, as usual. They were all happy with their recent payments from the money they had helped embezzle from Silver Lake banks, their counterfeiting and gambling ventures. They knew that the international security community must be looking for them but felt secure that their real identities were covered in layers of cyberspace pixels – clouds of confusing identities. They were over-confident, in fact. Everyone except the three Team members that had rolled Jason Bing out of the trash chute of the jet were content to wait for Jacob Wheeler to contact them with their next assignment. This was their usual procedure.

The three men that had plotted against Wheeler had been actively tracing his movements since he had left his villa in the Southeast for London. They had their covert telescopic internet sights on a woman they knew to be Wheeler's (now possibly former) girlfriend, Jessica Parker. They knew from her emails that she suspected that Jake was more into computers than he had talked to her about and that sort of put her off him. *"Into"* was the ludicrous word she had used.

They laughed at her naïve suspicions. She, herself, was a competent programmer and had not told him. She had also seen an extensive map of what he had done on her computer, so she knew that he had enemies in cyberspace. The insurgents also viewed what had happened to his home computers in London with interest. After watching her for a short time, they decided that it was unproductive to look into her further.

The mutineers had recently lost track of Jake's whereabouts, to their great frustration. In fact, for the last two days, they had no idea where he was. Drunk maybe. Clubbing? No idea. It worried them no end and they ramped up their hacking of his computer identities to no avail. It seemed he was not on the Net, either. It seemed as if he had dropped off the edge of the earth. They hadn't a clue as to how close they had gotten to guessing what had happened to him. Jessica didn't seem to know a thing.

Asia and Frankie slept late the next day. In fact, the stove was starting to burn down. It was Zucchini that finally attempted to wake Asia. She needed to go outside to take care of her business, no matter what.

She was not alone. Most of Frankie's dogs wanted out, as well. Asia walked over to the barn doors, unlocked the chain holding them closed and yanked on the handles. They did not budge. She tried again. Still, they remained motionless. Zucchini whimpered.

Asia looked down at her and said, "Frozen shut, girl. I'll have to call the Simmons boys."

She turned around and shouted, "Frankie! We're stuck here for now. The doors are frozen! I'll call the Simmons. They'll get us out."

"Better do that," responded Frankie. "Good thing you have your cell phone with you."

"Yeah. They're great in an emergency." The doors shook and rattled. Zucchini sniffed at them and barked. The doors banged again.

Rainier Voss met with his research colleagues at Langley. They went over all the possible scenarios for capturing and further profiling the hackers they were after. Most of the researchers felt there was at least one member of their fugitive group still undercover in Silver Lake. They voted to send a contingency back there to try and hunt them down.

Half of the CIA research group was to go to London as a European base of operations. Even if the hacker group was in eastern Europe, they would be closer to a possible source of information. Voss was chosen to lead the group flying to London. He called Asia and told her he would be leaving for London the next day from Virginia.

His trip to Europe was something they had discussed when he was staying at her home. He promised to email and give her updates on his travels.

He inserted the video game disc for *XCOM 2* by *Firaxis Games* into his CIA mega-computer. It was the furthest thing from his mind to fight an alien invasion, but it helped him relax and let his worries go. This computer had some amazing graphics and a huge screen. He had an old love of video games from his teen years.

He was off the clock and it relaxed his mind. This was a security-approved copy and in common after-hours use at the agency. Oddly enough, using some of their approved after-hours/pre-hours games were credited with solving some really difficult, time-sensitive agency problems. According to a recent, brilliant, innovative administrator, using video games gave operatives time to muse while engaging minimally in the usage of their muscular and reflexive thinking skills.

It wasn't like work, where their answers and actions affected real-time life and death situations.

She (by the way, that administrator was a woman) was right on. She even provided a flight training program, so interested operatives could learn the basics of flying. Voss had completed that training program, but still occasionally practiced flying on the simulator provided on the last disc of the program. There was also an accuracy program for gunfire in flight.

He switched to the flight simulator now, clicking on an .mp3 recording of Chopin's *Nocturne* which helped him *not* think while he flew flawlessly – practicing on a GPS simulation of a flight path from London to Dublin, Ireland. He knew the simulator could also imitate rough weather and some mechanical emergencies, as well. He coasted in his virtual airplane deep in thought inside his music. No real ideas came to him, but he really enjoyed seeing the real landscape of England and Ireland, even if it was animated.

Outside of having to delay a visit with Asia Reynolds, Voss looked forward to seeing London and maybe even some of the English and Irish countryside. There were two solid possible leads on the hacker gang that attacked Silver Lake: one—Jason Bing (the dead man who was English and had a record tracing back to when he was eleven, programming viruses, worms and cracking programs)—and two—the suspicions of Interpol based on witnesses to the gaming and counterfeiting cons perpetrated in Monaco last year. His favorite source of information for this case was the hacker community. They might even be personally acquainted with some of the personnel they were looking for.

The CIA group going to London also felt the hacker community there might give them even more leads, especially since their hacker allies here in the States had created intense and believable online hacking identities for Rainier and his fellow CIA operatives. The US authorities had given them a *carte blanche* to join up in London with the Symantec security corporation undercover people before both security groups dove into the local hacker population to gather whatever information they could on the group that had hacked Silver Lake.

Feeling exhausted and cold, Jake Wheeler pulled his aching, injured body into a medium large space between three boulders and two small, but strong, trees. Right now, there was no telling where, exactly, he was. He was confused and a little disoriented right now. Turned around. He had a good guess where he was from the terrain, but he wouldn't be absolutely sure until he checked his compass readings and looked at the maps he had in his backpack. He pretty much thought he had been blown off course by the ferocious wind that had kicked up. Yes, he damn well thought so. He couldn't sleep yet; he would die from hypothermia. He knew it. He was way too tired and emotionally wrought to care about his body temperature and that was dangerous.

He propped himself up on a boulder and took the whiskey bag and his backpack off, setting them both close to him. *"No whiskey,"* he told himself, strongly. No liquor until he was finished setting up his camp. If he did that, he would be in danger of falling asleep even on the cold, muddy ground. He couldn't risk that. He pulled the dome tarpaulin and folded up hammock, small fold-up stove, magnesium-flint lighter, coconut shell candle and a few other things out of his backpack, such as some of the smoked salmon jerky, apples and sandwich – which he ate right away.

He felt a little better and stronger and painfully pulled himself up to throw the dome tarp over the boulders. He used tent spikes to hold it down. It was a perfect fit. He had eyed the proportions of his small camp site well. He sat down and crawled out into a much lighter rain and gathered dead pine needles (which burn regardless of how wet they are) and very small branches that dry quickly. He peeled the wet bark off the branches and got two thick, strong sticks to weave into the ends of the hammock net.

He crawled back under the tarp and changed into a dry knit (warmer) shirt from the backpack. He slung the hammock low on two opposing trees fitting it through the two openings in the tarp in the front and back. He hooked his wet, muddy shirt on the bottom of the net. He had a cheap, ultra-thin, but huge (20' x 20'), lightweight plastic tarp to set over the dome tarp, giving him more dry space.

He got up painfully and limped around the dome, tying clothesline from one tree to another. He put the thin tarp over three clotheslines and pinned it with clothes pins. He could cook under that and protect his fire from droplets off the trees and the rain. It wasn't very good in the wind, but the wind had died down as fast as it had come up and he had two more such tarps in his backpack. New from the store, they were very small (about 3"x 3") or the size and weight of a miniature packet of Kleenex, very easy to pack and essential. If he moved, he would just throw away the one that he had used.

They were perfect for the light rain and extended far beyond the entrance to the dome tarp, so it kept his entrance and the cooking area dry. He was slightly protected from the wind, so the ultra thin tarp was okay right now and even in heavy rain. If there was only a light wind, it would keep his cooking area dry. He put the half coconut shell with old, melted scented candles and a waxed, hemp rope wick outside the dome, but still under the ultra-thin plastic. That lasted longer than his mag light (and batteries). He used it for bathroom purposes. It lit a large area around his "tent" at night. The shell would not burn or crack with the heat of a flame so it was safe and could light his sleeping area too. It was also a great way to conserve candle wax from his packet of new candles. He had a few extra lighters and waterproof matches to light candles with.

The magnesium-flint lighter conserved this equipment. He used that to light his campfires which could eat up matches or lighters unnecessarily. One just shaved some magnesium into dry pine needles or tinder of some sort, and scratched the flint with a piece of steel, generally the back of a hunting knife. The flint produced sparks, lit the highly flammable magnesium and ignited the tinder/pine needles. It was good in the rain because it was entirely water-proof. It was also very small, the size of a house key.

Night was falling. It would be dark in another hour or so. He stacked the dead and brown pine needles inside a rock circle under the little fold up stove, shaved the magnesium into the center of the needles and scraped the flint with his steel hunting knife. The flint sent out a couple of large sparks into the magnesium shavings igniting them and subsequently the pine needles. He quickly added a few small branches. It caught well. The small cooking fire felt heavenly. He silently blessed his father for teaching him these little tricks and giving him these small comforts that meant everything to him right now.

His leg was swollen like a balloon from standing on it and the pain from it still made him feel faint. He had not gone into shock, though. Probably since he had warmed up, not fallen asleep and kept his mind on what he had to do. Psychology was very important to him because of his injuries.

He used his bottle of water to make a small pot of hot tea. He would try and hunt tomorrow and look for clean water. When his tea was finished, he lifted the stove off the fire with a stick and added larger branches to the stone circle. He put a large stack of branches under the thin, plastic tarpaulin on some stones to dry out overnight. The fire really warmed him now.

He packed everything away in the plastic kayaking bag neatly and closed it securely. Finally, he opened his whiskey bag and took a couple of deep draughts from the Glenlivet. The pounding throb in his leg went away. He massaged it gently. He drank again and pulled himself up on a large staff he had found and easily lowered himself into the tarpaulin cover and onto the hammock. He used a dry pair of thick, cotton khakis from the backpack as a pillow and put the wet-pack under his knee to elevate his left leg. He fell into a deep sleep immediately.

The fire burned for a few more hours and radiated enough heat to comfort him and aid his slumber. His clothes began to dry. He snored loudly into the night.

A red deer was startled and jumped away from his camp, leaping into the setting sun.

Chapter Twelve

D
r. Rainier Voss and his CIA-Symantec research team debarked at Heathrow Airport in London. they had all decided to live in Brixton and use that area as a hub to contact hacker communities in Europe. The researchers wanted to create personal friendships with individual hackers. So, that night everyone went to the *Cannoniere* Club, a local Brixton computer gamer club during the day and an electronica dance club at night. It was a good start for their investigation since it simply meant dancing and meeting the regulars.

Rainier became popular with the *Cannoniere* day crowd right away. His gaming skills proved invaluable for making new friends with these computer-savvy young people. He even suggested upgrades to the *Cannoniere's* processors which were accepted and installed within a week, definitely increasing the speed of the club's gaming equipment, and the speed at which he gained friends among the youthful gamers in the club. The name of the club told it all, it was Italian for "gunships".

The CIA-Symantec group thought outright that they had nailed the right group for some form of computer wizardry, including some hacking. Unless, of course, the name only referred to the computer war games that were so popular right now. The club had a reputation, though, for cultivating app programmers, and that was real close to what the investigators were looking for in terms of contacts.

There was a locked back room at the club that Voss wanted access to. He was told, in confidence, by a young gamer that the locked door led to offices and a mega-computer room used for writing code by a very select group chosen by the *Cannoniere* owners and managers. Rainier asked by what process the club owners chose their elite members for this activity. The young kid shook his head and said that one had to allow the club to profile the person and place tracers on them and then come up clean. Plus, said the young computer geek, one had to be able to wield a computer like a light saber. He said he could do that but did not like hacking and that the club owners were corrupt. Just about everyone surmised that was what their codes were used for.

"Light saber?" asked Rainier, deliberately sounding incredulous.

"Yeah," said the boy. "They give you assignments sort of blind, and you have to solve the problems they give you. But me and my friends can see through all of that, and we know what they can do with the programming that we give them, and it is possibly not legal stuff. By the way, be careful if you are still interested or curious. They are really paranoid of spies and especially Downing Street."

Voss looked at the boy piercingly, questioning. "Downing Street?" he asked, seeming to be without comprehension.

The kid's shoulders shook with laughter. He said, "You really *are* an American. Downing Street is MI-6, Her

Majesty's Secret Service. The UK's version of the CIA. The *Cannoniere* doesn't like them, to put it mildly. If you *are* chosen to go to the back room, you can talk to me, but you would need to stop there."

Later, the next morning, Voss got a call from Asia. She wanted to join him in London. She had finished filming her piece on the history of Silver Lake and could edit the film overseas, or later if she could not find a studio in the UK in her price range. She wanted to combine her visit to Voss with research for a documentary on underground London and the caves of the UK in general. She wanted to visit an international donkey sanctuary she had seen online, The Donkey Sanctuary in Sidmouth, Devon. She planned on giving the piece to KANU.

She would be out of Rainier's way most of the time, doing library research and traveling to historical sites to film. He was delighted, but anxious.

The CIA gave him permission to spend time with Asia, but she was not allowed to move in with him or contact other members of the international investigative team, which now included MI-6. Her politics and notoriety as a documentarian, might be difficult for them or lead to them breaking cover and exposing them to danger. According to their very recent findings, Brixton had a lot to hide. Especially the *Cannoniere* Club seemed to be a nexus of possible illegal computer activity. The Brits did not want to move in on the back room until the American team had placed their man there and had some concrete findings in their own investigation.

The young boy that Rainier had met, Philip Overhouse, was well-known to MI-6 since his days in computer classes in secondary school. He had already spent time in jail for illegal mail activity and possible virus spreading through a gaming application he had created. That could explain his lack of interest in joining the people in the back room. Or, he was working for the club and keeping an eye on those interested in becoming one of the elite. Rainier would be careful of him. Being wary of possible threatening people was part of his investigative role anyway.

Rainier was to enter the back room at the *Cannoniere* tonight. He had passed the scrutiny of the administration at the club. They seemed curious and interested in his computer talent. Asia would be at Heathrow in another twenty-four hours. She had chosen a student rooming house area close to Oxford University to stay in, mainly because she planned on getting a pass to use the libraries there. She was hoping there were also a lot of interesting bookstores in the area to browse in. She was planning on getting a London rail pass so that she could travel freely and easily to places of interest.

Both Rainier and Asia had been disappointed that the US security agencies would not let them reside together. But they could see each other as much as possible. Asia was still snowed-in at her barn, so Rainier was worried about that, too. Asia reassured him that Jed and Jerry Simmons would get her and Frankie out soon.

Frankie and Elise were to share time taking care of Asia's dogs and the donkey while she was in Europe. There was food for the dogs, donkey and humans in the barn. She would stock up before she left. Jed and Jerry had other work they had to complete before they dug them out. The boys would be there today, and soon.

Rainier could hear Frankie complaining in the background of the phone call. She said loudly, "Yeah, if they ever get us out of here!" He could hear the banging of the barn doors clearly. Asia assured him that it was only the wind from the snowstorm.

He said, "Call me back as soon as you are safe."

She said, "I love you. I will call as soon as I get to the house. Don't worry. I think I hear the Simmons boys right now. Someone is scraping around the doors. It must be them and their snowplow."

"Okay," responded Rannie with anxiety. "Be safe. I will talk to you later."

"You be careful, too. Bye..."

"Goodbye..."

The scraping continued outside Asia's barn doors. Suddenly, a high-pitched scream was heard along with an animated, excited conversation. There was the roar of a truck and then silence. The barn doors rattled and shook again. Asia's phone rang. She answered it.

"Yes?"

It was Jed Simmons. He said, breathlessly, "We almost got your barn doors de-iced. The storm dumped about three feet of snow, so we have to shovel and plow all around your house". Cryptically, he added, "Even if you *can* get the barn doors open, I would not advise coming out behind your house right now."

"Wow," exclaimed Asia. *"Three feet?!* That must be a record for our area. The cornfields are seriously buried now. What was the matter? I thought I heard a scream. Why did you pull away? Why can't we come out? We need to get out of here."

"Oh, Ms. Reynolds, we are so sorry. Me and Jerry have to go home and get my rifle."

Asia tensed, remembering the troubles at her home last summer. "Maybe you need to call the police!" she said. "Don't take matters into your own hands."

There was a confused silence on the phone. "Um, ah, well I think we can scare him off ourselves. Or shoot him."

"Oh, no!" exclaimed Asia, concerned. "If it is an intruder, don't take that responsibility on yourselves. That is a job for the police. I can call them for you if you think that guy saw you."

Jed laughed a little, which Asia felt was a touch cavalier and inappropriate.

Then Jed said, "Ms. Reynolds, it was a *bear*, not a person."

"Oh my God," said Asia, covering her mouth for a second. "Ms. Franklin and I have been hearing the barn door banging around all night long. We thought it was the storm."

"Nope," replied Jed, still laughing a little. "The bear has probably been trying to get into the barn. He stuttered and continued, "I-I don't think he can get in if the doors are securely padlocked."

"They are," said Asia.

"We will return soon. I have a rifle that should take care of this. We'll just try and scare him off. I know you have a rifle in your house, too. So, if he comes back, you can just shoot into the air if you have to. If he won't leave, then we will get some fresh bear meat. I have a hunting license and bear is in season."

"Thanks, okay," answered Asia. "Call me and let me know how it is going and when you arrive."

Jed answered, "We will."

"Bye, then."

Asia called Elise who volunteered to move into her house when she left for London. She did not want her coming over too early. She could not even imagine what Elise would do if she saw a bear, besides the fact that *she* was still locked in the barn. Elise and Frankie were to care for the dogs and Pumpkin while she was gone. Elise was still a little wary of Pumpkin, so Frankie was going to come over to feed and groom her and try and show Elise how to do the same thing. It was Frankie Franklin that had the extensive livestock experience. In fact, she was hoping to bring her two goats, Thelma and Louise, over to keep Pumpkin company while Asia was in the UK.

Timid, little Elise was hoping to get her camera crew out to the barn, later, and get the goats and donkey on film for a little human interest piece for her *Mississippi River Journal* late night show. Harry ("the Hippie") Skylar was back home and Elise was hoping to get him to record some background music for the piece, especially since she had offered to advertise his new CD with Sage: *Skylar and Sommers – Rocky Mountain Music* which was all his own compositions and beautifully mixed and recorded by Sage's father, Antonio.

"Oh no. No way!" exclaimed Elise with a tremor in her voice when she heard the news about the bear.

She said, though, that she would send a news crew over to Asia's house with the Forest Service Rangers. "The crew is brave. They can stand at a distance. They can tell me when the Rangers have the bear tranquilized and put away safely in a cage and are transporting it far, far away into the Missouri Ozarks. I am *not* coming to your house until that bear is gone to his new home. That is *not* part of our deal—two dogs and a donkey—yeah, okay. But no bears. I might be country, but that does not mean the whole country gets to come into my home or that I am Mother Earth. I love Mother Earth, but she does her job and I do mine – as an admirer. I do not need a close up with a wild bear to prove anything."

"Okay, okay, Elise. I am sure between the Rangers and the Simmons boys; they will take care of our little bear problem."

"Our problem? *Little!?* Are you so sure it is small? How do you know? You've been stuck in y'alls barn all morning! *Hunh...!"*

"Good Gawd, Elise, you are such an alarmist. Just stay home until we call you back."

"You haven't even *heard* an alarm yet. I scream and yell, you know."

"Elise, just watch it on TV or your KANU monitor until I give you the all-clear."

"Okay, I'll be waitin' for you. Be careful."

Rainier's similar caution rang in Asia's ears. She could hardly wait to pack for her trip. "Don't worry, Elise. I'll be in touch as soon as they have Smokey packed up and on his way to his new home in the mountains." Asia heard sirens approaching in the distance and clicked off her phone. Soon, the sound of a plow (perhaps one larger than the Simmons) was scraping her driveway and back area.

"Ms. Reynolds?" came a deep, manly voice through the barn doors.

"Yes?" she answered.

"We're here to dart the bear and take him to Missouri. The Simmons boys called us. We think it is just a young male looking for his first hunting grounds, not an injured or overly hungry bear. Silver Lake town maintenance is helping the Simmons boys plow and open your driveway to the road."

"I understand, thank you all."

"We'll let you know when we have the animal caged and the Simmons boys can get your doors dug out and get you out of there. Elise Snuggles of KANU also called us for help and sent a news crew, so your bear will be on the evening news and her *Journal*."

"That's great. Thank you," answered Asia, relieved. She sat down with Frankie, who was now fully awake, and opened a can of vegetarian chili, heating it on the steel plate of her barrel stove. She kept a small store of food and water in a cabinet in the barn for just such an emergency. This was not the first time she had been snowed in. Sliding outside doors were not good in heavy snow or cold, they tended to freeze and jam. She really needed to install a smaller inset door that opened in. The kind that Elise was fond of commenting on in her joking way. (Doors that open in are not blocked by extreme snow fall. Doors that open out are.)

_____

Jake Wheeler woke up cold that morning and noticed right away that the swelling in his left leg had gone down by at least half. He felt that might indicate a bad bruising or sprain, but not a break. He grabbed his staff and swung carefully out of the hammock. He put the injured foot down gently. The pain, too, had lessened greatly. He stretched. He could stand and walk much more easily. No more crawling in the mud.

The rain had stopped, and the sun was out drying the mud. He felt a little cold, but for winter it was rather warm, maybe 40 degrees Fahrenheit. He was used to that kind of cold from his own experiences in Scotland as a child, so it did not bother him. Not much snow, if any. That gave him the impression he had been blown far to the west into the Outer Hebrides. That was an area known for its ferocious ocean swellings and sea disturbances during winter storms, like the one that brought his helicopter down. Rain, instead of snow, indicated that he was near the warmer tides of the Outer Hebrides, as well.

It had something to do with an unusually warm ocean current that passed by the peninsula and islands of these outer reaches of Scotland. He guessed he had been blown off course by about 190 miles or so, from Dornoch to the western coastline near the Isle of Harris or, more likely, the Isle of Lewis.

The weather, cliffs and proximity to the forest sparked a mental image of the Isle of Lewis, which was slightly off his flight path to his grand's estate. Maybe, maybe not. But for weather this clement, he *must* be pretty far west to pick up that current. He pulled his backpack and whiskey bag over, took a swig of Highland Park and set some breakfast things out, piling up dry, dead pine needles and putting them under his fold-up stove. Even though he might be on the Isle of Lewis, he was too far to be within walking distance of his grand's.

He was planning on cooking oatmeal and powdered milk with a packet of honey and some dried apple. He needed to find a spring or someone's house or cottage pretty soon to replenish his water supply. It was almost gone. He had only taken a small bottle of water with him. He tried his cell phone as the oats cooked. There was no reception. He smashed his useless phone on the rocks and carefully picked up the pieces, separating the SIM card and burying all of it.

He took the solar panel attached to his portable charger and pinned it on the top of his cap. When charged he could use this for his radio. He planned on looking for an abandoned Croft house today (and they were plentiful on both Isles), so he would need to walk around to get his bearings. He preferred to contact a home where someone was residing, but an abandoned house could help if it started to snow or rain too hard. For now, his camp was enough. The sun would recharge the lithium charger batteries. Neither Lewis nor Harris were known for good cell phone reception.

The cooking fire felt divine and Jake put his injured leg near the warmth. He had his leg elevated slightly all night due to the natural angle of the hammock and his wetpack. He shook his now dry jacket out and the crusted, dried mud fell off in chunks. It was mostly Polyester/Nylon outside and a warm pile inside. The pile was relatively clean. He felt lucky to have a jacket.

He got up and started walking through the woods. He had his Glock in hand for self-defense and hunting purposes and was using a small nylon laundry bag for a possible game bag. There were no worn paths, nor any indication of a coast-line road. Therefore, he was further convinced that he was not on the Isle of Harris which had an extended asphalt road along its coastline. That was both good and bad.

He sat down on a rock to drink some after-breakfast Glenlivet and look deeper into the woods. He had left his dry bag back at his camp but wanted at least one of the whiskey bottles with him.

It was stunningly beautiful here. That gave him some peace. He saw a large red buck and then four red doe follow-ing in a group. He wasn't prepared to shoot a deer just yet. He could dry strips of meat, but was not prepared to carry the deer with his injured leg ... if he could find an abandoned Croft house, though, he mused thoughtfully...

He wanted to be rescued, but he was truly enjoying be-ing obscure. He did not want, necessarily, to be found. At least not right now. He wanted his grandpapa, but almost no one else. If he found a friendly, inhabited residence he could call grand from there, or think of something else.

He looked up at a patch of bright blue sky and was won-dering how far the east coast of the Hebrides was, how far Stornoway was. It could be very far. Stornoway was a rather large village-township that was close to his grand's estate. He heard the rush of water and saw a sparkle of what could pos-sibly be a spring ahead.

A flash of sunlight attracted Jake like a magnet. He had found a source of what appeared to be clean water—a small pool that drained into a rock strewn stream going downhill. He filled his water bottle and put a water purification tablet in the water. It looked like a spring, the water was clean and clear – but there was no sense in making himself sick with *Giardia intestinalis* or some other invisible, tasteless water-borne bacteria.

Even if he found an abandoned Croft house, he didn't want to risk using any of the stoves there unless the weather forced him to. The roofs of such houses were usually faulty and leaky, and the chimneys and stovepipes could cause back-drafting smoke and a possible fire. The abandoned houses were usually still owned by family members and they would not appreciate having them burned down.

He preferred his camp or a kind person's house where he could at least write a letter. No one would know who he was here. He would give an alias for a name anyway. Getting a cell phone signal up here was sort of hopeless.

It was getting dark again. Daylight hours in the Outer Hebrides were short in the winter. Jake sat down to rest his leg. He had soaked his left foot and injured leg in the cool spring water to clean his wounds. The leg almost looked normal now. He was pretty sure he had a sprain, but he would need an x-ray to be sure there were also no fractures. He had been lucky. He had looked over the cliff he had crashed on and saw no refuse scattered anywhere. There was not even one scrap of his helicopter on the cliff. There was no sign of his having crashed there.

There was no trace of his helicopter below the cliff, either. It had washed away. Maybe he could wash away his past like that and become a new person. He thought he could.

He took a long drink of his whiskey. Even the crash was an epiphany for him, a revelation. He drank again and again.

Jake walked slowly back to his camp. The Aurora Borealis lit the night sky with amazing streaks of light – flashing violet, magenta and ephemeral, changing, glowing chartreuse. As screwed as Jake really was, he smiled, still in a little pain, drunk, but oddly happy. Happy within himself. Maybe he was becoming a new man in this heavenly light of the Scottish Borealis. He sat down in front of his dome tarp using his walking stick and lit a campfire still watching the Outer Hebrides light show above him as if it was a sign just for him. It was still in the 40's (Fahrenheit) but the fire gave him much more warmth and even inner comfort. He added some whiskey to that warmth.

He used a stick to put his folding stove in place and made a packet of dehydrated chicken and rice with garlic, olive oil and onion in cheddar sauce using his new, purified spring water.

It tasted grand and he took a drink of whiskey and poured some into the mixture and felt even better. This would taste even finer with roasted red grouse in it. He had more of the same dehydrated camping food in his backpack.

He watched the sky and drank even more. Still tired from his trials of the day before, he limped to his hammock, balled up his clean pants from the backpack for a pillow, put his dry pack on the hammock, and climbed in.

Sleeping on a hammock comfortably is an art that Jake had mastered as a child. It was a perfect emergency bed that stayed dry and folded up (without the end sticks) to the size of a pair of socks and could be used as a fishing net, too.

Tomorrow he would hunt for game birds – red grouse and woodcock, both very tasty roasted over an open fire on a stick. A deer would take more effort and mental preparation. He didn't think he was strong enough yet to carry one on his back.

———————

Asia heard a bang on the barn doors. She was finishing some hot *Numi* vegetable tea, but yelped, "Yes?" thinking that this might just be a human being this time.

A deep voice replied, "You can unlock your doors now, Ms. Reynolds, we have the bear sedated, caged and on his way to Missouri. Try it. The Simmons boys are right here and will help you pull those doors open if you need them. I am a Ranger Robert Sandoval with the Mingo Wildlife Refuge Forest Service, just in case you need anything else. There might be more than one bear roaming Silver Lake, we don't know. Nothing else around here right now, though."

Asia was shocked, but muttered, "Okay, Officer. Thank you so very much." The doors came open as soon as Asia unlocked the padlock. All the dogs raced outside at once and jumped around for joy. Zucchini walked over to Asia's back door, peed on it, and sat down elegantly and sedately waiting for her to open the way to the kitchen. Big Boy and Hunny followed her and sat down as well.

The snow that had been cleared with the one of the Silver Lake town plows was piled in drifts almost eight feet high. It was amazing. Her back area and drive were clear though. The Simmons' and Silver Lake maintenance had done a wonderful job. Her roofs were cleared over the door as well. She assumed they had cleared the front of her house too. The Simmons had left already, and the town plow was just now pulling out of her driveway.

She would have to watch the excitement that had ensued around her barn on TV in Elise's *Mississippi River Journal* program tonight after 10 pm. It would be re-broadcast on the six o'clock news tomorrow as well.

The men from the township had charged Frankie's battery and cleared her truck. She packed her dogs in it gratefully and threw a kiss at Asia saying, "I'll call you from Elise's cell phone. Have a great trip. I love you! Don't worry about Pumpkin, I'll entertain her like a royal princess!" Asia laughed and waved as her friend pulled down the drive.

She walked tiredly to her back door and let all three dogs in. Hunny and Big Boy could walk home to Frankie's later on. She fed all the big dogs Science Diet and Salmon Oil as a treat. They chomped away as she went upstairs to pack. She was booked on a flight to London in a couple of hours. She was glad that the blizzard was over, or her flight would have been canceled. It could have been impossible to get through the snow to the airport by the roads – what to speak of being held hostage in her own barn by a bear.

Elise was due at her house soon and she didn't want to tell her about the possibility of an "extra" bear. She thought if she told her on the way out the door, it would muffle her screams of objection. Frankie would be there with her rifle to protect Elise. Frankie would feed and groom Pumpkin and Fuzzy Bud. That would make it easier on Elise.

Asia's flight was approximately ten hours on an overnight flight to Heathrow. She packed all her camera equipment, maps of London and the British Isles. She was planning on traveling extensively when Rainier had to work. She assumed his hours would be odd, but he could not tell her much for security reasons.

She heard Elise call her name. She almost never knocked or used the doorbell. It was just a habit she had since grammar school. She simply walked right into her friend's houses. It was a habit she wasn't about to break, even if she could.

"Asia!?" came her loud voice. "Asia, where are you?" She heard Elise mumble to herself as she walked around downstairs, "I hope she didn't take off early. I need instructions." Asia heard Elise bang into something, maybe slamming a phone book down.

Then she said loudly, *"Dang, Asia?! It's me, Elise!"*

"I'm up here, Elise," yelled Asia from upstairs. "I just finished packing. I'll be right down." Asia dragged her small, hard-shell case-on-wheels down the stairs and put it by the back door. She gave Elise a "To Do" list and a hug, telling her Frankie Franklin would be there this afternoon. She showed her the food in the fridge and pantry and explained how to open the gun cabinet in the basement, just in case.

"Just in case of *what?!*" exclaimed the excitable Elise, concerned. "The bear is gone, *isn't it?*" asked Elise again, piercingly. Asia looked at the floor and avoided looking at Elise who frowned and looked at Asia suspiciously. *"Isn't it?"* she repeated, tenaciously.

"Oh, Yes. Oh, yes. It is caged and on its way to Missouri."

"Good!" said Elise with a look of relief.

Asia still could not meet her eyes.

"What about all these gigantic dogs? I don't have to take care of *all* of them, do I?"

"No, of course not. They are just visiting. You can let them out around ten pm or so and tell Big Boy and Hunny to go home after you let Zucchini back in. I do not want her to follow them. I want her to stay here..."

"...And keep me company. Yeah," added Elise, finishing Asia's thought.

"Yeah," echoed Asia.

Elise sidled up to Asia with a conspiratorial grin on her face. She said, "Elton and I had a secret, very private wedding over the holidays. It was so exquisite that we only shared it with each other. We are putting off our West Indian honeymoon until your return. So, I am officially Elise Jamison now. You know I could not add my maiden name; it sounds too weird to say Mrs. Snuggles-Jamison or Mrs. Jamison-Snuggles. Sounds sort of too close for comfort."

Asia was surprised but laughed and threw her arms around Elise and hugged her hard.

"You didn't invite *anyone?!*"

"Nope. It was gorgeous – all dark blue velvet and silver. Even Elton's tuxedo was blue velvet. My dress, too. It was so intimate. The flowers were intoxicating. You know, Christmas/New Year's weddings are difficult for guests anyway. We videoed it, I'll give you a copy. We're sending copies to folks we would have invited." Elise gave Asia a deep, sparkling look and said, "This was way cheaper, too. The big party was for our engagement anyway."

"Happy?"

"Oh, *pu-leeze*, you know it."

"I'll get you something nice in London. Something special."

"Okay," said Elise amiably.

Asia looked at her watch, considering what the roads might be like, she needed to leave right away. She bent over and gave Zucchini a hug and patted Hunny and Big Boy.

Elise said, "Better go. I'll email you if I have any news or need anything."

Asia answered, "Okay. Love ya' Elise," and opened the back door with, "Oh, by the way, be careful going outside, especially in the dark. The Forest Service said another bear might be in the area. This bear might possibly be the brother of the one they carried away."

"What!?" exclaimed Eloise trying to grab onto Asia's parka.

"I really have to go now, Elise. Just keep the rifle from downstairs loaded and ready – by the back door. Frankie will be here tomorrow and help you do that. She's a regular Annie Oakley with a rifle. She's a total sharpshooter and has bagged bear before. She's not so good with a handgun but comes into her own when handling a rifle. I think it comes from being short. Just don't go out tonight. Call Elton if you need his help."

"Oh, *now* you tell me. Like I need you to tell me how to get help from my own husband. *Damn it,* Asia you know I might have opted out of this if I had known about the second bear."

"Elise, I have to go. It'll be fine. Just don't go out until Frankie gets here tomorrow to take care of the donkey. If you see anything, call Ranger Robert Sandoval from the Mingo Wildlife Refuge Forest Service he is already looking for this bear anyway."

"Anyway!" exclaimed Elise. "Have a good trip and re-member— *I'll get you back for this!"* She gave Asia a long, deep, dark look. "I *mean* it." It seemed as if Elise had growled, but it was Zucchini, maybe being a traitor and taking Elise's side.

Asia laughed and said, "Sorry, babe. I gotta' go. Don't worry, just lock the doors and windows and keep Zookie close. She will sound the alarm if anything threatening is close by. Bear know how to use door handles and open win-dows, so the latches are important."

Asia felt like a fink as she rushed out to her Silverado. She could park and lock at the Silver Lake International Air-port. She did not know when she would be able to return, but trusted her home and animals to Frankie and Elise, de-spite Elise's not wanting to face a bear, but who does? In fact, she thought she heard Elise say, *"Asshole..."* as she was leav-ing. Friendship includes many ups and downs, just like life in general.

Chapter Thirteen: The Heart of the Problem – Cyber-Babble

The back room at the *Cannoniere* Club was a prize that Rainier Voss cherished as much as any young Brixton resident. He planned on showing off his hacker wizardry (of which he had a great deal) that evening. He was also looking forward to seeing Asia the next day. He was sure his competent girlfriend would resolve the bear problem.

He rubbed his palms together in anticipation of the event of this evening, and also because it was a cold and snowy day in London. Fog had held the cold in place for a while. He could barely see to the corner from the middle of the block. He was eating dinner with a young Symantec representative and would get some advance information from him about who he might meet tonight at the Club. He rubbed his hands together again. He needed gloves.

Rainier stumbled into the café where he was to meet up with Symantec. Symantec, as a corporation, was much more than a computer software or virus protection company. They were instrumental in researching and uncovering the true direction, in the past, of the notorious *Stuxnet* worm.

A worm (like the one planted in Silver Lake) was like a virus, but it could simply insert itself and sit there not doing anything but grow within a computer's internal programming and spread itself from computer to computer. (The one in Silver Lake had amazing geographic boundaries). It did not travel outside of Silver Lake despite all the international tourists operating laptops there.

After spreading itself, *Stuxnet,* like any other worm, could activate upon command.

In the case of *Stuxnet*, itself, it was aimed at an unusual target – Programmable Logic Controllers – or computerized machines that control some manufacturing processes. Because of this unusual indirect target (which was a clever subterfuge), researchers were confounded trying to stop it at first. Finally, they figured out that it was the PLCs that controlled the speed of Plutonium centrifuges (as in a Nuclear Reactor) in Iran. These were what the worm was aiming to disrupt. Therefore, Iranians could not enrich their Plutonium and decommissioned a reactor because of it.

The original targets of the *Stuxnet* worm were these Iranian Nuclear Reactors. The worm could speed up the reactor, making the danger of explosion immanent as a threat, or slow it down so that the Plutonium enrichment process would not work. Due to some resistance to Nuclear Reactors among the Iranian population, the government of Iran had placed their Reactors in the center of very busy cities. If anyone interfered with them, their own population would be devastated. It was a cruel move. The average Iranian had nothing to do with Nuclear decisions. Reactors are expensive and the Iranians, not aware of the worm, had replaced that one Reactor already that was not enriching Plutonium.

The computer virus had done its job of slowing down that Reactor to the point that it did not function. As one would know, any large government expense takes bread out of the mouths of the poor or even average population. Symantec, along with Japanese anti-hacker crews, helped to remove the worm and avoid the threat of this economic disaster. It was a populist move, although some blamed the USA and Israel for the virus intended to stop the development of Asian and Middle Eastern Nuclear capabilities. The original intent and aim of the virus was not known by the analysts at first, since it was a high-level government secret.

The *Stuxnet* virus, though, could not be entirely removed. It still exists.

None of the analysts from the Silver Lake disaster felt the worm infecting that town was only a one time threat. The actual programming of the worm was never really deciphered just like *Stuxnet*. Plus, the fact was, it was capable of infesting any communications satellite manufactured without the new hardware and software capabilities that Rainier Voss and NASA had put into their recent launch. Which meant that *any* other satellite was vulnerable except that one. That was a lot of expense and time put into protecting only one satellite.

What if the *.mbezzl* worm infected four or five satellites or more? It did not directly lead to an embezzlement scheme, but it was a serious sort of mechanical hostage threat. It did, though, make the advent of embezzlement worms and viruses possible, since all satellite and wireless towers could be shut down. The activity of these hackers had used the infected satellite to eventually shut down wireless towers in Silver Lake. They still controlled that satellite through using their own earth-based computers and the electronic controls of the spacecraft. Thus, when the infected satellite was being used unchecked by the new satellite, no cell phone or internet or internet-based news had been possible. And that included security warnings, inter-bank transfers and police business, as well.

The Symantec representative, Rufus Brown, detailed, as he and Rainier ate some wonderful vegan dishes at the café in Brixton, known profiles of the super-hackers possibly inhabiting the *Cannoniere* Club and assumed to be "working" in the infamous back room when not seen in the gaming arena. The *Cannoniere* paid the more loyal, quiet and talented programmers and hackers when they reached their required level of proficiency, and they paid well, very well. MI-6 and New Scotland Yard had people working in the *Cannoniere* for years. No one yet had been able to enter the back room.

Rainier Voss had an extensive hacker background and that excited local law enforcement. He was much more skilled at hacking than any of their undercover plants had been. He also had the help of some American hackers. The discovery of the group of hackers responsible for the blackout in Silver Lake would be a breakthrough for them, even if none of the *Cannoniere* hackers were involved. The chances that a computer geek there would have an idea who had done this would be high. MI-6 and New Scotland Yard had filled

Brown in on the information he was now passing on to Dr. Voss.

Lucky Rainier had even *found* the café where he was to meet Rufus Brown in this fog. It helped that it had a sort of glaringly pink neon sign outside. The two men went right from the café to the *Cannoniere* Club. Voss was met at the door by two large, muscular bouncer types and strong-armed to the back of the Club, leaving Rufus in the gaming area. They both knew this was *Cannoniere* protocol.

The security teams from America and England's main problems at the *Cannoniere* was knowing the real purpose of the hacks. They were not always able to put two and two together. The *Cannoniere* was famous for "blinding" its hackers so that each programmer only knew part of their target. Thing was, though, if any one group would know or intuit who the Silver Lake hackers had been, the people in that back room would.

The two bouncers pushed Rainier, rather rudely, through the locked back door into a dark, completely unlit hallway where he was met by two more armed, extraordinarily muscular, security personnel and again strong-armed to another locked door at the opposite end of the hall. In contrast to the darkened hall (which was also painted flat black), the bright central lighting of the mega-computer room made Rainier squint and shield his eyes at first.

He was introduced to the ten or so programmers in the large (and comfortable) room. Besides the computers lining the walls in cubicles with body-conforming, ultra-padded chairs, there was a nice central lounge area with two circular couches and a thick, shag rug – no windows. One programmer was asleep on one of the couches next to the remains of his meal.

Rainier smiled in a friendly way. The programmer in the cubicle next to his smiled back. They began a conversation as Rainier worked on his part of the "puzzle" as their pieces of problems were called. It started being productive right away. He was set to work all night if he had to, and it looked like he might have to.

He knew Asia would call as soon as she landed in London and that she was prepared to go directly to her rooming house in the Oxford area. He knew, if necessary, she could walk over to the University of Oxford and start familiarizing herself with their various research facilities and libraries. She could also start filming. He would need some sleep before he met with her anyway.

His fingers moved like lightning over the keyboard as he talked to the guy next to him. Around midnight, he took a break for hot organic peppermint tea (Asia was rubbing off on him) and some free house sandwiches. He had to admit the food here was fantastic. He also fell into a deep sleep and woke up again around 1am. The crew in the room seemed to have changed—as did the guy who had been sitting in the cubicle next to him. That was his nearest companion. The wall was on the other side of him.

The new programmer next to him was, maybe, fifteen. *At one a.m.?* Perhaps he was just really young-looking. He was even more talkative than the other fellow and interested to know who Rainier was. He was impressed with Rainier's skills and gave him a great deal of information, including a few birth names with online identities of some possible London hackers who were well-known to also work overseas. And that amazing bit of information revealed that one of the possible hackers might have worked on some of the preliminary programming on *Stuxnet* when he was in Holland.

Rainier could feel his blood pressure rise. There was an insistent pounding in his chest. He was excited to try and connect with the people described by the programmer in the next cubicle.

Since Jake had disappeared or been sucked into Middle
Earth as some of his former crew described it, the members
of ex-Team Wheeler had scattered to their respective hide-
outs and vacated Wheeler's villa. Three of them (the mur-
derers of Jason Bing) were actively looking for Wheeler. No
one else even cared. Everyone who knew Wheeler was puzzled as to what he was really up to. His payments to his
former crew had been more than generous, at least twice
what any of them had expected. Most of his crew wanted
to do something more independent anyway. The three mutineers: Kent Rockford, Jules Ridden and Raphael Case, wanted command of Wheeler's worms, viruses and trojans. They
were a greedy bunch, and not likely to give up without taking
quite a bit of Wheeler's fortune with them, if they could get
their hands on it. Not being paid angered them even further.

The three mutineers went scavenging around upper-class
London for Jake's residences. There was always more than
one place. They met the first day back at the club they had
first found each other in, the *Cannoniere* in Brixton. It was
the place to be when they were all poor boy computer geeks
in secondary school. They were still welcome in the elite
back room and went back to eat their lunch (still given to
them *gratis*) in the lounge area there. It had been re-decorat-
ed since they had worked in there years ago.

They all drank some ale to celebrate, shook hands all
around and questioned some of the more long-term members about Jake (whom they knew as *"The Spy"* which was
one of his monikers online). One guy said to try an address
he had for *The Spy* which was a condominium near St. James

Park in Westminster. So, the three ex-Team members piled into Kent's car and drove over there. But it was futile. The condo they had an address for was pretty much empty and up for sale.

A resident of the building said they had heard a helicopter take off from the roof last week some time. Jake's former condo was on the top floor and the men knew he owned a roof area and a 'copter. The resident said the man that used to live on the top floor was very closeted, very secretive, kept to himself and seemed to be rather wealthy. The three men inspected the roof and found an old hangar. They were pretty sure the former owner had been Jake and had left for parts unknown recently.

Jules remembered that Jake had a grandparent in Scotland somewhere, so they researched various older people named Wheeler in that national area. They found several older men that could be Jake's grandparent, but none of them really panned out, except one old guy.

That man said he had a grandson that was due there days ago but had not shown up or gotten in touch. He was worried that something had happened to him and said he was flying in on his own helicopter. All three men began to check for the helicopter. They also checked for flight plans and news stories. They pulled their net as tight as they could, unaware that there were others casting a net encircling them, as well.

———————

Jake took off from his campsite early the next morning after a good, hot breakfast. The purified water seemed fine (with no stomach aches present), and he had about 1,000 purification pills in his emergency equipment. He washed his clothes at a different spring from the one he had gotten his drinking water at. Many campers forget to put soap in their emergency kits, but Jake wasn't one of them. He took a cold bath in the same spring he had washed his clothes in and felt refreshed, if not a little too cold. He went back to his campsite and strung a wash line, pinning his wet clothes up. There was no need to shave and he thought his black beard line was chic, anyway.

He massaged his left leg and foot. They were healing rapidly. He had some scrapes and bruises, but they were also beginning to disappear. He brushed his curly long hair and wished he had gotten it cut before his ill-fated trip. He checked the mirror. He looked pretty good for a camper.

He readied his Glock. He was going hunting. Still using his walking staff, but not limping nearly as much as before, he went on the hunt for game birds: woodcock and red grouse mostly. As soon as he entered the deeper woods, he surprised a group of about four grouse. He bagged two of them and put them in his net laundry bag. He was now glad his dad had made him practice his marksmanship every weekend when he was ten. He hated it back then – but really appreciated it now. His accurate shooting not only brought him a healthy meal but saved precious ammunition.

He didn't think he would need his handgun for self-defense. Most of his Team was okay. Except for Jules, Kent and Raphael who he knew were the perpetrators of Jason Bing's murder – no one else was dangerous like that, that he knew of anyway. The residents of the Hebrides, he knew, would be friendly enough, especially if they learned that his grandfather lived there, too – although Jake really did not think it was wise to give any real identification clues to anyone. Best they didn't know.

But they admired campers generally and were usually willing to help someone if it didn't put them out too much. After all, most of them were raising livestock for a living, which was a lot of work and they might not have very much money. Let them think he was simply out camping and might like some help anyway, or a ride somewhere to get groceries. He could pay them, if he had to. He had cash so he did not have to use an identifying piece of plastic such as a debit or credit card. That seemed realistic enough.

He walked past a lovely freshwater pool. Fish jumped out of the water at him, startled by his presence. He sat down to rest and took a sip of water from his bottle and some whiskey. Soon he would need more whiskey. He was actually having a wonderful time and felt rather happy, even though his girlfriend Jessica might have rejected him. He felt no urgency to leave but would like to get a message to his grand letting him know that he was all right.

Maybe he could use a pay phone in some little town somewhere, or the phone in a store if there was no pay phone. There should be at least one in Stornoway, but there was no guarantee that the phone used coins and not a credit card as they did in America presently. It was common enough to use a store phone here and just leave some money for the call. Maybe. Or even a letter. That was more private and less traceable. Yes, he would write a letter.

He could net some fresh fish here, but not now. He could see smoke in the distance. It must be a home. He got up and charted a course in that direction. He had the grouse. His need to contact a local was more important than cooking more meat than he needed in one day.

It took him a half hour to walk to the cozy-looking, two story Croft house with the smoke billowing from its chimney. There were no other homes in sight, but the house was on an asphalt road leading outwards relatively following the coast. He might have been blown during the storm from his destination near the Isle of Lewis onto the rocky cliffs of the Isle of Harris (which had a very convenient road like this). He fingered the Glock in his jacket pocket and knocked loudly on the purple front door. One of the owner's sheep baa-ed loudly in response back at him.

The door was opened by an older man with a full gray-streaked beard, much longer than his. The man looked at him with questioning eyes, but a broad smile. "MacGregor," the man said, looking directly into Jake's eyes. "Alastair Mac-Gregor. And you are?"

Jake used his London alias, and his best Scottish brogue, "Joshua Handlin, out of London. I am camping rough nearby and wondered if I could pay you to take a shower and maybe clean my birds here."

Jake held up the game bag.

MacGregor grabbed Jake around the waist in a big hug and pulled him into the warm, clean, but sparse home.

"Of course! Can I help you cook and eat those, too?" he said as he welcomed him in a joking manner. He looked over Jake's thin frame and added, "I can make some potatoes and greens, as well. My daughter brought over some wild blueberry scones and a pie we can finish. We'll make a feast. It has been a while since I've been hunting. You go and take a good, hot shower and I'll start those birds and the vegetables."

Jake was clean, but another shower was just fine as an excuse to be here and the meal sounded great. He needed to write that letter. After dinner, perhaps. He had decided to send the letter to his grandfather via Jessica with a warning not to say anything about him to anyone. He would instruct her to mail it to Bernie. He thought he could trust her. She wouldn't know who Bernie was. He couldn't think of anyone from his Team that knew of her. If they did, he knew how evasive she could be. That was one reason he liked her. The hot water felt great. He shaved with the things MacGregor put out for him.

_____

In terms of how Jessica felt about Jake, she knew he had been brutally bullied as a grammar school student. He was very small, smaller than the usual boy his age and that was why he had problems. That was also why he had liked staying indoors with his computers. She seemed very sympathetic and he felt she would forgive anything that she had gotten angry about recently. Especially if he entrusted her with something important.

She would believe he had enemies that unjustly persecuted him. Seemed the story of his life so far. He got depressed again and took a deep drink of his Glenlivet. He brushed his teeth.

The smells from the kitchen made Jake salivate. He hoped MacGregor had whiskey. He sat on the edge of the tub and drank the last of the Highland Park, hiding the empty bottle in his whiskey bag. He could not break out the

Glenlivet to share. It was too expensive a bottle and would raise suspicions. He liked MacGregor a lot. He hoped his presence in his home would not cause MacGregor harm. He vowed to try and make himself untraceable.

Highland Scots had a reputation for being close-mouthed. The letter he would compose would simply say he was okay, but he needed MacGregor to send it to Jessica from Stornoway, which was quite a ways away, but central to both the Isle of Lewis (being the only town on Lewis) and also Harris. It was Scotland, but presumably far from Mac-Gregor and also his camp.

Even Jessica (as far as he knew) wouldn't be able trace him into the Highland forest. No one would, he hoped. Disappearing felt good. It was a second chance for him. Even if he had become a drunk, he wanted to turn his life around. He felt that Jessica could help him later if he thought London was ever safe for him again. There might also be other things she could do for him if she proved trustworthy.

He could ride to Stornoway with MacGregor by using the excuse of getting groceries. It was more real than an excuse. He could use some fresh produce and some dried things like lentils (which were lighter weight and faster cooking than other beans) and some rice.

He wanted a chance, he thought to himself, *a chance to change.* There would be no more hacking, only application creation, games and more helpful types of programming—if he ever even saw a computer again. He had been in on the original Dutch creation of *Stuxnet* but was not aware of its further government applications. The idea of helping to stop further nuclear threats (which is what *Stuxnet* was designed to do) made him feel good, though. He thought about the Q-bit micro-processing chips in his dry pack as the last of his beard disappeared.

MacGregor called him, "Josh, dinner's ready! Come when you are dressed. I have some whiskey for us. *That'll* warm you up." MacGregor laughed heartily.

"No shit!" thought Jake. He smiled to himself.

Asia was stuck with her head in large over-sized picture books with intricate maps in Oxford's Bodleian library. She knew Voss was embroiled with negotiations in London and could not come to meet her. He would call her cell phone when he had the time to come up to see her. She had been in England a full day already.

She loved it here. What she was discovering took her breath away. She planned on taking the train to the English countryside tomorrow if Rainier still did not have time to visit her. She was well aware this might happen even before she left Illinois. She knew his trip here was very important and he was working intensively. She had found a lovely, small vegan restaurant within walking distance and was getting ready to pack up her notes and go over there for lunch.

Rainier Voss went to the London Philharmonic the next day. It was not *directly* work related—but it *was* work related. He needed the rest that it gave him. He was still absorbing and integrating the information he had been given the previous night. He would take Asia here later. She would find him boring right now since his mind was not on the music entirely and he probably could not talk and think at the same time at this point.

There had been an unexpected break in the Silver Lake hacking case. According to Symantec, Jake Wheeler, *The Spy*, their prime international suspect, had not even sent an email in the last few days, let alone used his cell phone. Excited by their newest intel on Wheeler they investigated him immediately. They had found out about his being locked out of his own computers and that his past physical address in London was no good anymore. Also, they knew that he had been away during the Silver Lake attack and had just gotten back to London when it was over.

Wheeler was skilled and wealthy enough to be their man and had a crew of other skilled programmers and a private jet. Their investigation was getting closer and closer to Jake as the primary suspect, the more they learned of him and his crew. Voss had gotten his name and specs also from the programmers at the *Cannoniere*. He *was* their man – or so Symantec felt. He had been a suspect for a while and Voss's confidants at the *Cannoniere* just confirmed what Symantec had suspected all along. They needed to find Jacob Wheeler.

Despite all the international focus on Jake Wheeler, Dr. Voss was more concerned with catching Wheeler's former crew. He couldn't say why – it was just intuitive. As he listened to the Philharmonic play Beethoven's Fifth Symphony, his mind drifted. He somehow felt that Wheeler's disappearance was a good thing. Or that Jake had gotten wind of their presence in London and was running – or dead. So far, Symantec felt that Jason Bing's death was a signal that Wheeler was suffering some kind of unpopularity. That

Bing's murder was intended to challenge Wheeler's leadership and thrown purposely into his face.

As far as international security knew, Wheeler had no criminal record anywhere, nor any reputation for outright violence. Even when he stole money, he seemed oddly sensitive towards not hurting the common folk. He stole from the rich and gave to himself and his crew. Some of his crew had nothing before they joined him. He had made them rich. Still, Interpol had him on their radar, presently accusing him of helping to murder Jason Bing, who was a British citizen. The London police were also interested in him for that murder and computer crimes possibly initiated or controlled from London. Voss was not sure about all that but was glad enough for the help.

Rainier had been given the names of three of Wheeler's crew members (and had seen them face-to-face before he knew who they were) at the *Cannoniere* Club last night. The programmer who told him who they were also said that some hackers felt that these three men were prone to physical violence and therefore disreputable. Being a former hacker himself, Voss was always interested in honor among hackers and paid attention to the warning.

Right now, Rainier was more interested in catching Kent, Jules and Raphael than Jacob Wheeler. Any group of hackers which other hackers distrusted and didn't like could make Rainier very suspicious.

As sticky ethically as the hackers at the *Cannoniere* were, most of them were just young, talented programmers that needed a chance to do something reputable with their skills as opposed to learning how to steal with a computer. He knew they usually needed money despite their unusual creativity and obvious computer talent.

Theft that included physical violence was usually unattractive to hackers. This was obviously not true of Kent, Jules and Raphael. He drifted into the music again, turning off his mental analysis of the hacker problems he faced. They needed hardcore evidence, not just suspicions.

Jake Wheeler came out of Alastair MacGregor's bathroom refreshed and saw a long dining room table set to the max with roasted, seasoned grouse, bowls of vegetables and butter and milk. The smell of coffee was also permeating the room. He rubbed his hands together. MacGregor said, "Sit ye down, my laddie. 'Tis all for meetin' you. The milk and butter are fresh from my own dairy cow."

Jake sat down and they both dug in. When they were halfway through their meal, Jake spoke up and said, "You know, Mr. MacGregor, I could use a ride to Stornoway. I need some groceries and stuff. I also need to get my hair cut. It is too long for camping. And I must write to my relatives, so I also need the post."

"First off, laddie, I'm Al or Alastair or even MacGregor. No need for the Mister. And I'll sure cut your hair for you and take you into Stornoway. I drive up there in me pickup about once a week for me own food and stuff too. So, takin' you would be a pleasure for me. I can use some company for the ride. I'll be goin' tomorrow in the early morning, so you might want to consider stayin' over because I need to go right after takin' care of me animals. That suit you?"

Jake smiled and said, "That'd be fine."

"I have an extra bedroom upstairs all fresh and clean and made up for me daughter, but you can use it tonight. We can eat some fine leftovers for breakfast with fresh eggs from me layin' hens. It'll be like a holiday."

After dinner, Jake and Al cleared the table and began washing up. They packed some fine stuffing, potatoes, vegetables, deviled eggs and other treats into MacGregor's propane refrigerator. There was practically an entire roast grouse left over. Cold roasted grouse would suit Jake just fine in the morning.

Al called him over to a wooden chair set in the middle of the kitchen linoleum. He brandished a huge pair of sharpened, glinting scissors. "You know for a guy who sells wool, I usually know where to get the very best scissors. These'll do the trick in no time."

Jake thought the analogy to shearing sheep and cutting his long locks was so funny he could hardly stop laughing. He had put all his diamond studs in storage with the things from his home in London. He blessed himself for remembering to remove his earrings.

Since the crash, his vanity and egotism (which left him very lonely) had mostly fallen away and vanished like the fog over the Highlands. He had found happiness here, something he had not expected. He sat down, and Al handed him a mug of hot coffee. Jake tasted it and was surprised that there seemed to be a shot of whiskey in it.

MacGregor waited while they finished their coffee and said, "Best thing to keep you warm with the weather up here—damp and cold." Jake nodded and drank a gulp or two. The whiskey wasn't anywhere near Glenlivet, but it worked. Just as it hit the spot, Al took the first whack at Jake's hair. Away went his fabulous shoulder-length, glistening locks "How short you want it?" asked the old man.

"Short as you can cut it with those scissors. Just try and make it even."

"Okay. Sure, I'll give you my prize-winning sheep shearin' cut. Even all over it is."

Jake pulled away for a couple of moments and laughed loudly again.

Al was done in about ten more minutes to Jake's surprise. He held a mirror up for him. Jake fanned his remaining hair out with his fingers. Al gave him a brush and he brushed his hair in front of the mirror. It looked great. Curly and even, but only an inch or two long. Perfect.

MacGregor showed him where his desk was and offered him writing materials, an envelope and even a stamp. Then MacGregor tactfully went into his living room and put a DVD in his telly. The noise was comforting to Jake and he felt inspired to write a simple note to his grand. He began:

"My Dearest Grandfather,

Sorry I could not show up for our time together. I have some important business to take care of and it could not wait. I will get in touch with you as soon as I can. I am all right, doing better than usual, in fact. If anyone should inquire about me, please just tell them you do not know anything and find some excuse to end the conversation. Do not let anyone into your home that is looking for me. They are not friends, or they wouldn't be looking. Except for Jessica Parker.

Enclosed are instructions for clearing out my storage unit in London and my estate in South East England. Take every-

thing to your estate or take it to my storage unit in London if you are being followed and tell all my staff and employees (except Richie and those you really need to help you) to vacate my villa.

Get my favorite riding horse and Corgi (you know the ones), and bring them back with you, or put them in a rented kennel and stable for a while if you feel you are being followed. The estate is already up for sale with my usual real estate agency, but do not tell anyone about that.

You can trust Richie with my estate sale, but do not tell him where you live or about Jessica. You know how to collect the money from the sale. Let Jessica know my wishes for keeping quiet as to my whereabouts. She will respect that. I will write again later.

Your Loving Grandson, Jake—-

P.S. I know this is hard to understand, but for reasons of intellectual property, Jessica needs to think my name is Joshua Handlin and that you and I are not related. I will explain further when next I see you."

He added a note to Jessica essentially saying the same thing, plus he said:

I love you Jessica. Very much. This is a difficult time in my life, and I hope you understand. If there was anything that made you upset in the past, we can discuss it later. I am transitioning right now. In the past, I did many things for reasons of social acceptance. I already had enough money. It was not for the money. You know my background—my childhood experiences.

Things have changed for me. I will talk to you when we meet again. We <u>will</u> meet again. Please send the enclosed letter *to my confidant Bernie Campbell at the enclosed address in Scotland, but do not speak of it to anyone. My most beloved friends are not public knowledge and those who are close to me would know enough not to speak to strangers about me. I will be in touch. Do not worry. I am relying on you.*

Again, I love you and trust you, Jessica. 'Till we meet again, Josh

———————

Elise Jamison banged around in Asia's kitchen until she got the dogs so nervous that Hunny (who was looking very pregnant at this point) and Big Boy wanted to go home and went over to the back door, waiting and looking at Elise with longing and a little whimpering. She said (to the dogs), "All right. All right. I get the idea. Wait a second." She walked over and let them out the door.

Zucchini just stayed in the kitchen and sidled up to Elise, pushing her hand with her big head and snout. Elise looked down at her and said, "And I guess you want to make me feel better. Well, thank you, honey. You da' best, but then you have to make sure that bear stays away. I gotta go to work tomorrow. Maybe I can go in late – wait 'till Frankie gets here."

She sat down and put her arms around Zucchini's neck, burying her face in her long hair. "I'm
scared, Zookie. I'm scared of bear. I'm not that strong."

Then she said one word, *"Elton..."* She snapped her fingers in frustration, sayin, "I gotta call my husband." Zookie licked Elise's hand and she said, "You're one smart dog, Zucchini. You know, don't you?"

She walked to the wall phone and called Elton, telling him in no uncertain terms to come over and bring his loaded rifle. Then she turned the outside lights on in the back. When she did, she saw a large shadow run away into the darkness. It was way too big to be a dog. "*Damn*, Asia," she complained.

Elton Jamison came over and got in safely. The newlyweds embraced passionately. Frankie came over the next day as promised, going first to the barn to take care of Fuzzy and Pumpkin. After that, she went to the house. Elton pulled her in quickly, holding his rifle at the ready, pointed towards Asia's back yard.

Frankie said, "Watcha' doin' man?!"

"Seen a bear there last night," answered Elton.

"That all?" said Frankie, sort of sarcastically. "They live here, too you know." She eyed his rifle. "Cain't do nothin' with that pea shooter anyway. Asia's got a Remington and a Winchester that uses .338s and .338 Ultra mags down in her gun locker. I'll go and get the Winchester. That'll kill any size bear outright. You saw the animal yourself?"

"Elise did. She saw its shadow last night. Had to be a bear, it was way too big for anything else." Elton hesitated. "Elise wants to leave. She was just being considerate towards Asia and even postponed our honeymoon. But now she feels like a prisoner. Can you handle all this alone, Frankie?"

"Sure. I can come over every day. Ain't afraid of no bear, neither. Thing is, Hunny had her puppies last night—six of them. They don't require much from me right now—except for some cleaning up and feedin' their mom. Hunny does most of the work. Go on ahead. I can handle this. I think I'll even get me a cell phone from Walmart. With a bear checkin' us out, I think I might need the backup. Been thinking of it for a while anyway."

Elise walked into the kitchen dressed and ready for work, no need to check in with Frankie, she was ready to go, go, go. She had an overnight bag with her and handed Frankie Asia's list of instructions and her cell phone number. Next stop for her and Elton – the Bahamas.

Chapter Fourteen:
A View from the
Top of the
Mountain

As Alastair's pickup got closer and closer to Stornoway, Jake started losing his self-confidence. He wondered if he could really trust Jessica Parker all that much. He also had to trust Richie, his protégé, to strip his jet and pack his estate, removing all identifying information. He needed to break up the jet and sell or dispose of the parts. He knew he could trust his grand to follow his instructions about packing up his villa near High Wycombe in Buckinghamshire. He knew Bernie would save his horse and Corgi and bring them to his hideaway in the Hebrides. His grand's was the only house on the island.

Beside the house, there were caves on his property and an off-the-grid cabin. It was a very sturdy, winterized cabin with a fine, expansive loft and all kinds of comforts. Grand would find his instructions easy and could quickly get his things out of storage in London when the time came.

It still seemed as if Jessica was his kingpin. That's a lot of reliance on a person he maybe didn't know all that well.

He was sorry he ever thought of amazing his teenage friends with his capacity to hack into other systems. His palms became sweaty thinking about the risks he had taken. Well, he couldn't have little Richie pull off the entire scheme. He had to blindfold him. Give him only a limited piece of the puzzle. No real locations or addresses.

If Jessica responded and sent his letter to grand, all anyone could see was a letter from London that was not from him. By the time the three mutineers figured out they had to hack into the British mail system, it would be too late, anyway. It was too involved. Police agencies would be in the same position of being too late and not knowing anything about the existence of Jessica.

All that was left to dismantle and clean up was his surveillance equipment and one Team coordinator in Silver Lake. If he pulled Richie in with a complicated con involving the London Silver Vaults with an admonition to be quiet about the tasks Wheeler asked him to do, he could get him to remove all evidence of himself. Wheeler could then remain untraceable by even his own former team members as well as the international security forces.

He felt Richie was salvageable and that he could trust him to keep his mouth shut because of the Silver Vaults scheme. Everyone would be watching Richie (who they felt would inherit the leadership position in Team Wheeler). Richie would be salivating over the millions in silver in the formerly untouchable London underground Vaults which still had made the mistake of using computerized systems for inventory and sales. He could get away clean and no one would, in actual fact, physically touch the Vaults which had been owned by the same families for approximately fifty years, making their personnel virtually impossible to break into. It was an elaborate con. He had no intention of trying to break into the Vaults. He needed something to bind Richie's loyalties to him. The Silver Vaults con would do just that.

There were, presently, 27 stores and many vaults occupied by the original Silver Vault families. This concocted scheme was as good an excuse as any to end their business in America. The entire Team would assume that they would be included in the Silver Vaults heist if any word of it got past Richie. He perspired until the sweat dripped into his eyes. He knew how risky this sounded even in his own mind.

Alastair and Jake entered Stornoway. Bernie Wheeler's estate was very close by, but Jake did not dare go there until he had spoken to his grandfather. Bernie had a dock near Stornoway. Jake had no intention of exposing his grand or himself right now. It was back to the woods for him. Hiding was the best idea.

Jake asked MacGregor to drop him off at the nearest liquor store. All of this hinged on Jessica and Richie being able to cover his tracks for him. His camp in the forest and burgeoning relationship with Alastair MacGregor was good. It could save him despite the fact that he knew he was now a rampaging (but half-way rational) alcoholic.

Whiskey tasted good in his mind and in his mouth. MacGregor dropped him off. They would meet later at the Stornoway Main Post Office after Jake bought a few groceries and supplies.

The town of Stornoway was lovely and colorful, and Jake carefully kept an eye out for his grand. His grand also went shopping here very occasionally, but usually sent staff to do his errands. So, Jake was careful. He zipped into an alley and got a sip of only moderately expensive, locally brewed whiskey that he thought MacGregor would like also. He had two bottles, one for the both of them and one for himself. He could not afford anything extravagant right now. He also bought fresh bait for fishing. He was planning on getting back to his camp after today. He bought a heavier coat, sweaters, a heavy wool knit cap, gloves, wool socks, another change of clothing, two extra flannel shirts, and knee-high gum boots.

He was on a budget now since he only had 2,500 Euros left to last him until he felt safe using his bank accounts, cheques and credit cards again. He did not know when that would be, if ever. He had several offshore accounts in the West Indies and a safety deposit box in Switzerland. He could get clandestine access to all of those depending on how closely he was watched by security forces. He was good sleeping rough in the Hebrides right now. He figured he could survive many more months that way. His leg was completely healed, and he had no intention of calling attention to himself by seeking medical care. He kissed his letter to Jessica for good luck and dropped it into the outgoing box to London. He just *knew* she'd come through for him.

It felt odd not being able to use instant forms of communication. It would take his letters a couple of weeks to make their way to Jessica and then on to his grand. His grand could speak to Richie about the liquidation and sale of his villa near Chislehurst and the National Trust. The two would get along and Richie would accept his request to stay quiet. The London Silver Vaults heist would give Richie a chance to think he was special. He had always loved that. He, of course, included a note to Richie with his letter to his grandfather. He trusted Jessica to send that to his villa where Richie was still residing.

Asia Reynolds was going from library to library collecting maps and photos of the places that she wanted to visit. She didn't think most of what she was looking at was open to the public, but it fascinated her. She thought correctly that if she explained her documentary work to the librarians, she could gain more access than the public generally had. She was able to see what she needed to.

So, she concentrated on memorizing the maps of the mazes she was collecting. She had a good sense of direction, so she memorized whatever landmarks were offered in the photos she was able to copy. Using her camera and tablet to photograph pages from her research books worked really well. She could check the images immediately for accuracy on both devices. And what was a Xerox machine, anyway? Just a big, cumbersome, sometimes fuzzy camera. Using her tablet and cell phone to take photos, also offered her some privacy as to what she wanted copies of.

Most of what she was researching related to the Silver Lake investigation (possibly), as well as something she could video for a documentary. And, as the English would say, bloody interesting subjects, too.

There were many clandestine subjects in the history of London. And many new and mundane things that Asia found just walking around the town of Oxford. She even videoed her crossing of the English Channel and some of the more charming parks including her present favorite – the St. James Lake Park – which delighted her, even though it was another full day's journey back and forth from Oxford. It was a must see. It filled her days waiting for Rainier. The tradition of bird watching on the perimeters of London prompted Asia to buy a pair of binoculars and a good bird book.

For some reason, while she was waiting for Rainier, she also took a tour of the Tower of London which thoroughly freaked her out. There were so many gruesome stories around the place. She could feel the spirits of the dead a little too intimately. Lucky her, the Tower was less than a day's journey. It was only two hours away.

Rainier finally called her and asked her to meet him outside the *Cannoniere* Club where he would give her a miniature camera so she could film in the club while he worked a half shift in the back room. It was a breach of security protocol and could put Asia in danger, but no one could identify her with any security force, so he decided to try. He promised when they were done, he would follow her back to a hotel in Oxford. She was delighted to help him, although when she got inside the *Cannoniere*, the place frightened her. Rainier put a pen camera in the breast pocket of her jacket and told her to walk around with something to eat and drink and try and get the faces of as many customers as she could. It was a good day for that, many of the regulars were there. Full moon tonight. The gamers appeared like Were-wolves when the moon was full. He would film with a simi-lar camera in the back room.

Jake sat down on the curb outside of the Stornoway Post Office. He enjoyed the sunny, clear sky and the sharp smell of the salt air since the town was also an ocean port. He took a swig of the new whiskey. He grimaced. After Glenlivet and Highland Park, this was comparable to paint thinner. Yet, it was hot and opened his sinuses. He had bought a nice large sandwich which went well with the whiskey. He kept the bottle of alcohol covered inside a brown paper bag.

MacGregor pulled up in his truck, smoking a cigarette. He leaned over and yelled through the window, "Having a nip? Get in, mate. Need help with your packages?"

"No," answered Jake, capping the cheap whiskey and putting his purchases into the bed of the pickup. He had bought a large duffle with shoulder straps to carry everything back to his camp. He could wear the clothing and his new gum boots. He looked at MacGregor's cigarette. "I didn't know you smoked," he said.

MacGregor responded with, "And I didn't know you drank outside."

Jake looked embarrassed.

"By the way, I don't smoke habitually. Only occasionally, like now. Want one?"

Jake said, "Sure."

The two smoked in silence. "Send your letter?"

"Yeah," answered Jake.

"You can use my P.O. Box here as a return address, ya' know. If you need to."

Jake looked startled at the offer. After a moment's hesitation, he said, "Thank you, MacGregor." But he had plans to use a phone at some store when he was next in Stornoway if he felt the need to. Jessica should get his letter about a week from hence. There was a chance that no one would trace the call if he made it from a store. It would be unexpected and too short to get organized with any tracer and Stornoway was not that close to where his camp or MacGregor were.

A regular mailing address was too jeopardizing for Mac-Gregor. The last thing he wanted for himself or his new friend was to have him identified. He had used no return address on his letter to Jessica. MacGregor was part of his new life, as long as the friendship lasted. He would be delighted to introduce him to grand and Jessica when the time came – but not now. He was still terrified of being followed. He could not risk it, being so close to his family's hidden island estate. It tempted him, but this move was not safe, yet.

———————

Frankie Franklin played with Hunny's new brood of puppies. Their eyes had just opened and were still blue. They were beginning to crawl. She thought "*Seven St. Bernards!* They were magnificent dogs. They were a little mixed with German Shepard, it seemed. Good, then they were not a product of recent incest and also might be a bit smaller than their mother.

It was a good thing she still had the income from her rib shack. They would eat like horses. She would not put them up for adoption until they were trained, had all their shots and were spayed. With chemical spaying using Zeuterin, the males could be spayed as young as six weeks. It was not as attractive as surgery, but she had a dog over 12 that had been spayed by injection and that dog was very strong and healthy. No gray or health issues. She would consider it. But six weeks was still too young for her to offer them for adoption. Maybe four months. They would be large by then, but better trained.

Frankie delighted in such things. She would make a list of people that had offered to adopt one of them. She could have a little St. Bernard club! *Yes!* They were beautiful little souls right now.

Hunny was a conscientious and good mother. Frankie fed her organic chicken eggs, cow and goat milk and organic shredded turkey. She bought salmon oil and gave her a squirt or two of that in her base of slightly higher quality wet dog food. For kibble, she gave her a mixture of Science Diet and Wellness Duck and Oatmeal, giving her slabs of cold, cooked organic oatmeal for an extra treat. Hunny and her children flourished.

Frankie brought her two newly rescued young goats over to play with Pumpkin as she cleaned the barn and groomed and fed the donkey. Pumpkin, Fuzzy Bud, Zucchini and the goats had such a good time that Frankie decided to leave them together for the time-being. Maybe Asia would like to adopt the little goats, tentatively named Thelma and Louise. They were from her farm rescue collection. True, there were animals, such as her loving Newfoundland dog Big Boy, who she would never put up for adoption. For some of the others, she had revolving ads in the Silver Lake newspapers and advertisers, although she was *very* picky as to who she let take them home. She always insisted on unscheduled follow up visits. She had to be allowed to just drop by and see how they were doing. They had to agree to that in writing. If she saw anything funny, she had the right to take them back to her own ranch. Some of her animals had injuries from neglect and abuse and she was not about to let any animal go to an impractical, uneducated or emotionally unstable home. The animals who had health or emotional issues stayed with her as a forever home, anyway.

Should she die or otherwise need back-up, her daughter and family sometimes came over and helped with animal care and had enthusiastically agreed to inherit her farm with all the animals in it. And the rib shack restaurant, too. She had a good, close family.

Rainier and Asia were worn out after visiting so many places on the London Tube in what turned out to be an extended visit encompassing two days. Rainier's mentors felt he deserved and should also have an extended time off to absorb and re-organize all the information they had garnered and all the possible directions they could go in. One of his favorite sites was, like Asia, the St. James Park and Lake.

He took her on a walk, hand-in-hand, to the former address they had discovered for their suspect, Jake Wheeler, who used to live close to that park. They knew he had moved out. What a beautiful neighborhood! They, of course, couldn't see anything from the sidewalk. He shouldn't have even taken her there. It was against security protocol. But, since he was there, he wanted to case the neighborhood. One could see quite a bit just from a walk around. Mostly what they saw were an unusual amount of birds even for the winter.

There were, though, a group of movers in front of Jake Wheeler's former condo. They lounged about and commented how they were glad that they were almost finished. Some of them were still inside the building going to retrieve more objects, Rainier pulled Asia out of sight – away from the moving truck's driver and other workers. He used her binoculars to see what condo was being moved. It was the top floor – Jake Wheeler's old condominium. He called it in immediately to the CIA, New Scotland Yard and MI-6, so they could follow up. He had little hope they would get there before the truck moved on.

In fact, it pulled away while Voss was still there. He hurried Asia away from the scene.

Her last surprise on this whirlwind tour of London was an above ground visit to the Hellfire Caves in West Wycombe. Asia filmed the entrance which was an imitation Gothic brick church archway. Rainier was even more fascinated by the caves than Asia. They were man-made chalk caves excavated by Sir Frances Dashwood around 1748-52 next to the Church of St. Lawrence near High Wycombe in Buckinghamshire.

The surrounding countryside was beautiful and both of them wanted to rent their overnight Shangri-La there. Rainier nixed that though. As per his recent evidential findings, he felt that he and Asia were getting too close to hacker residences. An Oxford hotel (which was closer to his security force) was safer. Asia was disappointed but, seeing as her library research was within possible walking distance, and she had gotten a great deal of useful video the last two days – she agreed and took Rainier's hand as they disembarked the train back in Oxford and walked to a lovely vegan café for dinner – not only to eat, but to rest their feet. Important after two long days of intensive walking.

Rainier and Asia were totally unaware of how dangerously close they had gotten to an epi-center in West Wycombe. Good thing, too. Rainier would not tolerate Asia being put in harm's way. Rainier was curious about the caves, though, and thought he would like to go back with some of his security.

Asia explained that her interest was based on the fact that Silver Lake had a cave system as well. And there was another cave system (that might be linked to Silver Lake's) that coursed throughout Ozark country across the Mississippi in Missouri.

Jessica Parker sat in her London condo thinking about Joshua Handlin with her chin on her hand, gazing pensively out the window into the barren trees of the park next door. That was where she first met Josh, her heart quickened at the thought. She smiled to herself. It was summer, though, and the trees were in full bloom. There were many more birds.

Jessica wondered why Josh would trust her with so clandestine an errand. Why was Bernie Campbell was so important to him? She thought maybe she would protect Josh simply because he seemed so naïve as to trust her and find some solace in her. It made her feel more love for him than she had felt before. In fact, she felt she didn't really know him that well. What he had done on her computer, at least what she could decipher of what he had done, scared her. It was high-level programmer stuff even a geek would not know.

She also knew more code than she had told him. She created computer apps in her spare time and did not want to fight over her ideas, which *had* happened before. She hoped that no one had sent Josh to spy on her programming.

She thought, *"People are so damned dishonest."* Her programming was just a version of baby-talk to someone like him. So, he knew code. So what?

Yeah. So what, anyway? Sounded like he was in some sort of trouble. *Shit!* She hoped she didn't just do something illegal by mailing his letters.

She had kept copies of everything he sent her and her own responses. She figured she'd give him a chance. That was what he said he wanted. She could feel that he wanted to trust her, so she'd try and be true. He said he needed a chance to change. Change from *what*? Drinking too much? Something else? Something he needed to run from? The cops? That was the part that sort of freaked her out – she didn't know. Oh well, it was only a letter or two.

She had to get to work, so she showered and got dressed. Her job wasn't much, but it paid well. She was a top-notch secretary to a big investment broker. The work was easy. It left her free in the evenings and on weekends so she could write code and create new apps.

She was working on a game app that combined *Tetris* with *Scrabble*. She thought it would be popular. And it got her mind off Joshua. She liked him. She did. She figured he was offline somewhere, but she emailed her Beta version of *Tebble* or *Scrabbis* (she hadn't decided on a name yet) to him. She might love him. She wasn't sure. Remember – *"A friend in need,"* she mused.

When Rainier got back to Brixton, he organized a Swat team comprised of representatives from New Scotland Yard, MI-6, Interpol and the CIA. He had a solid line on who Kent, Jules and Raphael were and their connection to Jake Wheeler. All of this was from his fellow programmers in the back room at the *Cannoniere* sans any leaks to the administrators of the club. There were people who knew all three of them. He and Asia had gotten clear photos of them. They were "made".

Voss had recorded verbal testimony from a back-room programmer who was willing to testify in a closed courtroom that these three were the only Wheeler Team members responsible for the Jason Bing murder and that they were trying to frame Wheeler and other Team Wheeler members for it. From this testimony, they had "Probable Cause" and an American warrant was issued on two continents for Raphael Case, Jules Ridden and Kent Rockford.

Unfortunately, the warrant also included Jacob Wheeler, being the Captain and owner of the corporate jet that the murder was carried out in. Wheeler was wanted for questioning by the American security agencies following him. Voss, himself, was not sure that he was in any way involved in the murder. There might be other charges handed down from Silver Lake, though.

Their informant urged him to have them picked up as soon as possible before they killed or injured anyone else. He told Rainier that the three ex-crew intended to kill Wheeler's grandfather and girlfriend and were planning major embezzlement hacks of entire cities if they got their hands on Wheeler's programming. And they were darn close to that. Their young informant wanted them out of the hacker community. He also said no one knew where Jake Wheeler was, only that he was beginning to disband his hacking crew.

The international Swat team sent four security personnel to one of Bernard Wheeler's rented offices in Dornoch to protect Bernie while they searched for the three hackers who were presumed to still be in London. It took some work to find him since he was listed under his mother's maiden name, but they found him using old birth records. They were luckily able to convince him to let them in to his home. He genuinely did not seem to know where his grandson was. Although, security felt that even if he *did* know, he wouldn't tell them.

With his former hacking crew (Team Wheeler) disband-
ing, the international police worked 24-7 to track all of them
from identification gleaned from the *Cannoniere* and American hackers. Jake Wheeler, himself, seemed to have fallen off
the edge of the earth. So far, he was entirely a blank – and
presumed to be offline. No cell phone usage, no emails, no
recent records and no sign of his helicopter. *Vanished!* Or
dead.

Kent Rockford, Jules Ridden and Raphael Case were in
custody the next day. They, foolishly, had not gone into hiding. The three men had thought they were invulnerable and
their identities well-hidden. Obviously, they were wrong.

Their massive egotistical, obsessive-compulsive programming habits had led them to remain at Kent Rockford's
condo in London, planning more murder and mayhem.
They were easy to find, and New Scotland Yard led the way.
They were promised a hefty jail sentence on both continents.
The expressions of surprise on their faces when the Swat
team broke their door in was almost funny.

In America, due to their mutual complicity in the
demise of Jason Bing, they were all sure to get murder one
– plus added years for embezzlement and federal felony
charges within the statutes of the *Computer Fraud and Abuse
Act*, as well as counterfeiting charges. There was solid evidence that the three men had premeditated and planned the
murder of Bing. Extradition to the USA was pretty much a
sure thing. England had much lighter penalties, but not Illinois. They would be flying trans-continental within forty-
eight hours. They were toast. Burnt toast.

The entire international police team immediately refocused on finding the rest of the hacking group and even, possibly, Wheeler himself. The security on Bernie Campbell-Wheeler was now serving a dual purpose in both protecting him and looking for his grandson.

Jessica Parker had a surveillance team on her 24-7 without her knowledge. These people were good. So good, in fact, that they tried to befriend Jessica undercover. Unsuccessfully, so far. She was rather reclusive, on-the-street sort of friendly. But not up close.

When Rainier spoke to Asia, she, being her brilliant self, came up with multiple suggestions relating to his case. That was good, great actually, since Kent, Jules and Raphael were not talking to the police. Even after being offered an American plea deal to get themselves out of life sentences, they would not speak. It was well-known that they would try and implicate other Team Wheeler members and Wheeler, himself. They did this out of vindictiveness, so the court refused to give them any reduction in sentencing. The three were extradited to Illinois and given life sentences without parole.

The British detectives that had found Kent's address (it was actually Rainier and the *Cannoniere* back room informant that first suggested the address) were actively trying to get information about the various hiding paces of the Team and Wheeler. To no avail quite yet.

Yet Asia had some research clues that could pan out. Rainier was intrigued. He got permission to stay with her in Oxford and put together another Swat team for possible use as soon as Asia felt she could lead them to the places that Rainier and his American and especially *Cannoniere* informants felt were possible hiding places. He got several of the scanning wands that were used to uncover internet access in the case of the *Anonymous hacktivist*-sympathizer, American journalist Barrett Brown. They also had K-9 units and were going to include maintenance crews that worked in the fantastical places that Asia had described.

She told an open-mouthed Rainier about her ideas which started *underneath* the Down Street Tube (subway) Station in London. This subterranean area under the subway station was used by Winston Churchill during WWII between Green Park and Hyde Park Corner Stations and was still preserved and on display as an underground museum. There were other huge spaces that had been used by the British Air Force, shooting ranges and even a clean, dry and nicely decorated conference room and a huge multiple-stationed switchboard area. There were other disused areas that could hide a large number of people, as well. Some of the equipment was still in operational condition.

"Really?!" exclaimed the excited Rainier, begging her to show all of them these underground exhibits.

"Really," answered Asia. The Swat team was also present during this explanation. The British members of the Swat team already knew about these places and sort of guessed where Asia was going with this.

She stated, "The most interesting aspect of this is that, despite all of the maps I have photographed and studied, no one really knows where all the tunnels of the disused parts of the London Tube go to. There are more places that can be cleaned and put back into use. The electricity, and in some cases, phone line connections, are still usable. New water pumps were purchased every year to keep the tunnels dry.

"It is estimated that there are about thirteen abandoned underground stations in the London Tube. Here is the information I was able to find."

She handed the team copies of her maps and the list of closed stations. Like she had said, there was no complete map of where all the tunnels went to or what other tunnels they were connected to. There was plenty of ventilation down there also due to the many staircases leading above ground. And quite a few unused elevators.

The maintenance men from the London Tube agreed with her that they did not know the extent of the tunneling either and examined her detailed maps along with the Swat team. The security forces knew there were quite a few hackers that were running mega-computers out of London. Like the CIA and European security, they had never been able to pinpoint *exactly where* in London. Rainier felt the tunnels underneath London were a distinct possibility.

Asia also suggested a simultaneous examination of the chalk-flint caves in Chislehurst, Bromley. This was a very old set of excavations that extended into a maze of tunnels that was about 22 miles long. She felt that the Hellfire caves in West Wycombe were of no use for their purposes. They were well-known and finite.

Chislehurst, on the other hand, was different. Some of the Chislehurst tunnels could be extended manually, for one thing. Also, not all the tunnels were used for the tourist trade or visited regularly. Plans were made to send more Swat teams and K-9 units to Chislehurst, which would coordinate their timing with the raids on the London Tube. In fact, security forces planned on sending 13 Swat teams and K-9 units entering each of the closed stations and *all* Tube exits/entrances at the same time to avoid escapes. The dogs would help prevent this, too.

Times were set for the raids, and all the teams were co-ordinated at their entry points the next day. Each team had two or three members with internet detecting wands. They were all warned to be as silent as possible even during arrests. Tasers, pepper spray and combat knives were preferable to guns since ricochet was a serious threat in the hard-surfaced tunnels of the London underground. Above all, they were told many times to *be quiet and act silently*.

The police teams entered underground London simultaneously – exactly to the second. Above ground, multiple arrest vehicles awaited for transport. The largest sting operation England had ever seen proceeded like a huge Swiss clock.

The round-up was successful. Every single member of Team Wheeler was detained, including Richie Stevens who was still living at Jake Wheeler's residence near the chalk caves of Chislehurst in the South-Eastern countryside. Wheeler's estate was practically empty. It was up for sale. Richie had handled the liquidation and was living in a small cottage on Wheeler's huge, now defunct, estate.

The computer and survival equipment recovered from their successful raids on Wheeler's ex-hackers hiding underground was very high tech. They found all of this in the London subway tunnels and Chislehurst. It filled most of a Lon-

don warehouse. It would take the better part of a year to an-
alyze all the hard drives and external storage devices that had
been confiscated.

Wheeler's jet, horses and Corgis were never found. Nor
was most of the stolen money from the Silver Lake banking
system. The team was too smart to have anything on any of
their hard drives or flash drives.

In fact, Wheeler himself was not seen or heard from,
despite constant surveillance of his family and girlfriend.
Whatever became of him was unknown. Perhaps he just
stood on the peak of some mountain in the Scottish Highlands and observed everything in his new "kingdom". Maybe
that pleased him more than his old life as a computer wizard.
One thing, though, most hackers agreed – he also disappeared online, or he was moving and watching incognito like
a spy, like his nickname.

Was he dead? No one knew. The first year after the round
up, Jessica Parker moved to Bernie Wheeler's estate in Scotland (after Jake had agreed to reveal his real identity to her)
and was very much online. Innocently so. Her game *Scrabbis*
went viral with all the different levels of skill and an optional
maze attachment – and made her a millionaire. You could
beat the machine in *Scrabble*. Parker's app did not need two
or more players. There was another option where more players could play. She had been able to quit her job. Jake was not
seen anywhere. Even his grandfather began to wonder.

All the publicity surrounding the capture of his old Team did get back to Jake. He even watched the recorded take-down of his Team members on TV in a pub in Stornoway. You know he was a billionaire, actually. So, after the take-down, he took a private jet to Switzerland with false identification papers and passport and emptied his safety deposit box there and got state-of-the-art plastic surgery. He still loved living outside most of the time and that was his second "ace in hand". MacGregor became a "new" friend after his surgery. They both mourned the sudden loss of Joshua Handlin, since MacGregor had no clue that this new visitor (after plastic surgery) was actually his old friend Josh.

Never knowing what happened to Handlin, MacGregor was happy enough to have a new friend to take up that space. The "new" Jake was just another weird camper running away from the city, that liked living outside and brought him game and whiskey from time-to-time, knowing that he liked that.

Now, Jake could make trips to see his grandfather and also his devoted Jessica. Grand made Jessica his heir, since Jake would have to remain in hiding for the rest of his life and had inherited early anyway. *That's the price you pay*, he thought to himself with just a small sip of Glenlivet. He had pretty much quit drinking except for a little social drinking – very little social drinking.

Jake's *.mbezzl* worm is still being studied by the experts who hope it never resurfaces again in any form. Asia Reynolds and Rainier Voss were touted in the British and American press as genius investigators responsible for protecting whatever city might have been attacked with that intrusive virus. Still, Jake Wheeler had escaped into a seemingly impenetrable web of mystery and secrecy. His entire team, though, were all safely ensconced inside either the American prison system in Illinois or the English prison system in London.

Elise and Elton Jamison spent *two* months touring the West Indies and Frankie Franklin had a big welcome home animal party with Chico, Julio and Cisco Almonte, Sheila Rodriguez, Asia Reynolds, Harry the Hippie, Sage Sommers, herself and her daughter, (sans Joe Doe who still felt they were all Martians and had proof). There was a full range of rescued pets in Asia's barn during the party – nine full grown dogs, 10 with Zucchini and 11 with a rather shy Fuzzy Bud, plus six large and growing St. Bernard puppies, two goats, one very happy donkey – and no bear. They all had a great time playing with the animals wildly, but gently, and eating Franklin's Bar-B-Qued ribs and vegan alternatives.

Epilogue:
Separating fact
from fiction

Much of the technical information in this book is real. *Stuxnet* was a real worm/virus developed first in Holland (the name of the worm is Dutch and pronounced "Stucks net") and then further programmed by the two governments of the USA and Israel for use to limit the nuclear programs of Iran, Pakistan and other third world countries. Its connection with Programmable Logic Controllers (PLCs) is accurate.

Stuxnet never entirely disappeared despite Microsoft fixes. The code it was written in still confounds systems analysts. No one knew at first what the target of the virus-worm was and mistakenly (in the author's own opinion) neutralized most of it. Its use in this book is, of course, entirely fictional. It is true that it is federally illegal to use computers to hack into banks and other private and public institutions under the *Computer Fraud and Abuse Act. Anonymous* is a real *"hacktivist"* organization. Barrett Brown is a real person (former journalist) and his biography is real (see *The Hacker*

Wars movie on Netflix). The internet discovery wand used to arrest Brown also really exists.

In terms of *Anonymous*, some of the members actually *did* hack FBI credit cards, forcing the agents to donate to charitable organizations during one Christmas season.

The London underground Silver Vaults actually exist. There are approximately 68 vaults and 27 shops. The Vaults date from 1876 when they opened on Chancery Lane. The Hellfire and Chislehurst chalk-flint caves are real. St. James Lake Park is also authentic.

The 13 closed stops on the London Tube (subway) are also extent. Churchill's underground War Room suite underneath the Down Street Tube (subway) Station is real. The new water pumps installed each year, the kitchen, bathrooms, conference room, shooting range, electricity and phone connectors also exist. The fact that no one knows the actual extent of all the connections and tunnels, and that no complete map has ever been made is a fact.

Dornoch, Stornoway, the Scottish Highlands and Outer Hebrides descriptions are accurate, and the Isles of Lewis and Harris and existing abandoned and in-use Croft houses are authentic. It is a magnificent, unusual and beautiful part of the world and I invite you to visit there if you ever have the chance. The weather is benign and the average winter temperature in the lowlands during the winter of 2016 was 40 degrees Fahrenheit.

The Aurora Borealis in the area is featured on YouTube and is probably one of the most spectacular natural movies you will ever see!

———————

One note about the music that Rainier Voss plays on the piano – if you are curious what these pieces sound like, you can copy the names from this book and put them into the YouTube search bar. Generally, you will find the piece and you can listen to it. I recommend Daniel Barenboim's piano recordings when available. He is an exquisite classical pianist.

About the Author

SOPHIA WATSON LOVES to learn how to fix computer hardware, so she has a natural interest in cyber crime. She also finds it scary. She has an interest in researching this area.

She also loves to travel (see her Collected Poetry "Waiting for the Sunrise" written as Cathy Smith on Smashwords), so desktop traveling via YouTube, Facebook and Google for her novels is loads of fun.

She lives in the forests of New England, in northern Maine, so she loves to write about rural life. She also grew up outside of Chicago and has lived in Missouri in Ozark county (visiting the caves in Mark Twain National Park), so those areas are also familiar to her. The caves in the Cape Girardeau area are fictional, so is the little town of Silver Lake.

She lived in Boston during her college years, graduating magna cum laude from Boston University and attending Harvard for graduate school – so the fine points of gentrification are familiar to her.

The fourth book in the Silver Lake Cozy Mystery series is entitled *Solstice* and the exciting sequel to this book. It is also about international cyber-crime. We track Jake Wheeler down in the Outer Hebrides & look for the stolen money. He gets some amazing help from *Anonymous* the hacktivist group. Be ready for some fast-paced excitement, another perspective on cyber crime and Jake's conversion from wanted criminal to cyber authority and international cyber cop. This truly *does* happen in reality and has happened to a few notorious cyber criminals. Beats prison by a mile.

Sophia also writes under the name Zara Brooks-Watson (the Bonaventura Cozy Mysteries: *Jitterbug* and *Tie Dye*).

For all updates on her books, see: silverlakemysteries.wixsite.com/sophia-watson.[1]

---

1.   http://silverlakemysteries.wixsite.com/sophia-watson

Don't miss out!

Visit the website below and you can sign up to receive emails whenever Sophia Watson publishes a new book. There's no charge and no obligation.

https://books2read.com/r/B-A-SDVE-SIZO

BOOKS 2 READ

Connecting independent readers to independent writers.

Did you love *Snow Angels*? Then you should read *Solstice* by Sophia Watson!

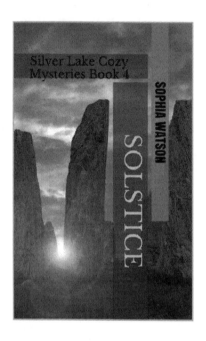

Solstice is the second of our Cyber-Crime mini-series within the *Silver Lake Cozy Mystery* series. The first being ***Snow Angels***. In this volume, former hacker criminal, Jake Wheeler almost gets corralled in an attempt to regain his normal urban life in London. He runs and succeeds in getting to his grandfather's private island in the Outer Hebrides in Scotland. Of course, he is not totally free, but does gain a couple of hacker advocates from the organization, *Anonymous*. He makes some very tough decisions helped by local Scottish royalty, the Earl of Sutherland and his Falconer.

Dive into the Deep Web with an Onion Browser & learn about Bitcoin, its machinery, software and its advantages. Interested in computer wizardry and the European experience? This book is for you!

Read more at silverlakemysteries.wixsite.com/sophia-watson.

Also by Sophia Watson

Silver Lake Cozy Mysteries
It All Comes Out in the Wash
Snow Angels
That Summer in Silver Lake
Solstice

Watch for more at silverlakemysteries.wixsite.com/sophia-watson.

Made in the USA
Columbia, SC
18 November 2024

46816316R00159